D1173312

Prologue

"It is my belief that we were never intended to know what life holds in store for us from one moment to the next, and I am convinced the Creator showed great wisdom in this. For if I had foreseen the day my world would begin to change, I would have said it was indeed a good day for new beginnings. I would not have guessed that from that time forward black would seem as white, and white black. That my own kind would turn against me. That enemies and strangers would be my only companions. There was nothing to warn me that all I held true would show itself false—that I would come to trust only those things I had neither dreamed of nor remotely imagined. As I say, the Creator knew what he was about. . . ."

— Aldair, late of the Venicii, aboard the free vessel *Ahzir al'Rhaz*

ALDAIR IN ALBION

by
Neal Barrett, Jr.

DAW BOOKS, INC.
DONALD A. WOLLHEIM, PUBLISHER

1301 Avenue of the Americas
New York, N. Y.   10019

COPYRIGHT ©, 1976, BY NEAL BARRETT, JR.

All Rights Reserved.

Cover art by Josh Kirby.

FIRST PRINTING, MAY 1976

1 2 3 4 5 6 7 8 9

PRINTED IN U.S.A.

ALDAIR
IN ALBION

ONE

I have no love for cities, nor do any of the Venicii. If it were not for the burden of honor I would quit myself of Silium and never look back. It is a place of narrow streets that shut out the sun, and tight little houses squeezed one against another. It is impossible to breathe here, and the water is not fit to drink. It is no place for a man born to the broad valleys of the Eubirones.

Still, many seem to like this life and would be lonely without the stink of their neighbors. They are a strange lot, and grow restless and uneasy without the presence of friends. If one man finds himself alone, he seeks out another. If two are together they search for a third. And they are happiest when everyone they know is packed together in the smallest quarter they can find. All of this is beyond my understanding.

I would miss the University, though, and Master Levitinus. He has been good to me, and there is much to be said for learning. Though what I will do with the knowledge I gain here I cannot say. When I return to the north I will take up the duties of a man. I already know these things, and can do them as well as any other. A sharp eye and a true arrow are required to keep raiders from the walls—I do not imagine the enemies of the Venicii will be impressed with my grasp of history, or the ability to do sums in my head. Still, it is the wish of my mother and my uncles that I stay in Silium and learn whatever I can. They say it will bring honor and respect to the clan, and this may be so.

Yesterday marked the second week into summer, and the heat that broiled the city from dawn to dusk lingered into evening. It was a moist, sucking heat that near melted the marrow and there was not enough ale in all Silium to turn it away. Toward midnight, though, a small miracle occurred. Dark thunderheads rumbled in from the south and poured out their blessings. It was a hard rain, lasting the night, and just before dawning the clouds scudded away and left Silium in a buttery glow.

So the rain had washed the city clean for the moment, and it did not appear as dismal as it might. From Highgate I could look down upon a sea of peaked roofs and yellow thatching clear to the white dome of St. Bellium's and the spires of University. Beyond that, the stone walls and towers that circle the town and protect it from enemies that no longer exist. And farther, the bright greens and browns of fields and orchards still sparkling with wetness.

It is not the capital of the empire, nor even as big as Culivia, which is on the sea and boasts a harbor. Still, if you are from the north of the Eubirones and within smelling distance of Stygianns, you can be excused for thinking Silium is as large as it needs to be.

It was a good enough morning, then. All you could rightly expect from a city. It seemed to me a fair day for drinking barley beer and swimming in the river past the gates. Or simply nosing about in small shops and inspecting interesting things I could not afford to buy. I would not do any of this, however, as I was not sent to Silium at some expense to enjoy myself. Instead, I left the Quarter behind, turned down Highgate, and cut across to Gildrow, where the street drops sharply away and winds like a cobbled river toward the gray walls of University.

It was early yet, but I was about with a purpose—having in mind the goal of filling an empty belly at the Quill before classes. Learning is not nearly as taxing as a day in the north, but the Venicii are used to eating well, and it is a hard habit to break.

A few tradesmen were about. A sleepy apprentice pushed a broom before his master's shop, and cookfires sent the odor of new bread to mix with rain smell. A wheeler's wife yelled at her husband from an upper window, and the fellow mumbled an answer without looking up from his work. On the corner near Crofters, two Cygnian slaves struggled to bring a small handcart up the steep alley. The cart was loaded with heavy bolts of flaxweave, and clearly more than they could handle. Their owner, though, thought differently. He cursed them soundly and beat them about the legs and shoulders with a stick. The slaves bleated loudly. One trembled and rolled watery eyes. The other shook his head dumbly and urinated down his leg.

Plainly, I thought, here was a lout as dense as his charges. Only a fool strikes a slave where work muscles lie. More than that, these creatures were still unshaven and summer was upon us. If they carried heavy coats of wool a month from now the heat would kill them. Then this worthy would cry out that a Cygnian would rather die than do a day's work.

My father used to say that you can tell a master by his slaves, and I believe this is so. The fellow here had the short snout and square head of the Belaturvi, and ears that hung nearly to his jowls. His body hair was auburn splotched with black and covered with a dirty blue tunic. The tunic marked him as a Belaturvi, for all that tribe were millers once, and they still take pride in this, though I cannot see why.

Turning my back on this scene I started down Gildrow again and remembered Master Theon. Two winters ago he penned an article declaring that slaves as well as freemen were children of the Church, entitled to the blessings of the Creator and passage to Albion. This document sent the Good Fathers scurrying, and eventually reached Rhemia itself. Word has it that a caustic note arrived shortly thereafter from that city, advising Master Theon of the wisdom of following scholarly pursuits and leaving religious matters to those who best understood them. That if he continued to poke his snout where it didn't belong, arrangements could be made to shorten it considerably.

The Church is jealous of its ways and it is best not to cross them. I know for a fact that some students are still discussing Master Theon's doctrine, but they are foolish to do so. Who can say whether the Creator blesses all creatures alike? And what's the use in debating the good and the bad of slavery? Clearly, the Creator does not greatly object to this practice, since he allows it to continue unhindered.

Down Gildrow to Bolters' Alley, then, and straight to the Quill, with a short stop along the way. Halfway up the narrow street of Greenstone is Master Chelsium's shop under the sign of the mended pot. And in the shop—hopefully—the Mistress Illycia, up and about for the day. Though I knew it was more likely she still slumbered in the room above. Illycia cares little for the morning hours. She is wide awake when the sun dies, though—when a student needs to study, or gain a night's sleep. Still, if *I* didn't take her time, she'd spend it with another. I had no illusions about that. Females are inconstant creatures at best.

At the glaziers, I stopped for a moment to peer in a pane of dark glass. I do not cut a bad figure, nor an overly impressive one, either. My clothes are worn but well made. They mark me for a provincial, but I am not ashamed of Venicii blood. I wear thick breeches caught at the ankles in the northern style, boots of Stygiann hide, and a loose blouse with sleeves cut at the shoulders. The blouse is diamond-patched in blue and red clan colors. A bronze brooch set with an enameled signet holds the plain woolen cloak about my shoulders, and there is a short iron dagger in my belt. When I arrived in Silium I was told that students should not be concerned with arms, but I find this idea ridiculous. A sharp weapon will pierce a learned man as quickly as a slave. Besides, the dagger was a gift of my father's, and he would turn over in his grave if he knew I'd set it aside for fashion.

I stood tall before the glass—though I didn't need to. I am nearly a head taller than these short, pudgy southerners who are much given to fat from easy living. My body is covered with a good coat of silver-white hair. The pink skin of youth still shows through in places but there's little I can do about that. My eyes are set properly close above a snout that is as long as it should be. The bristles on my jowls are growing as fast as can be expected for a man of seventeen summers, and I haven't been tempted to purchase the grizzly whiskers that can be attached with a clear paste. Some of the three-year students do this—more to mock fashion than show maturity.

I took a last look at myself, flicked a speck of lint from one ear, and stepped jauntily—I supposed—into Greenstone. Mystress Illycia, of course, was nowhere to be seen. A younger sister peeked at me through an upper window and giggled. This greatly annoyed me, and I moved quickly out of her sight.

One of the few things I like about Silium is the Market.

We hold this event in the north, of course, as do all peoples everywhere. But the small fairs of the Eubirones seem shabby indeed compared to this. They are held only weekly there, instead of every day of the year, and the wares are generally dull and uninteresting.

Morning is the best time to see this spectacle, when the sun first brightens the day and the rich collection of sounds, smells, and colors is fresh to the senses. Awnings of blue, amber, sun-yellow, and brown shield their goods from the sun. Sellers vie loudly for a customer's attention, and I have seen them fight openly over a well-dressed buyer. You can see people of all stations in this place—squat, sullen farmers mix with scurrying slaves, wealthy merchants on horseback and Church Fathers in dark linen cassocks. The smells of spice, bread, stale urine, and fresh vegetables mingles with the odor of horse manure and unwashed bodies. And ever present is the sour reminder of yesterday's business. It ever pervades the Market, and cannot be washed away by an evening's rain.

This day there was no time to see what new wares might be had, so I cut hurriedly around the maze instead of through it. I was more than a little irritated with myself. The sun was higher than it should be, and if my foolish prancing before Mistress Illycia's cost me breakfast—why, I *deserved* to start the day on an empty stomach!

Something had drawn a crowd at the far end of the square. I stopped, muttered an oath. All the scampering about was for nothing. Townsmen with nothing better to do blocked the way to the Quill to see whatever there was to see. I pressed a path through them, or tried to, one hand firmly on my purse.

This is a peculiar thing about Silium. For all their traffic with the world, these people have the curiosity of children. They will line up to watch fornicating mice, or a turnip on the end of a string. All distractions are equally amazing. And since I was in the midst of them now, with no hope of going further, I peered over stubby heads to see what wonder had drawn their attention.

I peered—then peered again, somewhat surprised. For a change, there was something to give the gawkers their money's worth. A Rhemian patrol had captured a Stygiann warrior. He was locked in an iron cage atop a horsecart—the bars so thick they'd have held an army at bay. I guessed the Rhemians were parading him through the southern provinces to show how well the Empire protected its citizens. I had to grin at the thought. The poor brute was either drunk or asleep, if Rhemians had taken him alive.

Stygianns were no novelty to me. They had come howling out of the woods of the Lauvectii as long as anyone could remember, and were blood enemies of the Eubirones. Still, they were a rare sight as far south as Silium, and it was likely none of these people had ever seen one. They weren't *quite* certain they wanted to see one now. The usually raucous crowd was strangely quiet. They watched, but said nothing, and no one ventured too near the creature.

The Stygiann paid no attention to us. We might as well not have been there, as far as he was concerned. He leaned against the rear of his cage, arms folded, red eyes somewhere beyond the walls of Silium. He was big. Even for his kind. The long, rangy form was covered in thick gray fur, but even the heavy pelt couldn't hide the hard belts of muscle corded beneath. His clothes, such as they were, had been badly torn. Still, I spotted the dirty yellow band on one sleeve. He was of some importance, then. A chief or subchief of his clan. The Rhemians probably hadn't noticed this, or didn't care.

Even these townspeople, who knew nothing at all about Stygianns, seemed to sense the brute's power. And certainly I was not fooled by the fact that he was relatively peaceful for the moment. Stygianns are clever and cunning, and good fighters to boot. They are dangerous at all times, but the darkness is their element. They are particularly at home in the thick oak forests of the Lauvectii, and when they melt into these woods it is impossible to find them.

Someone spoke beside me, and I looked up, startled for a moment. Without realizing it, I had moved to the very front of the crowd. The cage was no more than a few yards away. I could even smell the creature plainly. Clearly, my mind had simply gone blank for some minutes and I had forgotten what I was about—that I had classes to go to, and an empty stomach besides.

And then another peculiar thing happened. I cannot explain this, or say why I chose to do what I did. I merely took a step forward and spoke directly to the Stygiann in his own language.

"C'reef. Mahr a shinn, Stygiaar. . . ."

The Stygiann's furry ears flicked to a point. He turned slowly and gazed at me down his sharp muzzle. The townsmen on either side had heard me, of course. Now they gave me wide-eyed looks, and ample room.

The Stygiann grinned, showing razor teeth and a long tongue. "Well, young one. The dinner comes to speak with the diner."

"Not today," I said. "Today you eat iron, warrior."

The Stygiann laughed—that peculiar sound I have heard before from the edge of the forest. It is more a cough than a laugh, but there is no mistaking where it comes from.

"Right enough," he told me. "I may just do that, too, before the day is through."

He looked me over, and I knew he didn't miss the rough boots made of the hide of his kinsmen.

"You speak the True Tongue. By your dress you are a Northman."

"Eubirones."

"Ah . . ."

"Aldair. Of clan Venicii. By the river Rheinus."

The Stygiann nodded understanding. "I know the place. I will make it a point to visit the Venicii when I am able."

"They'll welcome you," I said shortly. "Come armed though. With sober warriors. The Venicii already have many fine pelts to warm their winters."

His gaunt face clouded a moment, then fell into an easy grin. "Well said, Venicii. It's likely enough, though, you won't get this one. Your brothers have plans for it."

"Perhaps you'll grace a Rhemian hallway, then," I suggested. "Or warm the floor of his bedchamber."

"Perhaps," the Stygiann said stoicly. His thick tail flicked at a bottle fly. "Or perhaps the god of the woods and streams will cleave these bars for me. Though he has not yet done so, and I fear I may be too far south for my prayers to be heard. If there *are* gods," he added grimly, "and they truly listen to such things."

"It's possible they do," I said. "Though I shouldn't think a Stygiann god would—"

I stopped there. One of the Rhemian soldiers guarding the cage had taken notice of us. He came quickly around the rear of the cart, a dark frown spreading across his features.

"You." He came to a halt and pointed a finger at me. "Am I wrong, boy, or were you trying to talk to this thing?"

I started to reply, but a helpful townsman answered for me. "He was talking to it, for sure. And it talked right back to him!"

The soldier looked at the townsman, then at me. "That right?"

I nodded. "I spoke to the Stygiann."

"What for?"

"I don't know," I said honestly. "I just did."

The soldier considered that. "He know what you're saying?"

"Of course he did. It's his tongue."

He raised a brow. "And you speak it?"

"Yes."

The man scratched his chest a long moment. He was short, probably a true Rhemian. He wore a painted bronze breastplate and a tufted helmet with a great deal of the tufting worn away. A tunic hung to his knees, and he carried the stubby gladius blade of the infantry. He was a veteran of some years, for his thick legs were bowed and scarred.

"I don't like the looks of this business," he said finally. He tilted the helmet back on his head. "Seems to me it's not proper for Rhemian citizens to be talking to beasts."

"Soldier," I said, certain this was an excellent time to keep my mouth shut, "it's not *proper* for citizens of Rhemia to find their cousins barbecued in the Lauvectii. But they do."

His eyes narrowed. "And you're saying what, then?" He knew where the Lauvectii was.

"That the Eubirones learn to take care of their own, as Rhemian legions are a rare sight in the north."

The soldier stiffened. Red flushed the curve of his jowls. "Listen—" he began, then changed his mind. A circle of townsmen had gathered around us, deciding this show was better than the Stygiann.

"Get on about your business," he told them shortly, "if you have any!" He gripped the hilt of his sword and looked at me. "I don't want to *see* you around here. Understood?"

I didn't answer. I moved back through the crowd—they gave me room, as is fitting for a man who speaks with beasts.

It did not strike me until some time later that the soldier was right—I *had* done a most unusual thing. And even after I realized this, I could find no explanation for it. Certainly, I had never spoken to a Stygiann before in my life. Few men have. But we all know their tongue in the north, for it has been laboriously pieced together through the years, from those rare Stygianns who will allow themselves to be taken alive. We believe it is wise to be able to speak to your enemies, even though the occasion seldom arises. For the most part, we kill their raiders when we can, and take their pelts—while the Stygianns murder as many of us as possible, and frequently roast and eat whomever they catch. This is not much of a basis for making conversation.

Still, I *had* spoken to this particular Stygiann. Why, though? I had nothing to say to the beast. And just as puzzling—what did he have to say to me?

I had to laugh at a sudden thought. By the Creator, was Silium as bad as all that? It was a sorry place, indeed, if the Eubirones and Stygianns could find no one to talk to but each other!

TWO

We pay for our sins, they say, in one way or another. I paid doubly for mine. My stomach remained empty for the day, and at the end of it I was asked by Master Levitinus to remain after the others had gone. We would discuss, he said, students who were too busily engaged to attend their classes on time.

It was thus I found myself on a hard bench in a cold hall before the Master's quarters, and overheard a conversation I was not meant to hear.

The door was not firmly closed, and the voices too loud to ignore. One, I knew, was Levitinus himself. The other, I soon realized, was Flaviun Sellenus. It was this voice—surprisingly—that was doing most of the louder talking. Surprisingly, because Flaviun is no more than a student himself, and he was not speaking in the manner a pupil uses with a Master.

I caught only bits of the conversation—not intending to hear any of this at all. Master Levitinus was chastising Flaviun for lack of attention to his lessons. For not attending classes. For not following the rules of the University. For half a dozen other infractions I can't recall. Flaviun hotly denied all this, and insisted he was being persecuted for no reason whatever, and so on. Levitinus warned him that another such outburst would see his dismissal from the University. There were several loud exchanges, and then the door burst open and Flaviun Sellenus rushed angrily past me —not so quickly, though, that he didn't see me there, and show his surprise.

The Master, needless to say, brushed lightly over my own trivial sins. I was in quickly, and out sooner than that. But

16

I was ashamed to have caused him even the smallest of worries. He was severely shaken by the encounter with Flaviun, and I could guess the reason for that. Sad to say, there are students, and then there are *students*, at the University. By that I mean that money speaks with as loud a voice in the halls of learning as it does in the marketplace. This is not as the Masters would have it, but it is true, nevertheless. Certainly, the school does not exist on tuitions such as Aldair of Venicii can pay. Those with money bear the greater burden —and, too often, feel they are entitled to greater privilege.

Thus, Flaviun Sellenus. A pudgy little bore he may be, but he is also the son of a wealthy townsman, and makes much of his father's Rhemian connections, and his family's full Empire citizenship. In truth, he is as much a provincial as I am. But gold nicely gilds the leaves of a family tree. So Master Levitinus could not be overly pleased with this business. Though Flaviun undoubtedly received far less than he deserved. It would have been an easier draught to swallow, say, if the student had been an Aldair, with coppers instead of silver in his purse, and no family to speak of.

I could have gone to the Quill and filled my belly. But Flaviun would be there, loudly exclaiming his own lurid version of what had happened in the Master's quarters. He would find a ready audience, because he buys wine freely for those who will listen. I could not bear the thought of listening to that. Instead, I walked back to the Quarter by the long way, and ate at a place I'd never seen before, and spent half the night digesting my mistake.

It was not the best of days.

"History," Master Levitinus was saying, "is not to be thought of as merely the chronicle of the past. It is not a record of the dead, as some of you may think, or a dry account of events that occurred long ago. History is the living story of people. We are making history now, young scholars." He paused, and favored us with a wan smile. "And if you do not wish students of the future to doze through their books, why it is up to you to create an interesting chapter for them."

The students laughed appreciatively. Some because they felt it was the thing to do, and others—like myself—because we genuinely respected Master Levitinus. He is a good teacher, and does, truly, make history come alive. When he describes a famous battle, you can almost hear the clash of ancient armor, and the cries of the victors and vanquished. The Hermian League marches again, and the Golden Kings sit upon their thrones. The city towers of Alticus gleam in the sun, and the birth pangs of the Rhemian Empire shake the world.

"We have come far and we have learned much," he said. "But we have only made a small beginning." He spread his short arms on the lectern. "Each of us, in the few years we have on Earth, can experience but a second or so in the long span of history. More than that is beyond our comprehension. Two hundred years? Five hundred?" Levitinus shook his head. "If we cannot imagine that, my friends, how can we conceive of the *whole* of recorded history—three thousand long years?" He paused again and looked out at each of us. "Yet, such a time is really *only the lifespan of thirty long-lived men. . . .*" He let the point sink home. "Thirty. Not so great a number. There are nearly that many of you in this small room. So if history seems to belong to the past—well, it does, in a sense. But never forget that history lives. That the years that have gone before are only a wink in the eye of time. That thirty men could tell it all. . . ."

"Master Levitinus?"

I knew that voice before I leaned forward to look. Flaviun Sellenus, of course. What was he up to now, then? Doing penance for yesterday's mischief? I had my doubts about that.

Master Levitinus hesitated, then nodded permission to speak.

"You say history began three thousand years ago, Master. And beyond that, then, is the Darkness?"

I glanced quickly at Levitinus. The old Master wasn't taken in by that one. It was a baited question, and he knew it.

"The Church tells us this is so," Levitinus answered evenly.

Flaviun appeared to be confused. And *I* was not taken in by *that*.

"I don't question the Church, Master," Flaviun said.

"No, young scholar. I didn't think you did."

"I know that Man was created in Albion, that he sinned

in the Creator's eyes, and was cast out upon the world," Flaviun mouthed the Scripture.

"This is so," said Levitinus.

"Man in Albion, then, is a part of the Darkness?"

Levitinus didn't hesitate. "That's a question you must ask a Churchman, Flaviun Sellinus. For this is a university, not a theological seminary."

A few of the students laughed.

"Then—" Flaviun, playing the ardent scholar, seemed to search for words. "Then, theology *ends,* and history *begins* the day—or the hour, if you will—when Man was banished from Albion."

Levitinus looked at the ceiling. "Since the Church still survives, I would assume theology did not end with that event. Theology and history move through the ages, side by side."

Good for you, I thought.

"But we can begin to speak of history, after the Darkness?" Flaviun asked. "From the Church's point of view, we are not interpreting Scripture after that."

"I suppose so," Levitinus said shortly. He was trying to repress his irritation. "What is your point, Flaviun? I assume you have one in mind."

"Master," Flaviun said with mock respect, "pardon my ignorance. I only wish to *learn."*

"I am pleased," Levitinus said dryly. "Unfortunately, we have little time to learn more today." He glanced at the big sandclock on his lectern. "Tomorrow, perhaps—"

"One question, then," Flaviun cut in, "or perhaps two." He didn't wait, this time, for Levitinus's permission. "First, what was the first event after history began? And secondly—*when did the blue fires first appear over Albion?*"

I sat up straight, and I was not the only one. A shocked silence fell over the room. I looked at Levitinus. He was pale, visibly shaken.

Flaviun had very cleverly sprung his trap. Even Levitinus hadn't seen it. Flaviun well knew that it was forbidden to even mention the blue fires that had once circled Albion. Even the Fathers themselves spoke of this in whispers, if at all. So Flaviun Sellinus had committed a serious heresy. Only he hadn't. A Master is responsible for his pupils—and Flaviun had managed to lay that responsibility squarely before his teacher. Thus: it was forbidden to speak of the fires. But our pudgy little troublemaker had pushed Levitinus into admitting that all events after the Darkness were history. He had not qualified his statement. Therefore, he had *allowed* Flaviun to mention that which must not be mentioned.

Levitinus pulled himself together. "I believe—that will be all for today," he began. "What has been discussed here— will not be discussed again. In or out of this classroom. We—"

"*No,* Master Levitinus, that will not be all!" cried Flaviun. He was on his feet, his eyes flashing anger. "I am a paid student, sir. I remind you, with all *respect,* that a teacher is obligated to answer the questions of his pupils!"

Levitinus flushed. "Young scholar, I remind *you* that—"

"Did you or did you not admit we could speak in the realm of history!" Flaviun shouted.

"Your question—"

"My question was a proper question. It was posed under the instruction and *guidance* of a Master. I asked about the blue fires, sir! Over Island Albion! Now, I would like an answer!"

"You have no right, Flaviun Sellenus!" Levitinus's jowls trembled.

"I have every right," Flaviun smiled thinly. "My Master gave me permission to speak of this subject. There are witnesses here who will testify to this."

My heart went cold at that. Levitinus's eyes widened. So that was it, then. Flaviun saw a need for witnesses. Witnesses give testimony, and there is only one body that would be concerned with testimony on such a subject.

"I ask again," Flaviun went on. "When were the blue fires first seen over Albion, Master?"

Levitinus stared at him.

"Would you tell me this is the *Church's* business?" Flaviun taunted. He shook his head. "No, sir—you have already said it is history's business. And if you will not answer one question, suppose we try another. Why do the flames *no longer* circle Albion? Why, Master? No blue fires have been seen for what—a hundred years? Two hundred?" Flaviun laughed harshly. "Only the lives of two long-lived men, is it not? Has the Creator forgiven us, then? Can we return to Albion, Master? Surely—"

"Get out!" cried Levitinus. His face was black with rage. "You are no longer a student at this university!"

"I am, sir," Flaviun said coolly.

Levitinus speared him with a trembling finger. "Not in this classroom, or any other."

"Now the flames, Master. As a Master Scholar, you—"

"Flaviun Sellenus." Levitinus's fingers whitened on the lectern. "I do not give a whit about your blue flames. Or how many saints can stand on their heads on—on the tip of a quill. Or whether—or whether there is more gold on the altar of St. Bellium's than in your father's pockets, sir! Or—or . . ."

I watched, too horrified to move. Moments before, Levitinus had been a fine, proud man—a teacher who had done much to open my mind to the world about me. Now I saw something happen that I would never forget. I looked into Levitinus's eyes and saw him grow suddenly old. The strength went out of him and he seemed to crumble and fall in upon himself. It was as if he realized, in that moment, that something very terrible had happened. That he had lost control of his world, and all about him. He was surprised—and then not surprised at all. And when he walked past us and out of the classroom he looked neither to the left nor the right. He left his greatness and his soul behind him, and he was no more, now, than an old man in a somewhat shabby black robe.

"Flaviun. Flaviun Sellenus."

I caught up with them just outside the Quill. A great many students were clustered about Flaviun, now. He was much in favor, having toppled a giant, and lived to tell the tale.

He turned and faced me, his mouth feigning surprise. "Well. Good Master Hayseed. Do you join us for wine?" He shot me a winning smile, and proceeded to inspect me from head to toe. Apparently, he could hardly credit the fact that I truly walked the Earth. This greatly amused the other students.

"Flaviun," I said, "I would not join you for a cup of water in the wastelands."

Flaviun rolled his eyes. "And I, sir, would not invite you!"

I took a step toward him. "You are a coward," I said. "Nothing more than that. You could not fill your purse with enough gold to give you the weight of a man."

"Oh?"

"A coward, and a weakling to boot. I call you out for your actions."

Flaviun frowned impatiently. "You do what, now?"

"Call you to answer. If you can, that is. If you know one end of a blade from the other."

Flaviun threw back his snout and laughed. The other students, though, showed no expression. The grins dropped from their faces and they moved away from Flaviun Sellenus.

Flaviun glared at them irritably. "Come now," he sighed. "You don't think this clod is *serious*, do you?" His eyes suddenly brightened. "All right, Master Aldair of wherever it is. You want satisfaction, do you?" He struck a mock-fighting pose and grunted like a warrior. "Dung forks at twenty paces, then. A weapon you're familiar with, no doubt!"

I was on him before he could move. I slapped him hard on one cheek and then the other. The blows sent him staggering. Tears welled in his eyes, and the tips of his ears went bloodless.

"There's your challenge, little beast," I told him. "If you can, take it from there." I turned, then, and walked away from them without looking back. Two stout Fathers in brown linen robes blocked my way and I moved past them without a glance. A tradesman scampered out of my path and yelled a curse at my back. I paid him no attention.

I was so angry I was near blind to the street under my boots. The little bastard was not done with his mischief, I knew that. His kind are easy enough to read. One taste of power is never sufficient. He'd humiliated his betters, and he'd carry the thing further if he could. Only, what more could he do? Nothing, surely, I told myself. The times were not so mean as that. A respected Scholar had nothing to fear from a vindictive student. Even one with gold in his pocket. Even the Church would have to see that Flaviun was in the wrong. That they'd hear of this business—or already knew—I had little doubt.

I walked on, placing one foot before the other. And wished I could be certain I was right.

The sun had dropped over the city walls, and the Market was cut neatly between brightness and shadow. The Stygiann was still in his iron cage. The word had passed quickly, though, and most of Silium had seen the Beast of the North. Only a handful of spectators wandered by. The Rhemian guards had been replaced by a trio of stout Tarconian mercenaries. They were big brutes, as are all of the Tarconii—double the height and four times the weight of any man of the Empire. They are good fighters, but more brawn than brain, and I have no liking for their kind. One stared at me blandly as I passed—a monster with a smooth black hide spotted with white. He shook his painted horns and rattled the gold ring in his nose.

I ate little. And slept none at all. My mind did not even conjure the image of Mistress Illycia.

Sometime in the night I rose and opened the shutters and leaned over the sill and searched the dark alleyway below. I could see nothing more. Instead of stars and the branches of trees, I had only wet stone and brick to look upon. In times such as these I sorely missed my mother and my friends and cousins, and the wilds of the Eubirones. It is not an easy life, but danger and treachery come at you in familiar forms, easily recognizable for what they are. . . .

THREE

Illycia was waiting for me in the morning, outside my quarters. I was certainly more than a little surprised. In the past, it is I who have done all the seeking—playing the small games females seem to enjoy so greatly. More than that, to find her up and about before midday was a wonder in itself.

At another time I would have been pleased with this attention. This morning, though, my mind was full of headier thoughts.

"You are going to classes this morning, Aldair?" She smiled, and cocked her head pertly.

"I am a student at the University," I told her. "It would seem logical that I attend classes, Illycia."

One brow raised painfully and I was immediately sorry. "Illycia," I said, "forgive me." I reached over and touched her arm. "I did not sleep well, and I have much on my mind."

"I understand, Aldair."

"Will you walk with me, then? If it's not our of your way."

Her face brightened and her snout wrinkled a pretty pink. Then she caught herself—remembering feminine wiles. "I *do* have some small purchases to make," she said thoughtfully. "It might be I could go as far as the Market."

"Fine," I said. "I would greatly appreciate that, Illycia."

She was full of town gossip, and eager to tell me the "simply terrible" thing that had happened during the night. I pretended I had not heard this news three times before breakfast—once from the old man who ran the boarding inn, and twice from the serving girl. The latter was so taken with the event she could scarcely keep from spilling barley cakes and

24

honey on the plank tables. It had been a different story each
time, and Illycia's version contained added embellishments.
The Stygiann captive had escaped during the night. He had
killed a Rhemian soldier. He had killed two Rhemian soldiers
and wounded a Tarconian mercenary. He had eaten a child.
Devoured a whole family. Another Stygiann had climbed the
city walls to set him free. There were a dozen, twenty, a
hundred of the creatures loose in Silium.

The truth, I knew, was lurking somewhere beneath this lit-
ter, carefully hidden. Probably the wily old devil *had* actually gotten away. And if it had been necessary to silence a
guard, he would have done so without hesitation. Beyond
that, he would not have been anxious to call attention to himself. I was certain he had not taken the time to eat half the
children in Silium, or dismember a Rhemian legion.

"I think it's dreadful," said Illycia.

"What is?"

"Why, that they just let him get away like that."

"They didn't just let him get away, Illycia."

"You know what I mean."

"He escaped. And I'm not overly surprised," I told her.
"They don't know anything about Stygianns down here. If
the Rhemians would bother to take a look at the provinces
they were so eager to conquer, they'd get some idea of what
we have to deal with up there. All they want to know is
whether or not the corn and wheat crops are better than last
year. They don't have time to count dead Venicii, or learn
that Stygianns have brains in their skulls like everyone else."

"Aldair!" Illycia's eyes widened, and she glanced quickly
about her. "You mustn't *say* such things."

"Why not? They're true."

"Well—maybe. But what if someone heard . . . ?"

"Then they'd hear nothing they don't already know," I
said wearily. I urged her along through Kingsgate and into
the Market.

There was nothing to be seen at the site of the night's disturbance. Even the Stygiann's empty cage was gone. Still,
this was where it had all happened, and there was a large
crowd on hand to remind one another of this.

"It makes me shiver just to think about it," said Illycia.
She shivered convincingly against me, and twitched the end
of her snout again. That perky little appendage was one of

Illycia's most appealing features. It had almost driven me crazy when I first caught sight of her in the street. I followed her to her father's shop right then, though it was three days before I summoned the courage to speak to her. This seems ridiculous to me now, though in truth, I would probably do the same thing again.

"Aldair," she said casually, "do you—have to go to classes today?"

I caught the tone of her voice and stopped and looked at her. The small black eyes had gone suddenly liquid. There was a peculiar curve around the side of her mouth. I felt a familiar physical reaction taking place, and I could have strangled her on the spot. She'd never done *this* before—and what a morning to start! Females are always ready when a man can do nothing about it. They plan these things carefully.

"Illycia. I can't miss the lectures."

"Well . . ." She shrugged one shoulder and inspected her fingers. "If you don't want to, Aldair . . ."

"You know very well I want to. I have been waiting for—"

Her brows rose. "Yes, Aldair?"

"Nothing," I said. "Nothing at all, Illycia."

"I'm surprised you even want to go," she said, gazing at the city walls. "I mean—this morning."

"What?" I studied her carefully. "Why wouldn't I?"

"You know. After what happened yesterday. At the University."

I stopped at a shop window and turned her to face me. "So that's out, too, is it? All right. What are they saying, Illycia?"

"I haven't heard much."

"I'll bet."

"What?"

"Nothing. What have you heard?"

"Just that Master . . . Master—"

"Levitinus."

"That Master Levitinus said things against the Church."

"That's not so, Illycia."

"And—that he near thrashed a student to death, and spoke in a strange tongue!"

I sighed and shook my head. "It wasn't that way at all. It

wasn't even Master Levitinus's fault. Illycia, don't believe everything you hear. Even if it's interesting."

She gave me a pout. "Is that what you think I do?"

"No. Of course not."

"Well I don't. Aldair . . ."

"What?"

"Tell me. What really happened, I mean." She bit her lip nervously. "You were there, weren't you?"

I am slow, but I eventually understand things. This, of course, explained my sudden desirability. Illycia wanted an eyewitness account.

"I've got to be going," I told her. "I'll be late."

"Aldair—"

I peeled her hand from my arm. "You will be pleased to learn, Illycia, that I plan to call upon Master Levitinus after classes. I will offer my services, if they are needed. He will be happy to learn you and the townspeople are concerned for his welfare."

Illycia stared at me, then her pink tongue crept over her lips in a knowing grin.

"I hope you *don't* call on Master Levitinus, Aldair."

"No? Why not?"

"Don't you know? Really?"

"Illycia—"

"You're hurting me, Aldair! All right—he's been—taken by the Church. Your fine Master Levitinus is a heretic! He's *sinned* against the Creator!"

I dropped her arm and bolted across the Market.

"Aldair, listen!" she called after me. "Did you really strike Flaviun Sellenus? Then—then carve the Sign across his back? Did you?"

Damn them. Damn them all! I'd been half afraid of this, but I could not make myself believe Flaviun would really go this far. Money, then. Enough silver, it seemed, would buy St. Bellium himself and a whole legion of Good Fathers!

I stopped before the gates of the University. Now that I was there, what was I to do? Go to class? It seemed more than ludicrous to do that. With Master Levitinus languishing in a cell somewhere. The Quill? They'd know something there, for certain. But—what if I faced Flaviun again? This time, I wouldn't be able to hold back. I'd surely slip a blade

in his ribs and join Levitinus. The faculty Quarter, maybe—
"Young Scholar Aldair . . ."

I turned, startled. And froze in my boots. I knew him immediately. One of the linen-robed Fathers. I'd nearly run him down after the business with Flaviun.

"Aldair . . ." He smiled easily, and I felt the color rise to my cheeks. He'd read my fear easily enough. "Why the long face, brother?" He walked to me and stopped. "Are your young sins so grave, then?"

"We are all grave sinners, Father," I said, and heard my voice catch.

The Father chuckled. "Now don't go quoting Scripture to me, Aldair. Though the Creator knows I could profit by it."

"Father. I didn't mean—"

"No, no, of course you didn't. I'm Father Tinius, by the way."

I automatically made the sign of the circle over my chest. I'm—honored, Father."

Tinius made a face. "Well, don't be. I'm a servant of the Creator, the same as you. And a poor one at that. Have you a moment to spare me, Aldair?"

What did the Church want with me, then, I wondered, but told him, "Gladly, Father." Then: "I have classes now, though, and—"

"Yes, yes." Tinius waved that aside. "Classes will wait, won't they? The soul comes before the mind, Aldair, and this won't take overly long."

Tinius gave me a familiar wink, as if we both knew the same secret. He moved jauntily away and all I could do was follow—though I liked this business not at all. The Good Father had never said how he knew my name, and didn't need to. I knew the answer to that one. He had witnessed my encounter with Flaviun, and of course the whole thing had to do with Master Levitinus. Young Goldpockets' hand was in this somewhere, then. I'd no doubt of that.

St. Bellium's is a rockpile of gray stonework. Its high, vaulted ceilings disappear in gloomy shadow, and it is no less depressing inside than out. I had never been in the place before, though I did not volunteer this information to Father Tinius.

The little room where he led me contained a plain bench, two stools, and a slit of a window. The window was no wider than a man's palm, and only the most determined beam of sunlight could have squeezed through to brighten the room.

It was a proper setting for Father Tinius. Like too many of his kind, he appeared to have been born in the darkest corner of his Church, and never ventured further. This has always concerned me—that the Good Fathers who praise the works of the Creator seem to ever shun the brightness of His day.

He was a pale, gaunt young man, then, with thinning body hair. His snout was so narrow the veins showed plainly on its surface. In the manner of the Fathers, he kept the coarse bristles plucked from his jowls. This practice added further pallor to his features. His small, pink eyes perched like afterthoughts atop his head, and there was almost no hair at all on the flaps of his ears.

Easing himself to one of the stools, he gave me a lazy smile. "I'll not waste time, Aldair," he told me. "I've asked you here to talk about Master Scholar Levitinus. You're a bright lad, and no doubt you've guessed this already."

I didn't say yes or no. Tinius held my gaze another second. "You were present at Master Levitinus's lecture yesterday morning."

"I was, Father."

"And are you aware, Aldair, that Master Levitinus has been detained by the Church?"

I held my expression in check. "Yes, Father. I had heard this." Detained, I thought. Now there's a fine word for it.

"And what else have you heard?"

"Only," I told him plainly, "that the Master has been charged with heresy—but that was just a street rumor, Father. I don't know—"

Tinius shook his head. "A wagging tongue is ever the burden of Man." He smiled. "No, Aldair. I am sure, by now, the good townspeople have Master Levitinus burned and quartered. This is nowhere near the truth, of course. I am well aware," he added solemnly, "that some would imagine the Church forever poking under house and haystack for heretics. I assure you we have better things to do."

Tinius squinted thoughtfully and leaned toward me. "I *will* say this, young Aldair. The Fathers are mortals like every other man, and subject to the same faults. Do you understand this?"

"I—yes, Father."

"And I will say further, and not for other ears, mind you —that there are overzealous men within the Church itself who are, shall we say"—he gazed at the ceiling, then back at me—"prone to see demons where only small imps abide?" He smiled at his words. "I fear this is what has happened in the case of Master Levitinus. What we have here, in my own opinion, is an unfortunate incident blown all out of proportion. An incident between a teacher and his student. One in which, I believe, Master Levitinus is entirely blameless."

I sat up straighter at that. "Yes," Tinius nodded fervently, "I know more of this than you imagine, young Aldair. You are not the first student I have spoken with this morning— nor the last. And I assure you I am quite capable of distinguishing truth from fiction, if you catch my meaning."

"I do," I told him, "and I am much relieved, Father."

"Fine." He leaned back and folded his hands. "Now . . . it is alleged that Master Levitinus, during yesterday's class, mentioned a certain subject holy to the Church—one forbidden to discussion. Is this true?"

I hesitated at that. "Yes, Father, in a way it is, but—"

Tinius raised a hand. "I know what you're going to say, boy. Let me ask the questions, Aldair. Wait. And you will see that I fully understand the situation."

"Yes, Father."

"So. Student Scholar Flaviun Sellenus admits openly, under question, that he, too, mentioned this—certain subject. But only after Master Levitinus affirmed that the topic was within academic bounds. Is this so?"

"Father—" I didn't care for the way this was going. "Flaviun is a liar and a coward! That's only the way it *seemed* to be!"

Tinius let out a breath and frowned impatiently. "Aldair. Please?" He flattened his palms on the bench before him. "Did Master Levitinus establish—one way or the other— that this subject was within the bounds of history?"

"Yes, in a way, but—"

"All right. And did he say"—Tinius made the sign of the Circle—"quote: 'I do not give a whit about your—certain subject—or how many saints can stand on their heads on the tip of a quill,' unquote?" Tinius looked up.

What could I say? He had heard it elsewhere already, no doubt. "Yes, Father," I said wearily, "such was said."

Tinius laughed so suddenly I sat up straight on my stool. "All right, Aldair. Relax, boy. Stop looking at me like that, will you? These were questions that had to be asked. Now, the *official* part of our visit is over." He leaned back and grinned at me. "And I am most anxious to get to the part that counts, Aldair. What really happened in that classroom? As you yourself saw it." There was a mischievous gleam in his eye that hadn't shown itself before, and I had to smile myself.

"I want to hear all of it," said Tinius. "Particularly the part I witnessed myself, and thoroughly enjoyed, I don't mind saying—where you set that pompous little moneybags Flaviun Sellenus in his place!" His grin suddenly faded. "It's high time," he said darkly, "that some people learned the Creator's blessing cannot be purchased for a handful of gold!"

FOUR

There was still an hour until midday.

But I had no heart for the classroom. I'd pay dearly, of course, for skipping lectures. Old Master Pelian is not as understanding as Levitinus. He would see to it I filled copybooks until my hands went numb. He keeps a fine stack of dry and deadly tomes on his shelves for just such a need.

Wealthy students like Flaviun Sellenus, it is said, can sometimes pay a fine for their mischief. But I have too few coppers in my purse for that.

Outside the dark cavern of St. Bellium's the light seemed warmer and brighter than ever. I stood for a moment and soaked in the sun. Then, I had the sudden urge to bound down the stone steps and lose myself in the chattering throng of the Market—to dive into that sea of color and motion. There was life there, and only death in that cold pile of stone behind me.

It struck me, suddenly, that this is a most peculiar world we live in. The same thought had come to me earlier, facing Tinius. The Church would call itself the light that kindled a man's soul, the guardian of his life on Earth. But as far as I could see, there was only darkness and the chill of death in St. Bellium's. Joy, warmth, and laughter were here below me, in the Market. Where traders cheated one another for half a worn penny, and town whores sold whatever wares were not available in the stalls. How could this be? There were some questions, I decided, that could not find ready answers in either the Church or the classroom.

There was no use visiting the Quill. There'd be few students there at this hours, and none I wanted to see. I thought of walking up the hill and seeking out Illycia. She had kindled my desires this morning—then dampened them just as quickly. But that's ever the way with a man—his body betrays him at the wink of a female eye, and he is ready and eager to forgive her faults. Illycia has a wagging tongue and a less than sensitive soul. But there is ample warmth and feeling in this maiden, if one does not care to probe too deeply.

Moving away from the church, I pressed through the busy stalls, glancing idly at cheap goods and wilted vegetables. My thoughts, though, were ever behind me. Had I said the right things? Answered questions in a manner that would help Master Levitinus? I had done the best I could, I decided —for whatever that was worth. And Father Tinius was decent enough, for a Churcher. In all fairness, he *had* given me the chance to speak my mind. In truth, there are good Fathers and bad ones—just as there are honest merchants and thieves. Those who have made their way to the northern provinces are a tougher breed than the pale Fathers of Silium. They risk their lives with other men, and ask for no special favors. Those who do not care for border life soon discover urgent callings elsewhere.

A traveling puppet show had set up its tent near the center of the Market, and I paused for a moment to watch. The story was easy enough to follow. Rhemian soldiers drove terrified raiders from paper walls. Grateful townsmen, including one beautiful maiden, cheered the brave legionnaires. One of the foes, I noted, was a motheaten, rather ineffectual Stygiann—almost a cartoon character. Would that it were so. In the end, soldiers, maiden, merchant, and benevolent Father joined hands and bowed to the audience.

Perhaps, I decided, this show is a true reflection of life itself. You are ever on a string, doing someone's bidding. Churches make the people dance to their somber tune, and Masters set you to learning dreary facts you'll likely never put to use. Everyone, it seems, is both puppet and puppeteer. Even a slave can scream at a horse, or swat a fly and kick a stone.

Is no one truly free, then? Wherever you are, there is a master somewhere in the wings. No doubt this is the true order of things. If the Creator had something else in mind, he would not have made the world the way it is.

Outside the city gates, Rhemian soldiers were practicing

with the bow. Or so they thought, I noted. I sincerely hoped this troop of archers never met foes larger than a hare, and I fervently wished I could magically drop them on the edge of the Lauvectii Forest for a day. Rhemians are fine soldiers —well disciplined and unbeatable when their enemies behave in the proper manner. There is no way to stop that solid line of shield and sword when it begins to move. But they do not know one end of an arrow from the other.

I bought cakes and honey from a vendor. There was a slave auction just inside the gates, but the offerings were less than impressive—shorn, bewildered Cygnians barely strong enough to move one foot before the other.

The sun was stretching its shadows and the gray specter of St. Bellium's darkened the square. I shuddered, and moved quickly into brightness. Could you ever walk out of the Church's cold reflection? It seemed not, and I wondered if such thoughts as that truly damned a man. We are warned that there is little difference between thought and deed in the eyes of the Creator. Perhaps my soul will never return to Albion, then. If it does not, no doubt I will have plenty of company elsewhere.

When I was very young, a child barely walking, an old man lived in our home. This was when my father was alive, and later I understood that the old man was my father's father. He had little to do other than drink barley beer and talk, and he did a great deal of both. Once, I remember, he spoke of Albion. How you could see its shores on a clear day from one of the many shrines that dot the coastline. To him, he declared loudly, it looked like any other shore a man could see—and if there were any souls hopping about over there they were too small to be spotted from a distance. He did, however, believe he'd seen a blue light in the sky, or something that looked like one. Though he admitted he had seen all sorts of lights before, blue ones included, when it was a fair, warm night and the ale was as cold as it should be. I heard no more, for my father stopped the old man from talking shortly after that, and sent me to bed with my brothers and cousins.

Someday I will make the journey to the coast and see for myself what there is to see. Perhaps Flaviun Sellenus is right. The mysterious lights have not shown themselves to men for some time, and it may be that the Creator has forgiven our ancient sins. Or perhaps the opposite is true. Perhaps he does not send blue flames into the sky anymore because he is totally disgusted with the race of Man, and wants nothing more to do with us. I could understand a decision such as this.

Sound broke through my thoughts and I stopped where I was and glanced about. There was a great deal of shouting going on somewhere, and I traced the Market with my eyes until I found its source. Finally my gaze rested on St. Bellium's. An uneasy chill settled in the base of my stomach. A throng of townsmen were gathering on the church steps, clear from the streetway to the high, vaulted doors. I moved across the square, pressing through the rear of the crowd.

"What's happening?" I asked an onlooker.

He gave me an elbow and a fierce glance. "How'd *I* know? I'm as far back as you!"

"They say it's a Declaration," put in a woman beside me.

"A Declaration?" She saw my puzzlement, and said something more—but I was past her, making a way for the front. I could see the Declaration over bobbing heads. A long, yellow parchment tacked to the big doors. The chill gripped my belly again. Someone grabbed roughly at my tunic.

"You've got a nerve, Aldair!"

"What?" I turned and pushed the hand aside. I recognized the angry face—a student who'd been friendly enough in the past, and no cohort of Flaviun's.

"What's the matter with you, Dherius?" I asked him. "Stand aside. I want to see whatever's up there."

"Hah! He already *knows* what it says!" jeered another student.

"He should," growled Dherius. "He helped the Good Fathers *write* it, Amion!"

I stared from one to the other. "Dherius—"

"Dherius—" he mocked me. "Don't pretend with us, Aldair. It was a fine little act you put on with Flaviun Sellenus —but the Declaration spells the truth. It's *your* hand that's murdered Master Levitinus. *Flaviun's name doesn't even appear on that thing—only yours—Aldair of Venicii!*"

I heard them muttering oaths behind me, and I was dimly aware of other angry hands and voices. But I had eyes only for one other, now—a familiar figure posed before the high door, gaunt and solemn as St. Bellium himself. And then I was alone, past the throng and up the gray steps, my hands closing about a pale and scrawny neck. Tinius went down beneath me; hands clawed air and little eyes widened in pain and surprise. My grip tightened until fingers near met each other. The face below me turned scarlet, but I didn't let go.

Then my whole body went suddenly numb, and I heard my own voice cry out. The sky tilted. Something sharp dug a hole in my side. A soldier was down over Tinius—another kicked me soundly in the ribs again and grinned broadly.

"I *know* this one, by damn," he shouted. He pointed a finger at me and called to the crowd. "He talks to Stygianns. In their own tongue!"

The crowd howled.

"And the devil talks *back* to *him!*"

"Heretic!" someone yelled, and the crowd took it up.

"Heretic!"

"Heretic!"

Hands grabbed at my legs. I lashed out without looking and heard a satisfying grunt. I was on my feet, pain forgotten, the iron dagger in my hand. The Rhemian lashed out with his sword. I felt its wind whip past me, ducked, ran the little blade home, and pulled it free. The soldier staggered, backed away, and I turned and bounded down the stone steps. The crowd shrank before me, making a path. Fun was fun, but they wanted no part of the real thing.

Raised voices and the clang of armor were behind me, but I didn't look back. Instinctively—for a moment—I ran for my quarters. Then I stopped, moved quickly away from that direction, and took a random path down one street and then another. They'd expect me to go for familiar ground—that way was closed, and I could forget about my small bundle of possessions.

Where, then? I paused in an alley to get my breath. There was no safe place in the city. No one in Silium would give me shelter. I was in the open, with another four hours or so of daylight before me.

FIVE

Stop running, I told myself. Stop running, and *start* thinking. This is the way hares end up in stew pots—they bound aimlessly about until fear, and not the skill of the hunter, brings them to ground.

So I made myself crouch in the alleyway and picture the scene before St. Bellium's. Rhemian soldiers have a particular way of doing things. They are no better than other men, but they have order, discipline, and training. These are three important factors, and they have enabled Rhemia to conquer most of the known world. And somewhere in the Rhemian drillbook, I guessed, there was a special procedure for gathering fugitives like myself into the net. It would be an orderly and systematic procedure. Start at the square, then. Quarter the city in an ever-widening circle while the quarry flees ahead of the hunters. And finally—

Of course, as a safety measure, riders would be sent around the perimeter of the city, to make sure I didn't try for the walls. Though they would not really expect me to get that far.

I was ahead of them, and still outside the circle for the moment. If I ran, though, they would have me. And if I stayed where I was, they would take me all the sooner. They would not stop until they had methodically turned over every stone in Silium.

I came to my feet. My heart was moving at a somewhat steadier pace. That was the answer, then. There was no running before the Rhemians. Only death waited there. Life lay behind their ranks. *Inside* the circle . . .

The blue-and-red diamonds of my blouse wouldn't do at all. I might as well have lit a signal fire and shouted my posi-

tion. Turned inside out, though, the garment showed a
shabby gray lining to the world. The same, then, for the
cloak. It was darker on the inside, and could be slung over
my shoulder in a different manner. The baggy pants gathered
at the ankle were a problem. They branded me as a norther-
ner to every child in Silium. Take off the pants, then—wrap
them around the waist and the result is not unlike the knee-
length Silium skirt. Not too bad, and I decided the extra
bulk made me look shorter and fatter.

The Sygiann boots? Best to bury them in the alley. There
wasn't another pair in Silium. Only, I couldn't do that. A
man has to hold on to his honor, or what's the use in living?
I had killed the Stygiann myself when I was barely fourteen.
The raiders broke through the men on the walls and came
for the houses, and I was there with five younger brothers
and cousins. I took the creature with an arrow through the
chest as he stood in the doorway and thought about all the
tender meat before him.

They were blood-boots, then. First kill. And I wore the
arrowhead that had done the job hanging from a red-and-
blue tassel on the right boot. No, the boots would not be
discarded in this southern dungheap.

They ended up hung about my shoulders, under my arms.
Then I took off one stocking and stuffed it under my belt.
Going about barefooted was conspicuous—but one foot bare
was something else. Or so I hoped. Thus, I picked up a piece
of kindling for a cane, to ease my newly "crippled" foot.
And if I didn't look much like a Silium native, I decided I
did not look a great deal like Aldair of the Venicii, either.

With a last, quick inspection, I walked out of the alleyway
and into the street, toward the circle of Rhemian soldiers.

I cannot recall a longer day.

By the Creator, was the sun against me, too? I am certain
it remained in the heavens an extra hour or so. By then, I
had crossed the Market a thousand times and peered into
every stall and shop until I knew the goods as well as the
owners. And I was certain, every moment, I'd walk into
Flaviun Sellenus or someone else from the town or University
who knew me.

By nightfall, it was not necessary to pretend the role of a

cripple. The strain on one leg had brought the role painfully close to reality.

There were no truly *good* places to hide. I settled on the low roof of a bakery just off the square. The gate was in view, and I could watch the Rhemians' progress, and make a guess at what they might be about. Clearly, they were less than enthused about this project, now. The night could be better spent in drinking and whoring. There was no glory in poking torches down holes and stumbling through musty cellars. The Church wanted this Aldair. Let them spend *their* off hours looking for him, then. Certainly, though, I did not delude myself. The search had slackened, but it had not come to an end. Rhemians do not take kindly to civilians who stick daggers into their bellies.

I watched the gate. And tried to ignore the warm aroma of fresh bread from below. When the stars turned over in the sky and the warder called the third hour, I dropped from the roof and followed shadows across the square until I was under the wall, far from the city gate. It was an old wall, patched and mended over the centuries, and there were footholes aplenty between the stones. It was a wall that would keep out an enemy if it was fully manned with warriors and weapons. But it was too long to guard every foot of such a structure in peacetime.

I crossed open fields until I came to a tangled copse of whitethorn. There I dropped to the ground and pulled my cloak about me. I looked once at the far yellow lights of Silium, and the low campfires of the Rhemians outside the walls. I would not miss that city, and no one would greatly feel my absence. The innkeeper would fill my room quickly and overcharge some other poor fellow. Illycia would find another lout like myself—a fellow more than happy to fondle the twin rows of soft nipples on her rosy belly. And perhaps one day she'd tease some lad beyond his patience, and he'd uncover the curly pink tail and other delights I'd dreamed about. Then, if I knew Illycia, her father would quickly have another daughter off his hands.

I would miss Master Levitinus. And, sir, I promised him silently, I shall not forget you. No doubt, your head is perched on a pole above St. Bellium's by now—but I vow that if it is in my power, I shall return to Silium one day and match it with two more. . . .

I sat under the wide boughs of a big oak and let the morning sun warm my face. A small freshlet chattered at my feet. Past the stream, and the stand of elm beyond, lay the farm and the thatched cottage where I had stolen the stale loaf of bread from the kitchen and the still-warm potato from a dying hearth.

I never stole much. I know better than most that food is sometimes hard to come by. Also, I did not wish to leave a trail for the soldiers to follow.

I had taken sparingly, then, on my three-day trek from Silium. Until this morning, that is. For when I had taken the bread and the potato from the farmhouse I had also taken a hunter's bow and a quiver of arrows. The food might not be missed, but the weapon surely would be. I could only reason that my life might depend upon this treasure, whereas the farmer could survive without it. The coins I left in its place were more than I could spare, but they would cover the cost of the bow. This payment might or might not, seal the fellow's mouth. Of course, I would have to assume that it wouldn't. So I bolted down the bread and stuck the rest of the potato in my belt, and followed the stream away from the house and the farm.

In a day, the stream widened and emptied into a river. It was a blue lazy river that mirrored the sky. Willows grew up to its banks and leaned dizzily into the water. In less than an hour I saw nine trading sailers pass—all but two moving downstream.

The river and the boats made up my mind for me. Though I knew little about this part of the country, I was aware, certainly, that I was walking westward, toward the coast. That direction had been incidental at the time. Now, I decided, it was a deliberate goal.

The night before I arrived at the river I took a dangerous —but necessary—risk. I stopped at an inn well off the main way, and bought a cup of wine and purchased writing paper. I then set down the story of what had transpired in Silium, and asked my mother's forgiveness for bringing shame upon her. I posted the letter with the innkeeper and paid extra for the promise that his boy would take it to the nearest village by morning. I was certain the letter would reach the north in less than a week, for the Rhemians run an efficient postal service. And I did not think they would cause my family any trouble on my account. There are advantages to living in the provinces. Gaullia, the Eubirones, and Trientius have been a part of the Empire for more than a hundred years, but Rhemia has given no more than lip service to these lands. Her legions have problems closer to home. The terrible Nicieans are ever a threat, though for the most part they stick to their own shore of the Southern Sea. There are always troubles within the borders of Rhemia itself, with one great lord plotting against the other, and there are a hundred other sore spots to plague the Empire. They can barely keep the Bataavi in check, or the Vikonen sea raiders—and both these peoples are much farther north than the Venicii.

So if the Rhemians offer little aid, they present few problems, either. Eventually, a rider going in that direction will ask the whereabouts of one Aldair. But no legions will march to the north. If they did, they would wish they had considered another direction. The Venicii take care of their own. A full-scale rebellion over one errant boy is hardly worth the trouble.

I dozed for a while, the hot sun warming me to sleep. I lay on my back on the last of a long train of barges coasting lazily toward the sea. The cargo was mostly timber and pottery, and the crescent-sailed boat leading its charges was too far ahead to notice whether a nonpaying passenger was aboard.

When the sun was near to setting the barges were pulled in close to shore and the sailing vessel went about its business. Evidently, I decided, someone else would take over the task of unloading cargo, probably in the morning.

I noted the river widened considerably ahead, and remembering my geography guessed the sea was not far away. I imagined I could smell salt in the air—as I had heard you could do this—but this may have been only in my mind.

When it was fully dark I jumped ashore and walked along the bank of the river. There were lights ahead which might be boats in a harbor. That meant a town, too—and it wouldn't be as easy to steal food there. More than that, there is no town or village in the Empire that does not have several Rhemian soldiers about.

Hungry or not, then, I decided to wait until the town slept. There were many small boats tied to the bank, bobbing in a gentle swell. I chose one, and stretched out on its small deck, hidden from the shore. Cold stars lit the sky.

And after a meal and a night's sleep—then what? I had no idea where I was, really. I only knew that the sea was nearby. I wondered. Could I see Albion from here? There was a spot along the coast where the Dark Island was only a few leagues away. Perhaps this was the very village my grandfather had visited.

I looked at the stars once, then closed my eyes. And if I could see Albion—what would I see? The souls of the dead? Grandfather said it was too far for that. Blue lights in the sky? No. There were no blue lights anymore.

I opened my eyes, certain I hadn't dozed more than a minute or so. I started to sit up, then froze. Something was moving along the shore. Two shapes. Three. Flowing from one dark patch to the next, part of the night itself; and nothing in the world moved like that except—*Stygianns!* "Creator's Eyes," I moaned, and clutched the hilt of my dagger—what was a Stygiann doing on the far western shore of Gaullia!

SIX

I moved only a fraction. Noiselessly. Just to bring my legs beneath me. It was enough, though. A black form was on me, incredibly fast, before my hand could pull the dagger from my belt. Hot breath burned me and red eyes looked into mine. A long blade flashed in starlight, plunged for my chest.

"Khairi—*hold!*"

The blade paused.

"Hold? Hold? What *for?*"

I tried to move. A strong arm absently drove my shoulders back to the deck.

A second form loomed beside the first. "Ah, I thought as much. I know this one, brother."

The first Stygiann glared, tightened his grip on my throat. "You'll know it some better, Rheif, when it's properly carved and spitted."

"No." The other stared down at me. Night eyes over a gray muzzle. Ghost-white teeth. "It's bad luck to eat someone you've talked with, Khairi."

"Then don't talk to it," Khairi grunted.

The one called Rheif bent down on his haunches. "Well, little warrior. We meet again."

"You look some different, Stygiann," I said. "You were a finer sight with bars about you."

Rheif laughed softly. "I found it hard to move about properly in iron. My brothers found a softer cloak for me."

"Rheif," Khairi pleaded, "stop talking to it so I can cut its throat. We've no time for this."

"No." Rheif shook his head, his red eyes on me. "This one came to me in a dream, brother. I'd know why."

"Everyone dreams about food," Khairi shrugged. "What of it?"

"This was not a food dream."

"It is *char'desh*. That is the only way it could figure in a true dream."

"Maybe. But perhaps it was a god-dream."

Khairi looked at me in astonishment, then at Rheif. "About *that?*"

"Khairi. Go watch with Whoris."

"We haven't time. . . ."

"Khairi."

Khairi growled to himself. "What about this?"

"Let him go. Do you doubt I can take care of him by myself?"

Khairi looked appalled. "Him? You call it *him?*"

"Go, brother. I will not be long."

Khairi shook his furry head and released his grip, then muttered to himself and slipped past Rheif to the shore.

I sat up and rubbed my neck.

"I trust you'll keep your hand from that splinter of iron, which I suppose is a weapon of some sort," said the Stygiann.

"I am not in a fighting mood at the moment," I assured him. "You are perfectly safe."

The Stygiann raised a brow. "I'm pleased to hear that. I greatly feared my life was in danger."

He looked out over the dark waters, then back to me. "What are you doing here, Venicii? I find it most strange to come upon you again."

"And I find it stranger still to see you. This is not the road to the forests of Lauvectii."

"It does not lead to the Eubirones, either." He left the question hanging.

I saw no reason not to answer. Eventually they would kill me anyway. I was as surprised as the one called Khairi that this one wished to talk—though perhaps I should not have been. Why was a second encounter between us any more unlikely than the first?

"I left the walls of Silium rather hurriedly," I told him. "It is hard to say whether those good people would treasure your skin more than mine."

The Stygiann looked at me quizzically, and I told him briefly what had happened, hitting the high points of my troubles. It is sometimes difficult to read the expressions of these creatures—finally, though, when I was finished, he chuckled lightly to himself.

"We are both among the hunted, then," he mused, "neither of us anxious to meet Rhemian soldiers."

"So it would seem."

"What were you doing on this boat, Venicii? Did you plan to steal it?"

"I had no such thought in mind," I told him. "I was sleeping. Too soundly, it seems. I had planned to wait for the late hours, then look for food in town."

"And then?"

"A fugitive is not the same as an ordinary traveler, Stygiann. As you must know by now. He is seldom sure where he will be tomorrow."

"True enough," he agreed. He scratched his muzzle and looked at me thoughtfully. "Venicii. Could you make this boat move properly if you wished to? Do you know of such things?"

His question startled me somewhat. "Could *I*? Why?"

He let out a breath. "Must I remind you that I am doing the asking and you the answering?"

"I know nothing about boats. I have crossed small rivers in the North when I had to. This is a different kind of boat, however. It has fabrics to catch the wind, and that is a skill that must be learned like any other. I suppose I *could* learn it if I wished. The Venicii can do anything they set their minds to. However, I have neither the time nor the desire to learn boatsmanship."

The Stygiann looked past me and sniffed the air. "Perhaps not," he said. "I do, though. . . ."

I stared at him a moment. "You? Why?"

"Because I have no wish to be skinned. It is as simple as that." His red eyes bore into mine. "There are Rhemians about, Venicii. A great many of them. Unfortunately, we have caused a slight disturbance in the area. They know we are somewhere about. They have not looked for us here because they believe Stygianns fear the water."

"Don't they?"

"Yes, They do. Though it is less a fear than a strangeness. But no stranger, I think, than becoming a pelt. I am hoping the Rhemians will not imagine a Stygiann would take to the river."

"I shook my head at that. "I would not believe it myself."

"Good." The Stygiann grinned broadly. "Then it is done. And you will come with us, Venicii."

"What!" I sat up straight. "Why?"

"Because I might find you useful." He looked at me with amusement. "Would you rather die here, then? At once? Khairi would happily take care of this for you."

"I am in no great hurry," I told him. I looked him straight in the eye. "Though I have no doubt you will kill me sooner or later."

"Well," he said cheerfully, "later is always better than sooner, is it not?"

"Rheif, I do not like this," Whoris grumbled. "It is not a natural place."

"Be still, brother," Rheif said softly. "Your voice moves quickly over the waters. There are no trees or hills to stop it."

"And none to hide behind, in case one is seen," Whoris added.

"Or to cling to, in case the water should wash in upon us. Which, no doubt, it will," said Khairi.

Rheif didn't answer. He sat aft of the two, who were at the oars on either side of the boat. I was behind him, working the small tiller.

It was the first time anyone had spoken for more than a quarter hour. None of us had dared do more than breathe as we passed the town, which Rheif said he had overheard the soldiers call Erdantii. This bit of information confirmed something I had already guessed. That Rheif spoke Rhemian as well as I did. His captors, certainly, had not known this. He was not an ordinary Stygiann, for sure.

The lights of the town were safely behind now, but there was no time to rest easy. Torches moved along both shores, and occasionally the clang of armor and a shouted command rang out over the waters. We had not been forgotten.

There were clouds in the south and west. So far, the moon had been good enough to stay behind them. I was in great hope this situation would continue. There were enough foes against us, without adding the elements to their ranks.

"This is slave work," Khairi grumbled. "Let the *char'desh* row, if you wish rowing done, Rheif. It is more suited to such labors."

"*It,* as you say, is busy," Rheif explained patiently. "It is working the guiding thing behind the boat, so that we may remain in the middle of the river."

"You had no business bringing it along," Khairi complained. "This is not a seemly thing. Did you see those boots? *I* know the Venicii, too—and not through conversation, either. Those boots may be my brother's hide! Or a cousin, at least."

"And you, Khairi, may have roasted this one's uncle in the Lauvectii," Rheif sighed. "So you are even. Shut up, please, and row."

"Stygiann," I said, "I know this may be of no concern to you, since you are much at home on the water, but have you noted that we are getting further and further from both shores? That the water is no longer as calm as it was?"

Rheif turned and looked at me without concern. "So? Is this important?"

"Taste the water over the side," I told him.

"Why?"

"Just taste it."

Rheif did. He spat and looked sourly at me. "It is somewhat salty."

"Yes. It is somewhat salty because we are moving *out* of the river. That's why the shore is farther away, and the waves are higher. The river is emptying into the sea."

"The *sea?*" Khairi moaned and shook his head.

"Quiet," said Rheif. He turned and gave me a sober look. "Venicii, I do not wish to take the boat to the sea."

I laughed. "Where did you think the river went, Stygiann?"

"I knew there was a sea somewhere, of course," he said thoughtfully. "I did not realize it was quite so near." He searched the shoreline with night eyes. "There has been no sign of the Rhemians lately. No torches or foolish shouting to show us where they are. Make the boat go closer to the shore. To the right, I think. If we have to sail in the sea for a while, we will. But we will always know where we are, and we can land wherever we wish."

I shook my head. "Rowing in the river is one thing," I explained. "The sea, as I understand it, is something else. Your brothers are already pulling harder. When we reach the sea, they may not be able to keep us moving in the proper direction."

Rheif raised his muzzle and sniffed. "There is a wind coming up. No doubt it will be stronger when we reach the sea. Then, Venicii, you can put the thing of cloth atop the pole and catch breezes in it, and Khairi and Whoris will not have to row." He spread his hands and gave me a patient smile. If you have any more foolish problems, it said, let me know and I will solve them quickly.

This was nothing but nonsense, of course. But there is no profit in arguing with a Stygiann.

I turned the tiller and brought the boat closer to the shore. This made the rowing somewhat easier for the two Stygianns, but not a great deal. Whoris kept mostly to himself, but Khairi grumbled continually. No one in the Eubirones would believe this, I told myself. My mother and my brothers and my cousins are asleep in their beds in the north. Each, no doubt, believes young Aldair is at his studies in Silium. Instead, he has attacked a Father of the Church, stabbed and perhaps killed a Rhemian soldier on the steps of St. Bellium's, is wanted across the land for assault and heresy—and now guides a boatload of Stygiann warriors out to sea. Most probably, I decided, this is not what my poor father planned for his son.

"That's close enough," Rheif whispered. "It is as dark as the woods of the Lauvectii out there." He grinned. "I can barely see the shoreline, which means they can see nothing at all, as they do not have the eyes of a Stygiann."

In another few moments, though, the sea rushed in with a vengeance to fill the river, and I had to move closer still, or Khairi and Whoris would not have been able to row at all. Now a great promontory loomed ahead of us in the darkness—a broad finger of stone stretching halfway across the river. And for the first time we saw the white-tipped waves of the sea, rolling in to beat against the land.

"Well, that's something I never thought I'd see," Rheif announced.

I gave him a wary look. "Now what, *Captain?*"

Rheif grinned. "Now, I think, you must catch the breezes for us. While I still have two live warriors aboard."

As I have said, a Stygiann hears only what he cares to hear. "I told you I know nothing of that art," I explained.

"You will learn," he said darkly. "And quickly. You also told me the Venicii can do anything they set their minds to."

"Rheif," Khairi broke in. "I do not feel right. There is something *wrong*."

Rheif scowled at him. "You do not like the sea, brother. I do not like it either. We will keep to it a while longer, though. And when we go ashore north of here, the Rhemians will no longer know where we are."

"No." Khairi turned and shook his head adamently. "It is *not* the sea, Rheif. It is something else." His nostrils flared and his pointed ears lay flat against his skull. "There is something wrong. You know that I feel these things. . . ."

"Khairi—"

"Rheif, look!" Whoris half rose and pointed.

I saw nothing at all, but Rheif suddenly cursed. "To the oars, quickly—row as fast as you can!"

"There's no way to go faster," Khairi moaned, "if there were—"

Something whistled through the air. Khairi grunted, and I saw a quick flash of silver as the long javelin passed completely through the Stygiann's body. He touched his chest, looked surprised, then dropped lazily over the side and was gone.

Shouts rose across the mouth of the river, and the moon chose that moment to sweep the clouds aside. I turned and saw the two long, high-prowed boats almost upon us, their oars churning the water white.

SEVEN

"Tarconii!" Rheif growled, and bounded over the small cabin to take Khairi's place at the oars. I saw that he was right. There was no mistaking the bulky silhouettes of the big mercenaries. Moonlight made cold patterns on their armor, and glinted off the tips of their horns and the sharp points of their weapons.

"It was a lucky throw that took poor Khairi," Rheif shouted over his shoulder. "They're not *that* good!"

"They're good enough," I said, but Rheif didn't hear. The Tarconii howled, beat their shields, and plunged closer. I ducked as another missile whispered overhead.

"We'll never outpace them in this sea turtle," I told the Stygiann. "That's for certain."

"Then we'll die making a try at it," snapped Rheif. "We— here, what are you about, Venicii?"

I caught his startled expression and laughed aloud. I had dropped to the bottom of the boat and searched out my bow and quiver. "If this was for you, friend, you'd know it by now. I could have put an arrow in your back ten times over in the last minute or so! As it is, there's a greater need, I'm sorry to say."

I nocked an arrow and tested the bow. Another javelin shivered into the water only scant yards from Whoris's oar.

"Can you hit anything with that toy?" Rheif asked soberly.

"How do you think I got the boots, Stygiann?"

"You push me too far, Venicii," he grumbled.

"And you push little enough. Row! Or they'll have us!" I sighted down the arrow, raised it a hair for distance, and the taut string hummed.

50

A short cry rose from the nearest longboat. A big shadow flailed the air, dropped over the side.

"By the wood gods!" Rheif stared over his shoulder in amazement, his big muzzle hung open. "I'd never have believed it!"

"It is not necessary that you believe or disbelieve," I said shortly. "It is the Tarconii we must convince." I set another arrow. The first boat had stopped short, forty yards or so away. The Tarconii were jabbering to one another in the bow, where my first shot had gone home. Clearly, they were without supervision, and this was a fair break for us. If a Rhemian had been along to guide their actions, they would never have slowed their pace—even if half their number had been felled by arrows.

I carefully loosed another shaft in their midst, and heard it hit wood, inches shy of the mark. Nevertheless, the Tarconii thought it was close enough, for they ducked their heads under the high bow. I tried again and heard the arrow sing off armor.

"Get the rowers if you can," said Rheif, breathing hard. "They're the ones who'll kill us with that pace of theirs!"

I shook my head. "There are about six to a boat, three on either side, a man at the back to steer, and but two in the bow to toss missiles." I aimed, watched the arrow flash over the water in a high arc. A Tarconii dropped his weapon and tumbled back into the boat.

I laughed in the wind. "See, Stygiann? Now a rower has to take the fellow's place, and likely he's not as eager now to give up his oar!"

The second boat pulled alongside the first. Two warriors launched missiles at once. The first went long, into the sea. The second crashed with a great shudder into the little cabin between myself and the Stygianns. Wood splintered, shaking the boat, and I prayed it hadn't plunged deep enough to pierce the hull below. I quickly loosed two arrows. Neither hit the mark, but they discouraged the mercenaries for a moment.

The headland was just behind us now, and the high swells tossed us about like a wood chip. Rheif and Whoris were losing three lengths for every one they made. I measured the distance between our own craft and the Tarconii. The sleek, narrow boats seemed little affected by the high seas. I had seen such craft before—they were not of Rhemian origin, or Tarconii. The design was adapted from the Vikonen of the far north, who were said to be the best sailors in the world —equal, even, to the Nicieans of the Southern Sea. And now the boats were eating up the yards steadily, gaining on us with every stroke of the oar.

"Things seem . . . terribly quiet . . . back there," breathed Rheif.

"They've learned a lesson," I told him. "The warriors are staying low and keeping an eye on us. They are letting the oarsmen work for them now. Tarconii are slow-witted, Stygiann—but they've found the answer nevertheless. Simply wait until they're right on top of us before they expose themselves. And that'll be the end of that."

Rheif didn't answer, and I listened for a moment to the Stygiann's strained breathing, and the pitiful wash of our oars against a powerful sea. We could never hope to outdistance them now. In another moment or so . . .

"You've arrows left, Venicii?"

"Four."

"Make them count, then, when the time comes."

"I'll do that, Stygiann."

"What an . . . end for me." Rheif sighed. "To labor upon the . . . sea . . . like a slave, while a Venicii plucks Tarconii off my hide. It is not the warrior's dying I'd imagined. . . ."

"Stop your death-song and row," I told him. "You're not cold in the grave as yet."

Rheif gave a hollow laugh. "You are . . . as great a fool as you are a . . . fine archer, Venicii. What are you called? You spoke your name once in Silium, but . . . I have forgotten."

"Aldair."

"I see. A peculiar name, but not among your own, I suppose. You understand that I cannot . . . speak it aloud. To do so, and call the name of an enemy, would not be seemly."

The Tarconii were no more than two boat lengths away. I could hear the creak of timber and the grunting of oarsmen. It annoyed and angered me that they seemed in no hurry now. They were merely playing with us, until the time was ripe.

"You will not be disgraced for long," I told him soberly, and loosed an arrow at a curious Tarconii. The shaft buried itself in the high prow.

"Can't you pull faster?" I asked.

"It is not as difficult as . . . it was," said Rheif, "for some reason. The higher sea seems closest to the shore. But we do not race across the waves, Venicii, if that's what you mean."

"I'm sure you are doing the best you can," I told him, and turned back to watch the Tarconii.

"Venicii!" Rheif cried, "I told you our time was near! *The sea-gods have decided not to wait for the Tarconii!*"

I turned, and my heart stopped for a moment, then took up its work again. The Stygiann was right. A great cold-white cloud was roiling in upon us from the sea—a silent death-mist sending gray tendrils out before it.

Rheif rested on his oars and started his death-song. The eerie sound brought me back to my senses. "Row!" I shouted. I leaned forward and pounded on the Stygiann. "Damn you, don't stop now!"

"There is little use in defying the gods," said Rheif. Whoris had stopped, too. He stared woodenly ahead and waited for death.

Behind us, the Tarconii came to life. Javelins sang about the boat once more. Rheif jerked up with a start and ploughed water with his oar.

"Straight into it," I told him. "Get there, and we're home, Stygiann."

"Home with our fathers is what you mean. . . ."

"*That* thing has nothing to do with the gods," I said. "It's no more than a mist—the same as fills the forest hollow, or clings to fever water. It hides the hare, friend, and it'll do the same for us!"

I loosed an arrow. Then another. One found its mark, and I had the satisfaction of seeing a big Tarconii with gold-scaled chest armor stare down at me a moment, then fall into the sea, a shaft buried deeply under one eye.

The mist curled long fingers out to greet us, then swallowed us in its chill maw. Cold droplets clung to my face. Rheif changed our course silently as soon as we were out of sight, and I moved the tiller and took us at a wide angle to the right.

I kept my last arrow nocked in a loose bow. Rheif and Whoris rested on their oars, and we all sat in silence and listened.

It was a strange feeling. Like floating in a great cloud

above the Earth. There was neither sound nor sight here. Nothing. Only the cold breath of the fog that wrapped heavy gray fingers about us.

Finally, the Stygiann reached out and touched me lightly and pointed. I watched, and saw a dark prow slice through the whiteness without a sound. A ghost ship with shadow crew. It was there, then it was gone. I let out a breath. It was so close, I could have near touched it with a northern bow. In seconds, the other boat followed, this one further away, and nearly invisible.

"It might be well to move us farther to the north," I whispered. "But quietly. They'll likely quarter back—and more than that, if we let ourselves drift like this, the sea'll put us back to shore."

Rheif nodded. He turned to touch Whoris, and in a moment turned solemnly back to face me. "Whoris is gone," he announced. "There is blood on his oar, and the bench is soaked with it. It is a great deal of blood, Venicii. He took a missile and rowed as long as he could, and said nothing to me."

"He was born a warrior," I said, "and died laughing at his enemies." It is an old Venicii prayer, and though Rheif didn't know this, he sensed honor in it. He stared at me a long moment. "I thank you for that," he said finally. "I think there would be no shame if I called you by name now. For though it has always been so with us, it is hard to see you as an enemy. Come, Aldair of the Venicii. You will have to get good Stygiann blood on your hands now, for there is rowing to be done. . . ."

After half a night on the water, I realized it was hopeless to even guess where we might be. There is no way to gain a sense of direction in the midst of nothing. It is impossible to keep track of the countless twists and turns and the subtle currents that move one about. We might have been leagues out to sea, or a dozen yards from shore.

"It does not matter greatly where we are for the moment," Rheif said quietly. "We cannot be seen, and we can hope for no more than that. However, the mist lifts from the forest in the morning, and likely it leaves the sea as well. I trust the sun-father leaves us in a seemly place when he strips the waters bare. . . ."

We took turns at watch, though by the early hours we both admitted that neither of us had been able to sleep.

"Rheif," I said finally, "the fog has a brightness to it."

He nodded. "The sun has touched it, then." He sniffed the air and the end of his muzzle twitched. "There's a breeze. Or the beginning of one." He snapped a thread from his cloak and let it fall. It drifted to the bottom of the boat at a slight angle. "Not much," Rheif grunted. "But it should rise soon." He looked at me then, and our eyes met in silent agreement. We had not heard the Tarconii during the long night, but that did not mean they were not nearby. When the fog lifted, we would be no better off than the night before if they were still about. We had not been able to outrow the narrow longships then, and we would do no better now.

I busied myself as quietly as possible with the unfamiliar ropes and fabric of the sailing gear. Rheif watched me. "It has been a long night," he said. "I can't remember one longer."

"The day may be somewhat shorter," I said, "unless we instantly master the art of sailing. There will be little time to practice our skills."

Rheif grinned tiredly and looked over my shoulder as I tried to puzzle out a tangle of rope that appeared to be important but, as far as I could see, belonged nowhere in particular.

"We need a pennant, Aldair," Rheif said solemnly. "It would not be proper to set forth without one."

I didn't look up from my work. "Your pelt should do nicely," I said. "It would catch the breeze and flutter prettily."

"Don't joke about such things," Rheif said nervously. "The Tarconii may hear you."

"They've already considered the idea, I'm certain."

"Hmmmph. It'll be a fair sight," he said. "My hide flapping in the breeze, and your fine pink head perched above the mast. We'll—"

I stopped him. The fog was quickly burning itself away. A small patch of slate-green water appeared. Then another.

"Never mind the silence now," I said. "Help me get this bloody thing together. I've saved the noisiest part for last."

Still, I bit the end of my tongue when Rheif pulled the

ropes as he had been instructed and the little brass rings squeaked loudly against the mast and raised the sail high.

"It doesn't look like much," he said glumly. "It just—sits there."

"It won't," I assured him. "There's a wind coming."

The fog was drifting swiftly away now, and there were more patches of green water, and a growing brightness. I took my place at the rear of the boat, and tried to pretend I knew what I was doing. Suddenly, a veil of mist parted and thrust us into full sunlight.

"There they are!" Rheif cried. I squinted into the light and spotted the two Tarconii vessels. They were several hundreds yards to the south, close together. They saw us, and beat upon their shields and cheered each other loudly.

"Aldair," Rheif said solemnly, "do something."

"I'm trying." The gray cloth hung listlessly, like so much wash on a line. There was a breeze of sorts, but the sail made no attempt to catch it.

The Tarconii set their oars and churned water.

"I don't understand this," I said.

"Maybe you're not doing it right."

"No doubt," I said shortly, "since we are not moving. Would you care to try your hand?"

"No thank you," said Rheif. "The Stygianns know nothing of this art."

"The Venicii, of coure, are born to the water," I said darkly. "I don't understand . . ."

I looked, and my stomach tied itself in a knot. The Tarconii had already halved the distance between us.

"Do you suppose we should row?" Rheif suggested.

"There's no use in it."

"Then we spent a long night for nothing."

A few missiles fell twenty yards short of our bow.

"You have one arrow?"

"Yes."

"That will not be adequate," Rheif announced.

I looked at him and shook my head. Foam shattered against the sides of the longboats. The Tarconii sped through green water, and our sail hung listlessly. I dropped the guide ropes and picked up my bow. This is the way it ends, then, I thought. As good a way as any, perhaps. Beside me, the Stygiann had pulled a long, ugly blade from his belt. I nocked my last arrow, and waited. Then the Tarconii stopped beating their shields. The longboats slowed, then rested in the water.

I looked questioningly at Rheif. He looked at me and shrugged.

There were no more cheers from across the water. The helmsmen were turning the boats, and Tarconii oars were churning water, each vessel seemingly racing the other to get under way.

"There is something peculiar in this," said Rheif. "It's hard to believe the two of us struck fear in their hearts."

"Something did," I said. Like Rheif, I was more than bewildered by the Tarconii retreat. I looked away from the boats and glanced up at our sail. It still hung there, doing nothing—though some wind was billowing the fabric now. I looked past the sail, at the low fog bank, far to our right. The sun had nearly burned it from the sea, and—

I stared, and gripped the mast. A cold chill struck the base of my spine. The mist lifted, vanished before my eyes. No one had to tell me what it was. Gray cliffs topped with dark and somber foliage. The morning sun was shining brightly, but no light seemed to touch those shores. Albion, for certain. And no more than a league or so away . . .

EIGHT

"There is your answer, then," I said, unable to take my eyes from that cheerless sight. "The Tarconii have abandoned us because they do not wish to offend the dead."

Rheif studied the dark island. "I have heard of this Albion. It does not appear to be a pleasant place at all—though I have no fear of it, as you do."

I turned to face him. "It is no disgrace to fear Albion, Rheif. It isn't the same as fear in battle, and there is no loss of honor in it. Besides, you would do well not to flaunt the Creator so near to his kingdom. No doubt he has a keen sense of hearing."

Rheif frowned and picked at the thick gray matting on his chest. "Aldair," he said finally, "I mean no disrespect, but this is the island of *your* dead—not mine."

"What?" I stared at him. "What are you talking about?"

"Simply"—Rheif sniffed—"that it is most unlikely that there are Stygiann souls on that shore."

Stygianns can be most irritating at times. Without even considering all their other obvious faults, it is no wonder they are blood enemies of the Eubirones.

"You are quite right, Rheif," I said shortly. "Stygianns are heathen, and therefore barred from Albion. Some say the Creator is more merciful, and occasionally allows a special heathen to cross his shores. Not many believe this, though— it is an unpopular opinion. I certainly do not hold with it myself!"

Rheif laughed and showed his teeth. "I am not speaking of being *barred* from anything, Aldair. Merely that Stygiann dead would not be cavorting about on the same island with *char'desh*. It would be unseemly."

I felt my face go hot at that. I knew the word, of course. Rheif's friend Khairi had used it often the day before. It is not a translation of my race, or of Venicii, or anything of the sort. It means simply *meat*.

"I see you are offended," Rheif sighed. He spread his long arms. "There is no need to be."

"No. You would not think so."

"And what I said is only logical, Aldair."

"It is nothing of the sort. There is *one* Creator. He is responsible for making all creatures."

"Then he made Stygianns, too?"

"Of course."

"Then why does he bar them from Albion?"

"What?" I looked up at him.

"I said—"

"I heard what you said. And there is a simple, *logical* answer. The Stygianns are heathen. They are not sons of the Church."

"But if we were sons of the Church, our souls would go to Albion?"

"Yes."

Rheif grinned and shook his head. "Aldair. Tell me the truth. What do you think those Good Fathers of yours would do if I walked into that fine church in Silium, which I could see from my cage, and said I did not wish to be a 'heathen' any longer? That I wished to join the others who come there of a morning? And suppose I brought a hundred or so warriors, females, and pups along with me?"

I stared at Rheif, much taken aback by his words. A Stygiann horde in St. Bellium's? It was an appalling thought, at best. And more than ludicrous. Everyone knew Stygianns had no desire to join the Church. Still, I could see what Rheif was trying to do. He had taken my words and twisted them about—Stygianns are good at this. Because I had told him the Creator made all things, he would argue that *all* souls could enter Albion equally. A fine argument, if it were not for the fact that it is clear all souls do not have the same value to the Creator. This is the same premise that put Master Theon in danger of losing his snout. I decided to pursue this no further. It makes little sense to argue religion with a Stygiann, who knows nothing of such matters. Clearly, I am not in agreement with all of the Church's teachings, but there are basic truths even the Good Fathers and an accused heretic can agree upon.

"Never mind pondering the matter." Rheif sighed. "I have no intention of marching upon Silium to meet your Creator."

"I will think upon this," I promised him, though I had no such thing in mind.

"There is no need," he assured me. "Stygianns and—your people would not get along, even if they were dead. They would fight continuously, just as they do now."

"No. There is no fighting in Albion."

Rheif twisted his muzzle and raised a red eye. "None? Then what do people do?"

"There are other things to do besides fighting."

Rheif glanced warily at Albion. "Not for Stygianns, there aren't."

"There is rowing," I suggested.

"That is not amusing," Rheif said darkly.

"Perhaps the Creator furnishes small boats—"

Rheif gave me a look of disgust and turned away.

For a while, heavy seas swept us alarmingly close to Albion's shores. Rheif paid no heed to this, but sunned himself on the roof of the small cabin and dozed. I did not take kindly to his attitude. Rheif, though, said there was nothing *he* could do—that if my Creator wished to dash us upon the sharp stones of his island, he would do so. In spite of anything either of us could do to the contrary.

He was right in one respect. Rowing was completely useless in such waters. The currents were capricious and uncaring of our fate, and pulled us one way and then another without reason. So it was up to me to struggle with the puzzling array of ropes and fabrics, and master the art of sailing before Albion claimed us, or an errant wave foundered us and sent us below.

I was more than uncomfortable in the shadow of that dark island, and anxious to be away. Sometimes I felt I could hear the souls of the dead moan upon the wind. Still, the business of sailing eluded me. I could not imagine why the craft's equipment should be put together in such a manner. The wind blew in one direction at a time. Suppose one did not wish to go in that particular direction? Did he simply go there anyway? Or wait until a favorable wind arose to take him to his destination? Clearly, this could not be, I decided. Few people would bother with such a troublesome art. Obviously, I was doing something wrong.

Once, through some combination of my actions, the big crescent sail snapped to life and suddenly billowed with air. The long, horizontal bar that held the bottom of the sail swung about and knocked Rheif off the cabin, nearly sweeping him overboard. The boat tilted at a dizzy angle and I quickly loosed the proper rope just in time. Another moment and we would have turned over in the sea.

Rheif, pale beneath his heavy fur, and drenched in salt water, solemnly stated that he hoped I would not do such a thing again.

Finally, a swift current seemed to grip the boat and pull it away from Albion. By the time the sun was low the gloomy island was no more than an ominous shadow on the western horizon. We appeared to be somewhere in midchannel again, and as the light faded we glimpsed the other shore, and imagined we could see the faint lights of a town, or another boat.

"I have a great thirst, Aldair," Rheif announced. The sun was gone and the first stars winked above the eastern sky.

"No doubt," I said.

"And a hunger, too."

I looked at him.

"For a small hare, Aldair, or a bush hen," he said soberly.

"You will find neither in the sea," I informed him. "Why don't you catch us a fish? That would be a useful thing to do."

Rheif gazed at the dark waters with little interest. "I have never caught a fish before."

"This would be an ideal time to begin."

The idea seemed to grow on Rheif and finally intrigue him. He found some light cord in the bottom of the boat and asked me if I would fashion the head from my last arrow into a hook. I protested strongly, stating that we might be glad to have that arrow in the future. I agreed, finally, to sacrifice the fastening from my brooch.

"We cannot catch a fish," Rheif announced. "We have no bait. It is my understanding that fish require this."

"Don't look at me," I said.

"I wasn't. At any rate, you are much too large for the

hook." After a great deal of complaining, he fashioned a lure from a tuft of his own gray fur and a bit of bright cloth from his jerkin. He showed it to me, and seemed very proud of his art. Later, something below did snap at this, but when the Stygiann tried to haul it aboard he pulled too hard and the line broke in two.

"The cord was rotten," he muttered. "That would have been an extremely large fish, Aldair. I could tell by the way he was pulling."

"We shall never know," I said.

The night breeze was gentle, and I no longer feared to try my hand at sailing again. Rheif agreed that this was a good idea only after I pointed out that our sole source of food was to be found on the land.

I took great care this time, remembering what had happened before. I recalled something else, too. When that sudden gust had caught us near Albion, the wind had *not* been behind us. It had come from the southeast, to our right, and it had caught us and turned us in a tight circle, sweeping us almost *against* the wind. It was an intriguing thought—that you could make the wind work for you, if you did not fight against it.

While Rheif slept, I practiced patiently, trying first one thing and then another. I learned that sailing was basically a matter of catching the wind at the proper angle in the sails, while operating the little guiding rudder at the rear of the boat. Even when the breeze was not at your back, you could move in another direction, simply by taking a zigzag course through the water, instead of trying to forge straight ahead.

When the first fair breezes of morning caught our sails, I almost forgot that I was weary, hungry, and thirsty. Moving the small boat swiftly over the sea, watching the green water churn to foam around my bow, I felt a freedom I had never known before. Here, on the open sea, a man could cut the strings that ever bound him to others. I thought of the wooden puppets in the Market at Silium, and laughed aloud. You will never hold me again, puppet masters! Not if you be the High Father of the Church or the Emperor himself. Aldair of Venicii, I vowed, is free, and has his own small boat with a sail that captures the wind—no matter in what direction he may be going!

"I suppose you will claim to be Captain, now," Rheif said, when he awoke and saw what I had accomplished.

"I think you could say that. At the very least, Master of Sailing."

Rheif muttered to himself. "I suppose there is nothing for it. Everything else has happened to me. My brothers are dead, I have come to call a Venicii by name, and my captive is now Master of Sailing. Little else can befall me." He watched me with his muzzle downcast. "When do you plan to end this voyage? May a mere passenger ask?"

"I thought to the south. You can see the shore there in the distance. There is nothing but world's end, of course, beyond Albion, which is now far behind us. But in the south we can safely go ashore after dark for food and water."

Rheif looked at me. "We are both from the north, Aldair. And you are taking us farther from home by the minute. What is for us in the south?"

"Mainly," I explained, "an absence of Rhemian soldiers and Tarconii longboats. The northern coast is thick with towns, harbors, and shipping. The channel is narrow and we could be easily spotted. And—even if we could land there undetected, I doubt that we could make our way across the whole of the continent, nearly, to the northern provinces— and farther still, to your own lands. *I* could, perhaps. But they have never seen a Stygiann in most of these areas, though they have heard of you. I doubt that you would be welcome."

Rheif was silent a long moment. He searched the far shoreline, scratched himself carefully, then gave me a puzzled glance. "That's a most peculiar thing for you to say, Aldair," he said solemnly. "Why would a Venicii care whether or not a Stygiann safely reached his home?"

"You are right," I agreed. "It is a most peculiar thing to say."

"We have always been enemies."

"True."

"We have nothing in common."

"No. Only hunger, thirst, and a price on our heads."

"Still," Rheif reasoned, "in spite of the fact that our blood is set against such a thing, it is possible that we can be temporarily useful to one another."

"It seems that we will have to for a while. I don't think we will see our homes soon, Rheif. And speaking for myself, though I certainly plan to return to the north someday, I am no longer in a great hurry to get there."

Rheif looked surprised. "No? What would you do instead?"

"I would see what there is to see."

"Sailing south."

"Yes. For the moment, at least."

Rheif lapsed into silence, and I tended the sails. I thought of the north, and home, and the south, and lands I had never seen before.

Strange, I thought. My success with the art of sailing had brought dreams of far places to mind, but I was truly as surprised as Rheif at the idea of going adventuring far from home. The thought had simply come to me only moments before I said it aloud. Not an overly unusual thing, perhaps. It surely couldn't be the first time the sea had set a young man's thoughts a-roaming.

Later, though, I leaned back in the rear of the boat and looked up at the stars. They were cold and white, like a million chips of ice studding the black sky. And another thought came to me then. This one slipped silently into my mind like a dark bird coming to roost, and I sat up, startled to find it there. *Someday,* I knew, *I would again sail to Island Albion.* More than that, I saw clearly that I would walk upon its forbidden shores.

The thought brought a sudden chill and turned my blood to ice. Why would I do such a thing as that? No man in his right mind would dare set foot on that place! Yet I knew with a cold certainly that this would be. And I wondered if one could ever really escape the puppet master. For even our thoughts sometimes come unbidden to mind, and chain us to a destiny we would not set for ourselves. . . .

NINE

When I came through the brush down the low hill I caught the faint light from the shielded fire, paused a moment behind cover, then walked into the clearing.

"I thought we said a fire wasn't a good idea."

Rheif looked up, his eyes red in the flickering glow. "It isn't," he agreed. He picked something from his sharp teeth and wiped his muzzle with the back of his hand. "However" —he gestured me to sit—"it is not seemly to eat raw meat. Only barbarians do that. I saved you a hare. It's still warm. What do you have there?"

I dropped my wares and reached gingerly into the coals where the hare lay wrapped in wet leaves. The meat smelled good, and after the first bite my stomach felt a little less than hollow. My people are not big meat eaters like the Stygianns, who seldom eat anything else, unless they have to. We subsist mainly on grains and vegetables and fruits, and prefer these things—but a fine roast hare, fish, or chicken is welcome on occasion. I devoured the hot flesh down to the bone, and didn't ask how the Stygiann had managed to catch two fat hares in the dark with no snares. I wasn't at all sure I wanted to know.

"I didn't find much," I told him around my food. "There's not a great deal around here to steal. A farm on the other side of the hill but nobody lives there. Burned out. I got the two jugs, though. They'll hold a few-days' water if we're careful."

I reached behind me. "And a bunch of wild onions. They're not too bad. I was so hungry I ate a few right out of the ground—while you were downing roast hare."

Rheif looked dolefully at the onions and turned up his

nose. "Plants. You people are always eating plants and things made of mush. Such foods are not good for you, Aldair."

I ignored him, and chewed on alternate bites of hare and onion.

"I've been thinking," said Rheif, stirring the fire. "I do not share your great liking for the water, and it occurs to me that if the boat should turn over while we are on the sea, we would die in a rather unpleasant manner."

"True."

"At least, on the land, one knows there is solid ground under his feet."

"And many enemies in his path," I added.

"No doubt. But a Stygiann knows how to fight his enemies on land."

"Rheif"—I leaned forward—"what is it you are trying to say? That you do not wish to continue the voyage? That you wish to strike north on foot?" I shook my head. "We would never reach our homes."

"You don't know that."

"I know it is most unlikely. And so do you."

"I do not care for boats," Rheif said stubbornly.

"Oh? May I remind you that it is *your* boat? That it was your idea to become seamen? I was merely sleeping on its decks when I was taken captive."

Rheif waved me aside impatiently. "You know very well that it was a means of escape for the moment, and nothing more. I never intended to take up boating as a profession."

"And that is exactly what we are doing," I pointed out. "Escaping."

"Yes. In the wrong direction."

I shook my head and turned away from the fire and pulled my cloak about my ears. "You must do what you feel is best." I yawned. "I will search the sides of barns and castles for your pelt, when I return from seeing the sights of the world. Though I will not bother to recount my adventures, as you will no longer be greatly interested."

Rheif was silent. But some time later he woke me and asked just what *kind* of sights we might expect to see.

"Rheif," I said sleepily, "how do I know? I have not been there as yet."

"You have been to the University," he insisted. "You must have learned something about the world."

"I did. I learned that it was best to be content with what you have, and not seek after knowledge."

Rheif's muzzle fell in disappointment.

"All right." I sat up. "There was a map, I recall, in Master Pelian's study. You were not allowed to touch this map, but it was all right to stand back and look."

"So?"

"Mostly it outlined the extent of the Rhemian Empire. In red. A great deal of the world is red."

"Not Stygia," Rheif said darkly.

"No. Not Stygia. And there are other unconquered areas as well." I closed my eyes a moment to think. "There is a big thrust of land just to the south of us. This is the homeland of the Tarconii. We will round that, turn eastward through a narrow strait that divides this continent and the one below. We will then be in the Southern Sea."

"And what is in the Southern Sea?"

"To the north," I told him, "is where we are, and the lands we know."

"And below? You spoke of another—"

"Continent? It is a dark land, and I know little about it. Except that it belongs to the Nicieans, who are said to be another race—unlike you, or me, or the Tarconii, or the Cygnian slaves. It is said their skins are green and shiny, and scaled like armor. They live in a sandy place without water, and cannot be conquered—even by the Rhemian legions. All of this may or may not be so. There is little about Niciea on the map, and I have never spoken to anyone who has actually seen a Niciean. It may be that people who know this race do not wish to talk about them."

Rheif stared at me, his red eyes bright in the coals of the fire. "Aldair," he said evenly, "now I understand what you mean by seeking adventure and seeing the sights in new lands. You would sail us past a thrust of land which is the home of the Tarconii, whom you no doubt remember. Then you would guide us in a small boat into the Southern Sea—if we are still alive by then—a sea ruled on the one hand by Rhemians, and on the other by terrible green things with shiny armored hides." He shook his head. "I have heard of such beings myself, and I am not sure they exist. I think they do not, but I have no desire to find out." He gave me a look of great disgust and turned over toward the fire. "If I am not

here in the morning," he said, "please do not hold the boat
for me, Aldair. . . ."

The coast remained much the same for the next four
days, and we were blessed with calm seas and fair winds. I
noted that we were making good time, and Rheif muttered
that each day took us that much further from the thick
forests of the north, and the many fine, cool brooks there,
which, he pointed out, was all the water a person really
needed.

There was no problem finding campsites for the night. The
few coastal towns we passed were small, and could be easily
avoided. Sometimes we spotted other boats, most of them
hugging the shore. Once we sailed quite close to a large fleet
of squat, ugly fishing vessels. Each sported billowing yellow
sails brightly painted with the silhouettes of various fishes.
Rheif didn't like the idea of being so close to other boats,
but I assured him that as long as he stayed out of sight, no
one would pay much attention to us.

On the fifth day we passed one of the high, rocky head-
lands that seemed common along this section of the coastline. It was no different from any of the other dark promon-
tories, but once we rounded its point a gleaming white city
sprang into view. It was nearly as large as Silium, but much
more delightful than that drab collection of narrow streets
and strangled allys. Houses of pink, yellow, and pale blue
climbed the green wall beyond the harbor. Great banks of
multicolored flowers hung from red-tiled roofs.

For all the city's beauty, however, there was one sour
note, which dampened our interest. Clearly, there were a
great many Rhemian soldiers about. Their golden banners
snapped in the breeze, and among the many vessels in the
blue harbor were two enormous Rhemian warships—dark,
ungainly shapes with more banks of oars than I could count.
The decks were topped with high, armored towers. A
great battering ram in the shape of a shark protruded from
the bow, and I could make out the latticed framework of
large catapults and trebuchets on both forward and after
decks.

We sailed past the harbor with our hearts in our throats.
One of the warships hoisted its blood-red sails and moved
ponderously out behind us. I did not look back, but I could

feel the shadow of this monster and hear the slaves chanting at their oars. It was quite some time before Rheif emerged from the cramped cabin to stretch his legs on deck. Neither of us spoke of the harbor or thè white city. It was a chill reminder, though, that it was not an easy thing to escape the long arm of Rhemian law. Even here, on this barren coastline, the Rhemians had built a city finer than either of us had ever seen.

The coast began to angle north and westward and I kept the boat well out to sea during the daylight hours. I decided this was the beginning of the large peninsula that jutted above the Southern Sea, and was the homeland of the Tarconii mercenaries. It was a place to be avoided, certainly. The Tarconii are a peculiar race, of mixed temperament. A brooding, moody people for the most part, they care for no one but their own. Left alone, they would tend to their own lands and never venture farther. But their giant stature and great strength mark them as natural soldiers. Under proper direction, nothing can stand in their way—even Rhemian legions, as the Rhemians well know. If they were not so lethargic and dull-witted, they could wrest the Empire from their masters. In truth, though, they are not as bright as Cygnian slaves, and have no bent for conquest.

Still, the Rhemians pamper them like children, and give them shiny armor to wear, and meaningless medals and decorations. Some of their leaders have even been granted citizenship—a fact that galls many Rhemian-born no end. But those who rule the Empire know what they are doing. A good soldier takes care of his weapons, and the Tarconii will ever receive proper attention.

TEN

At last the rugged coastline began to veer to the south again, and I assured Rheif we could not be far from the straits that led to the Southern Sea. In my own mind, though, I was not so confident. Evidently, the world was a great deal larger than I had imagined. That, or Master Pelian's map was not entirely accurate. A whole seven-day had passed since we had sailed by the white city—and we had only now rounded the big hump of the Tarconii peninsula. I could have covered the whole journey on that map with the width of one finger!

Rheif worried me.

He was becoming a less-than-pleasant traveling companion. He stayed to himself at the far end of the boat, scowling out to sea. When he said anything at all, he was short and surly, and his voice was a low growl in the back of his throat. Sometimes, in camp, I felt the Stygiann's gaze upon me, and once I turned and found those gleaming red eyes staring thoughtfully into my own.

I had turned away then, and made nothing of it. But sleep had not come easily. Rheif's thoughts had been plain enough. And I suppose I should not have been surprised. We were strange companions, indeed. It was a bizarre friendship at best—natural enemies with a common foe. And how secure was a bond such as that? Old angers were buried for the moment, but they could be brought to light quickly enough —in the time it took for a blade to flash. And Stygianns are without honor in battle. If it came, I would have no warning.

Even though this was the land of the Tarconii, we spotted none of those creatures on the shore. I decided their towns were farther inland. There was little to draw anyone to such

a barren coastline, and the Tarconii did not make ports of
their own. The boats that had pursued us in the north were
Rhemian-made. The Tarconii had been trained to use them,
but such craft was beyond their own skills.

Still, we made careful camps on their shores.

Rheif's spirits greatly improved two days later—though
the reason for this change in the Stygiann's mood near sickened me. I had brought the boat to shore on a rocky beach
and made an early camp. The beach had little to offer, and
there was much against it. There was no cover for ourselves
or the boat. Anyone who cared to look would spot us immediately. Still, Rheif's sharp eyes had caught a trace of
green on the dark crags that tumbled toward the shore, and
he argued that the chance of finding fresh water overshad-
owed the faint possibility of discovery.

I couldn't fault him on that. We needed water badly. And
food, as well. The few seeds and berries I'd put in my mouth
the last few days had done little more than remind me that
I did, indeed, still have a stomach, and that it was fast
shrinking to nothing. I kept these complaints to myself,
though. Food was not a subject I cared to discuss with Rheif.

The spring was halfway up the black cliff, and hard to
reach. I fell back twice, landing in a tumble of loose shale.
Rheif made the climb with ease and grinned down at me
sardonically where I lay asprawl on my short legs, covered
with dust and bruises. He volunteered to bring water down to
me in our jugs, but I would have died of thirst before that.
I was determined to make the climb, and did.

The water tasted good. It was slightly metallic, but fresh
and cool. I filled the jugs, momentarily despising the Stygiann
for cavorting about the cliffside and leaving the work to me.
I wondered how I would get back down to the narrow beach
without breaking my neck.

A pebble bounced off my shoulder and I glanced to see
Rheif gesturing excitedly. My stomach made a knot. We'd
done it, then—landed in the middle of a nest of Tarconii. At
any rate, I scrambled up beside him as quietly as I could, and
peered cautiously over the tumble of stone.

I was surprised and relieved.

"Slaves," I said. "Runaways, no doubt, to be so far from a
town or settlement."

Rheif gazed silently at the Cygnians and said nothing. There were a dozen or so of the creatures, and a miserable lot, indeed. They'd paid dearly for their freedom. They were gaunt and dirty, and they'd tried to sheer the winter wool from each other with sharp stones. The effort had left patches of filthy fleece and slow-healing sores. Their only shelter was a series of shallow burrows dug under stunted bushes in the scorched hollow just below the other side of the cliff.

"They won't bother us," I said. "We can be certain of that." I started down the cliffside, and in a little while the Stygiann followed.

I found a few shellfish in the shallows just before the sun went down. They tasted like fish that had been dead a long time, but I ate as many as I could find. Rheif squatted on the shore and watched me. He made no attempt to find anything to eat. He turned over and slept as soon as it was dark, and since it was hot now, even at night, we made no fire. There was nothing to cook over it, anyway.

Three hours into the night I opened one eye and watched Rheif disappear into the shadows of the cliff. He appeared for a quick moment once more at the top—a gaunt, furry shape bent dark against the darkness. I tried to stay awake, but closed my eyes sometime before morning.

Rheif was full of good cheer at dawn, and praised my seamanship, my prowess as an archer, and a number of other qualities I suddenly seemed to possess. I ignored him as best I could. I did not blame him for what he had done. If I had been a Stygiann, no doubt I would have done the same.

But I am not, and now it was my turn to be distant and moody. . . .

"I do not like the looks of that," Rheif said warily. "It does not seem a pleasant thing to me."

"It isn't," I agreed. The dark bank of clouds had rolled over the horizon only moments before, and I had immediately turned the boat toward the shore. But the storm was moving in at an alarming rate of speed. Already it blotted out the sun and left us in a chilling quiet at the bottom of a dark gray bowl.

Rheif gave me a questioning look. "The shore is not overly far away."

"No. Neither is the storm," I said shortly. Then I turned

away and concentrated on the boat. The winds were blowing in short, confusing bursts, from a number of different directions. It was hard to get any of them to sit still long enough to fill the sails.

Thunder started low in the east and rumbled across the sky for a full minute. We could almost follow its path with our eyes. Rain began pelting the sea in heavy, pendulous drops. Lightning blinded the heavens—the wind picked up ominously and I dropped the sails and scrambled to help Rheif with the oars. I was sure that if we had been another twenty yards or so offshore we would never have made it to the beach.

The storm raged throughout the rest of the day, fell to a deadly calm just before nightfall, then gained new strength and howled through the dark hours. The shallow cave was safely off the beach, and we were blessed with a dry, sandy floor. Still, there was great power in the winds, and cold fingers of rain occasionally sought us out even in the farthest corner of our shelter.

The dampness made Rheif's pelt smell worse than usual, if such a thing is possible. But I endured this, having no other choice in the matter. Besides, there were greater worries at hand: had we pulled the boat high enough among the rocks to save it? It was heavier than it looked, and we had done the best we could. That would be no consolation, though, if we were marooned forever among the Tarconii.

"I have never seen anything like this," Rheif announced.

"It storms in the north," I reminded him.

He shook his head morosely. "Not like this, though. There are no high waves crashing about outside."

"That is because there are no seas in the forests of Lauvectii, Stygiann. Seas are necessary for the presence of waves."

Rheif made a face and swept spray from his muzzle. "I know that, Venicii. I am not totally ignorant, even though I have not attended a great university and learned to read a map on the wall, and count on both hands." With that, he turned away and stared out at the storm. This was nearly the full extent of our conversation during the night, and perhaps it is well we said no more than we did.

There was nothing to do but wait out the morning. I tried to sleep, but couldn't. Mostly, I thought about food. During flashes of lightning, I studied the walls of our cave. Nature had laid down interesting patterns here—thin, horizontal bands of black, orange, and yellow that looked all the world like a finely made bolt of wool. These bands were perfectly straight, as if they had been drawn by a rule. To pass the time, I counted each small line, noted the number of times a color occurred, and generally strained my eyesight. Still, the cold hours passed more swiftly. . . .

The sky was leaden gray at dawn. The storm had passed an hour or so before, but we were still under its shadow. We stretched tired muscles and shook the life back into our limbs. Rheif surveyed the beach and sniffed distastefully.

"Everything smells bad," he announced.

The reason for this was clear. The beach was covered with dark, curly plants and piles of slimy green things lifted from the sea bottom. All of this attracted great swarms of flies.

While Rheif complained about the smell, I hurried to check on the boat—it was safe, but covered in more odorous garbage. It would take a full half day to get it in shape and back into the sea. I didn't have the heart for such a job as yet. Instead, I walked along the beach studying the strange objects the ocean had tossed ashore. I decided there was, indeed, an awesome world out there beneath the waves.

Our beach was curtained with a high cliff of weathered stone, the common backdrop along these shores. Usually it was fairly regular, and extended as far as the eye could see. Here, though, one small section had stepped forward, out of place, and nearly touched the sea. I walked around it, expecting to find a beach much like the one behind me. Instead I came up against a wall of stone—but not at all like the stone of the cliffside. It was as high as my head, and though it was worn and irregular in places, it was curiously smooth as well. I scratched away at its surface and found my fingers tracing a regular line—a shallow, horizontal groove. I brushed away loose soil and found another. Then I pulled myself up and peered over the top of the wall. There were other walls beyond—some higher, some only nubs of rock above the beach.

I felt a peculiar sense of excitement at this discovery. I have come across such places before, in the north, but they are difficult to find, and not overly common. And I have never known one to be as extensive as this.

Rheif was not impressed.

"It is simply a place where a city used to be," he said. "Anyone can see that."

"Anyone with eyes in their head can see a great deal more than that," I said. I found his attitude most irritating. "Did you ever see brick or stone such as this?" I kicked at the base of a wall. "Those parts that are exposed are extremely smooth and well made, Rheif."

"True," he agreed. "I can't see the need of such perfection, though. Too much smoothness is unnecessary."

"And all the *same . . .*" I was talking to myself, now, for the most part. "All nearly *exactly* the same."

I wandered a little way into the ruins, trying to imagine, in my mind's eye, what the city might have looked like. The bricks fascinated me. That they should all appear to be so strikingly alike. Kings might require such perfection. Had this been a place of royalty, then?

The city was old, for certain. Old enough to be quite frightening, I thought. Poor Master Levitinus. How many of his hypothetical centenarians would it take to span the years that lay upon these walls? And who had lived here? Certainly not the Tarconii, who now called this land their own —not unless they had fallen from greatness.

It was not only the age of the city that intrigued me. It was built in a most peculiar manner—or so I imagined. And I tried to sketch rooms where there were no rooms, and draw streets and alleyways in their proper places. Nothing, however, seemed to go where I wished it to go. It was as if—

I stopped. A shadow passed over my own and I looked up quickly. There was a blur of motion on the cliffside— something appeared to pause there, flail about, then drop from sight with a little shriek. I caught a flash of color out of the corner of my eye, then something hit the sandy ledge just above me. A shower of dirt and stones clattered down the face of the cliff. Then I was aware of Rheif moving swiftly past me—a grim smile on his gray muzzle and a light in his eyes.

ELEVEN

It was not hard to read the Stygiann's thoughts.

Fate had dropped supper handily into the larder. Whatever this fine morsel might be, it had temporarily stunned itself on the ledge above, and it was only necessary to retrieve it quickly before it came to its senses.

I fervently wished that I was somewhere else. . . .

Rheif was already up the cliff. He had scaled that obstacle like a bird, his feet scattering only the tiniest of pebbles. At the top, he gazed down at his prize a moment, then jumped the few feet to where it lay and scooped it up. He stood there a moment and grinned at me. Then the grin faded, and he stared dumbly at his feet as the ledge began to crumble and give way under his weight.

Rheif clawed for air. His fingers found solid rock and jerked him up short. He hung there, swinging slightly, his meal clutched tightly under one arm. The top of the cliff was out of reach. It was much too far to drop to the ground without breaking something.

"Aldair," he called, "are you doing something to help or are you still standing there?"

"For the moment, I am still standing here," I told him. "I'm not at all sure what to do."

The Stygiann's prize was coming alive again. It was squirming, and making small frightened sounds. I could not see it clearly, as it was half hidden by Rheif's body. What I could see, though, disturbed me.

"I cannot hold on much longer," Rheif said. "It would be best if you caught this thing and gave me the use of both hands. Aldair—are you *there?*"

"I'm here."

"Then why do I keep thinking that you aren't?"

I didn't answer. I could see Rheif's prize better than he could. It was fully awake. And fighting. And green.

Green?

That, I told myself, is not a good color. I suddenly wanted very badly to talk to Rheif about something. I moved a step closer to the base of the cliff.

Three humming sounds reached my ears.

Zip-zip-zip. Like angry bees.

Three arrows stitched a neat fence an inch ahead of my toes.

In a way, I was greatly relieved. Now I knew exactly what to do. I stood very still and did nothing.

The three archers on the cliff were much larger versions of the thing under Rheif's arm. Green, hideous, and frightening. And it was not necessary to have seen them before to guess they were Niceans. . . .

"Our adventures have come to a sorry end, Aldair." Rheif stared at me with sad red eyes and shook his head morosely.

"We are still alive," I reminded him. I fingered the iron collar about my neck. "And if they intended to kill us, I don't think they would have bothered with these."

One side of Rheif's muzzle raised disdainfully. "Perhaps you consider this living," he sniffed. "For a Stygiann, death is infinitely more desirable than slavery."

"Perhaps if you mentioned this," I suggested, "one of these creatures would grant your wish."

"I would. But it would be unseemly to do so. I am a Stygiann warrior, and a leader among my own kind. It would not be proper, Aldair, for me to beg a favor from these monsters, who are clearly of some lower order."

I didn't answer. For creatures of a lower order, the Niceans seemed to do quite well for themselves. I was much impressed by what I could see. The camp was in a dry, narrow cove, ringed by sentinels of stone, and in sight of the sea. There were twenty or so white tents scattered about, in no particular order. Set well apart from the others was a larger tent, nearly as big as a small country house. It was elaborately made and well fashioned. There was even a brass chimney rising through one of its double-spired peaks. Green pennons spangled with golden eyes fluttered overhead.

The tent itself was pale green, and patterned all over with the same golden eyes that graced the banners.

Clearly, this tent, which could hardly be called a tent at all, sheltered some important personage. That would have been obvious even if a dozen Niciean archers in ceremonial garb did not surround its perimeters night and day.

So far, I had not been able to glimpse anyone I felt might be the owner of this fine shelter. In truth, though, I may have seen this worthy half a dozen times without knowing it. These hideous creatures all looked much alike to me.

I watched two of them cross the cove toward one of the smaller tents. They wore common Nicieans robes wrapped about their slim green forms. Hoods were attached to the robes, and these could be raised to cover their flat heads from the sun.

We had seen Nicieans closely only twice. Once when we had been captured and taken to the cove to be searched and collared. Again when a guard had set a jug of water and a pot of food near the tall rock that gave us partial shade.

The thought brought me shame, but there was no denying the truth of it: the Nicieans had frightened me badly. They were beings one could not have imagined in the most troubled nightmare—things that did not seem to properly belong to this Earth of ours. Their flat, expressionless faces seemed all the more terrible for the lack of true features. They *did* have eyes and ears and a nose and a mouth, but they might as well have been missing entirely. The eyes were dark and lidless, like little black shiny balls, and the nose and mouth were mere slits and gashes.

They smelled, too. A sweet, dry, and dusty odor. Rheif stank, now—but that was something else. Stygianns smell bad because they are Stygianns and hold water in disdain. It is different with the Nicieans, who smell as if they have lived all their lives in holes under rocks.

"Aldair, what is *that* supposed to be?" Rheif pointed a suspicious finger at the pot of food between us. "I am near starved, but I could not possibly manage to bring such a thing to my mouth."

I sniffed at the mess. It was gray and sticky and full of black spots. I stirred it and poked it with a twig and brought a small dark glob under Rheif's nose.

His eyes widened and he shrank back in alarm. "By the gods—is that what I think it is?"

"I'm afraid so," I said. "It is the leg of some insect. A beetle, perhaps, or a hopper." I looked at Rheif. "This whole pot is a kind of bug stew, for the most part."

"And—this is what they eat?"

"Either that, or it is what they feed their slaves. And I am quite certain that they eat it, too, Rheif. They smell very much like this pot themselves."

Rheif's eyes rolled in dismay. "Then we are done for, Aldair. We will shortly starve to death. The sooner the better, as far as I'm concerned."

I stuck a finger in the pot and made myself bring some of the stuff to my mouth. "It isn't too bad," I told him. My stomach rolled over uneasily. "Once you forget what it is."

Rheif turned away. "Maybe not for you. The Venicii eat roots and vegetables and all other sorts of garbage, anyway. But it is not fit for a Stygiann." He folded his shaggy arms and stared maliciously at the big green tent. "You may live if you like, Aldair, and become a fat and happy Niciean slave."

I stopped, a finger halfway to my mouth. "Look," I said darkly, "kindly keep your thoughts to yourself, Rheif. It's not easy to forget that *your* appetite brought us to this sorry end!"

Rheif looked deeply hurt. "Aldair. How did I know it was one of their young? It didn't look like *any*one's child to me!"

"I hope they'll believe that," I said. "I'm a Venicii, you'll recall, and you are wasting your innocence on me."

"Those stories you tell in the north are greatly exaggerated," said Rheif. "Stygianns rarely eat the Venicii."

"Stygianns rarely catch them napping," I added.

In the evening, two soldiers dressed in elaborate ceremonial robes came for us, and led us to the far edge of the camp. A large wooden tub had been set up behind an outcropping of stone. The tub was full of water, and I could see steam rising from its surface.

Rheif looked horrified. "Aldair, they intend to drown us, for certain!"

I tried to hide my amusement. "It is not as simple as all that," I told him.

Rheif entered the tub at swordpoint, and howled when the

water hit his skin. He refused the bar of rough soap, and complied only after a soldier angrily pressed a long curved blade across his throat. I waited my turn, and bathed without complaint. It was a luxury I hadn't expected.

Rheif dismally inspected the white robe he'd been given to replace his clothing. "I can never return to the north," he said. "My brothers would scorn me and drive me from the clan."

"I think not," I said. "You would be a most valuable warrior, because your foes would not sense your presence until you were well upon them. . . ."

Certainly I did not believe the bath and new clothing were gestures accorded all newly captured slaves. For some reason, we were receiving special treatment. We had not been allowed to mix with the other slaves in camp. More than that, we had not been given any work to do. I was, then, very wary of the whole thing. When a slave is well treated, he knows for sure there's trouble afoot.

I was certain this was so when we were marched to the big green tent and told to wait until we were called; to stand or squat as we desired, but to stay clean and presentable.

After some time, a soldier came outside and stared at us, went back in, then came out again and spoke to us. "You will soon be in the aura of the Aghiir," he hissed in passable Rhemian. "You will address the Aghiir as 'Lord'—that is, if the Aghiir wishes to be addressed. If he does, he will indicate his desire. If he does not, you will say nothing." He looked at both of us with flat black eyes, then pushed us ahead of him into the tent.

It was too much to take in in a single glance. To my mind, the Aghiir's quarters looked all the world like a mad merchant's showroom. Patterned rugs in outlandish colors covered the bare ground. Lamps of all shapes and sizes hung from chains of bronze, silver, and gold and flickered under panes of colored glass. Elaborate chairs and tables of every fashion were scattered about the room in no particular order, and lattice screens were set here and there to divide the space into little half-rooms and corridors that led nowhere at all. The air was thick with the sweet, cloying odor of Nicieans, and the smell of burning scent.

A Niciean who looked like all other Nicieans sat in a finely carved chair and rested his legs on a pile of colored pillows. His green robe was sewn with golden eyes. He studied us in turn, then let his gaze fall on the guard.

"Which is the one who saved my nephew?"

"The taller one, Lord," said the soldier. "The heavy-pelted creature."

Rheif's jaw dropped momentarily, but he snapped his muzzle quickly shut and tried to look solemn.

"Your name, then?" asked the Nicie an. He gestured idly for the Stygiann to speak.

"Rheif. Rheif of Stygia, Lord."

"Go to your knees then, Rheif."

Rheif's eyes rolled, and I saw him swallow hard—but he did as he was told. The Nicie an pulled a heavy gold chain from his own shoulders. The chain held a blood-red stone in its base, bigger than a hen's egg. There were other, smaller stones along its links. He dropped this chain over Rheif's neck and told him to stand again. Then he turned to the soldier and did not look at Rheif at all. "And which limbs touched the young Dhar'jeem?"

The soldier bowed. "Both, Lord, in all truth. The one called Rheif used both arms to save the Personage—though he later utilized only one to cling to the rocks above."

The Aghiir glared crossly at the soldier and waved him off. "No matter." He sighed. "It would not be seemly to remove both the limbs of a slave who has served us. Not very practical, either."

He looked down, suddenly remembering Rheif was still present. "No reason *you* shouldn't decide, is there? Which arm do you use the least of all, slave?"

TWELVE

Some time after our interview, I learned the Niciean in the green tent was a high lord indeed—being the brother of the Emperor of all the Niceans. Rheif and I were given extra clothing and a tent to ourselves. We did not even have to take our meals with the other slaves.

"We are most fortunate," I told Rheif. "Evidently, we are attached to the high household itself. At least, this is what I gather from the soldiers I can understand. Most of them speak poor Rhemian."

"Perhaps you are fortunate," Rheif said gloomily. "You have your arms, and the prospect of keeping them. Whereas I shall shortly lose one, and be of no use to anyone. Stygianns do not look kindly upon cripples. This is seemly, of course, since they are a burden to the clan."

He fingered the new gold chain about his neck and shook his head in wonder. "I do not understand these Niceans, Aldair. First they reward me graciously for the service I have rendered their people. Then they tell me I must lose a limb for having performed this act. It is a very fine chain, but it is hardly worth an arm to me."

I had been resting in the shade of our tent, watching the Niceans move about the camp, doing whatever it was they were doing. At Rheif's words, though, I sat up and stared at him. "What *service* is this you have rendered the Niceans?" I asked him. "I don't seem to recall that incident."

Rheif looked down his shaggy nose in surprise. "It is strange that you should ask, Aldair. Since you were present when I rescued the Niciean lord's young nephew—the child who will one day become ruler of an empire."

I shook my head, finding it hard to believe what I was hearing. Of course, I had forgotten for the moment that Stygianns have the remarkable ability to remember those things they wish to remember.

"Rheif," I told him, "it is fortunate you did not rescue this prince any more than you did. The loss of an arm is not a good thing, but you would look strange indeed without that hairy muzzle attached to your face. . . ."

Later in the morning, a troop of archers marched to the center of the camp and came to a halt. An officer drove a green banner into the ground and stood at attention before his soldiers. In moments, a small crowd had gathered around this troop—Niceans with no duties at the moment, and even a few slaves who saw the chance to pause in their work. Soon another troop of archers marched into this circle and left three Niceans in the officer's charge. The officer spoke to each of the three, returned their salutes, and stepped away. The three soldiers removed their ornaments and robes and folded these articles in neat piles by their sides. Then they knelt down and touched their heads to the ground and extended their arms. The officer drew a long, curved blade and stepped behind them and took off each of their heads in turn. He was careful to do this from the proper position —even so, the severed necks released great columns of blood upon the sand, and some of this stained the officer's robes.

We learned that these three unfortunates were the same trio of archers who had captured us initially. They were members of the Nicean household guard, and the young prince had been in their charge when he wandered off and fell over the cliff into Rheif's care. A soldier explained that the Nicean lord, whose name was Tharrin, had forgiven the three, and granted them a full pardon, as they had served long and well in his service.

Since Nicean law stated that an offending member was removed in such cases—in lieu of the penalty of death, which the Niceans do not believe in—it was decreed that the three would be set free after the loss of their heads, that being the offending member in this case, as it housed the seat of reason, which had evidently not functioned properly during the moment in question.

Rheif and I were given no particular duties, and we often found ourselves with nothing to do. Occasionally, we worked about the camp with other slaves assigned to the household. There were beings of all races in this group—Rhemian soldiers captured in battle, miscellaneous citizens from every corner of the Empire, and even Cygnians and Tarconii. The Tarconii, being powerful creatures, were kept heavily chained and guarded most of the time, and it occurred to me that it was hardly worthwhile to capture them as slaves.

I spoke to some of our fellow slaves and learned that they were not overly unhappy with their fate. All of them preferred freedom, of course, but they reported the Niceans were not harsh masters unless one became rebellious or unruly. The Lord Tharrin, it seemed, was particularly easy to work for. I also learned that the Niceans do not enslave their own kind, as the Rhemians do, on occasion.

A few days after we witnessed the pardon and execution of the three archers, Rheif and I were taken to a tent near the royal lodgings. Here, a household slave who was a former Rhemian officer questioned us exhaustedly about our families, experiences, backgrounds, and so on. He seemed especially interested in how we happened to be where we were when we were captured. A scribe took all this information down. He seemed able to write as fast as a person could speak.

All this seemed very peculiar to me. Who cared where a slave came from, or what he thought about? I was to learn, though, that Niceans do not necessarily reason in the same manner as other beings.

One morning just after dawning an archer came for me and led me away from the camp and up the side of the rocky cliff that guarded the rear of the cove. Steps had been laboriously hacked from the hard stone there, and the going was relatively easy. Such a task seemed quite wasteful to me, even though there were plenty of slaves on hand to do the Niceans' bidding. Even the Rhemian legions would not exert such efforts, and they were well known for their ability to set up a complete defensible position after each day's march. Whatever these creatures were doing here on the lonely Tarconii coast—and I had no idea what that might be—the camp was clearly only temporary.

My answer lay just beyond the top of the cliff. And when I stood upon that ridge and looked about, I was struck with sudden wonder. The ruins on the beach paled before this great marvel—for the grave of a whole city lay before me. The morning sun caught its crumbling walls and broken spires and set them aflame, and for one quick moment I felt as if I had been swept back in time to watch the death-fires of this ancient place. The mood passed, and left me chilled to the bone.

A hundred or more slaves labored here, uncovering further levels of the city. They worked under the direction of Niceans, for the most part, but some of the slaves had become proficient in certain areas, and now supervised their fellows. Guiding this whole affair was the Lord Tharrin himself, and for the second time I found myself in his presence. He looked up as the guard and I approached.

"I am told you have an interest in such things," he said. "This is so?"

My mouth opened, but no words came out. Finally, I managed to get my wits about me. "Yes, Lord. I—do."

And there it was again, then. What did the brother of the Emperor of the Niceans care what *I* thought about anything?

The Lord Tharrin worked under a shaded tent, open to the occasional breezes on three sides. There were comfortable cushions about, and slaves to bring him cool drinks at his bidding. Still, the tent was clearly a work area. Charts and drawings were scattered around on wooden benches, weighed down by brick and stone samples from the city. A number of cloth bags were stacked in disorderly piles, each properly labeled in spidery Nicean script. About the tables lay dusty artifacts of all shapes and sizes. I was fascinated by these items, but could identify nothing that I saw. Most intriguing of all was a large plaster model of the ruins themselves. This display rested on a table made for the purpose, and occupied a full third of the tent.

"You like that, do you?" I looked up, startled, to find the Lord Tharrin's eyes upon me.

"Lord, I have never seen anything like it," I blurted out, forgetting no one had given me leave to speak. "One could imagine small creatures walking about in there, it is so finely done!"

This seemed to please the Nicean. His slit of a mouth creased in a half-smile. "It is accurate in all respects," he

said, moving toward the table. "Note. The white indicates
the state of the ruins at the point of discovery. This"— he
touched a section of the model and lifted it deftly in his
fingers—"shows what we have uncovered beneath."

I leaned across the table and saw there was a lower
level under the area he had removed. There appeared to be
a room there, and the suggestion of a hallway. This exca-
vated area was painted a light orange.

"Now," said Tharrin, "there is yet another piece to the
puzzle. The white is what is seen, the orange the discovered
—and the black the unknown." With that, he reached beyond
the model and selected a polished piece of black wood and
set it atop the white area in question. The piece fit perfectly. I tried to visualize the whole in one color. Extending
both the orange and the white in my mind, and joining it
with the black, the structure assumed the shape of a small
building.

"Ah, you see it." Tharrin nodded. "Of course," he added,
"this is only conjecture." He removed the black piece and
set it aside. "It is difficult to envision what was, from what is
left. But it is most satisfying to try."

He looked up then, and his black eyes bore into mine.
"This model shall be your responsibility," he told me. "You
are called Aldair, I believe? You may retain the name. It
is satisfactory. You will study this until you know it as
well as I do. You will accompany me to the ruins themselves
and take notes. It will not take you long to learn the
Nicien tongue, and our written script. It is not the bird-
scratching it appears to be to barbarians, but is really quite
lovely, as you will see."

The Lord Tharrin closed his hands behind him and looked
past me to the ruins. "It will be a satisfying life's work for
you, I should think, and worthy of your abilities. I have
always felt it is foolish to waste a creature's mind, be he
freeman or slave." He turned to me then, and touched me
with his black eyes.

"Well, Aldair—shall we get to work, then?"

THIRTEEN

I fell into my work easily and enjoyed it immensely. Lord Tharrin worked long hours, sometimes well into the night if a particularly knotty problem challenged his mind—but it would have to be said that the slave labored no longer than his master. And if I sometimes appeared for work bleary-eyed, with a head full of cobwebs, I did my best to hide my fatigue from Lord Tharrin. The Niciean thought sleep was a slothful habit that wasted precious work hours. There was much to be done, he told me, and little enough time in which to do it.

"We can all sleep in the Afterworld," he said stiffly, "though I assure you I do not intend to spend eternity in such a foolish manner. And none who work for me should expect to do so, either."

This statement amused me, though I did not dare let a smile cross my lips. Lord Tharrin, born to the nobility, blandly assumed that his staff would accompany him in death as well as life. He could not have imagined that it might be otherwise.

A two-month passed quickly. The days were shorter now, and a chill wind sometimes blew in from the sea after dark. Lord Tharrin found the changing weather discomfiting, as did all the Nicieans. This race cannot tolerate winter temperatures, and I learned that the expedition would soon have to close down and retreat to the Southern Sea until late in the spring. A garrison would be left behind to make sure the ruins were not disturbed, and it was said that many of this number sickened and died every year, before the ships returned from the south. Discipline in the camp was faultless—as it was understood that the winter garrison would again be chosen from among those troopers rated lowest by their officers.

Impatience, I found, was my greatest enemy. I was absorbed in the puzzle of the ruins, and frequently irritated that the work went so painfully slowly. I was dismayed to learn the Lord Tharrin had already devoted seven years to this project—that he foresaw another ten-seasons' work ahead before any real understanding of the city could be expected. The fact that he himself was already into his later years did not concern the Nicean. Naturally, he would complete the project. That was his desire. And who, indeed, would say that those desires would not be met?

I seldom saw Rheif anymore. The few hours we did spend together were often less than pleasant, for the Stygiann had fallen heir to moods of deep depression. A Stygiann is a rare creature outside his home forests, and Rheif was quite a curiosity in the Nicean camp. Ironically, the young Dhar'jeem was totally delighted with Rheif. The child would scream with joy when his "rescuer" was nearby, and howl with alarm when he was absent. Thus, to his horror, the Stygiann found himself assigned as the prince's permanent companion.

I took care to hide my amusement when Rheif appeared outside the royal tent, the small Nicean astride his back shrieking with pleasure. The Dhar'jeem's tiny hands clutched the long fur around the Stygiann's toothy muzzle, and his short green tail whipped the air as Rheif galloped grimly about until the child tired of his play.

Somehow, the Stygiann had decided I was totally to blame for his misfortune.

"This is where your adventuring has led us," he said sourly. "If we had abandoned the boat as I suggested, no doubt we would be home by now." He sighed and sniffed the air. "I am certain the first snow has covered the Lauvectii forests. There is frost on the trees, and crackly ice on all the ponds. Only I will never see these things again."

"Rheif," I assured him, "we will not always be slaves of the Niceans."

He raised a brow and put on a show of great surprise. "What? I cannot believe I am hearing you correctly, Aldair. Surely you do not wish to return to the Venicii? Why, it is well known that you happily follow the Lord Tharrin about like a proper slave, sniffing at his heels and placing small stones in little sacks."

I felt the heat rising to my face then. "Look, Stygiann," I told him, "I am a slave the same as you, and I do what the Niceans tell me to do. I do this because I wish to stay alive. It happens that the world as it was before holds an interest for me, and as long as I must be a slave there is no harm in filling my days with useful hours. I have *not* chosen slavery as a profession. And when the opportunity arises, I will rid myself of this damnable iron collar quickly enough!"

I think Rheif was somewhat taken aback by my anger. At least he scratched his hide with great interest and would not look me in the eye.

"At any rate," I added, "I am engaged in some meaningful task, and do not find myself consigned to a Nicean nursery. . . ."

Perhaps this last was unnecessary, but so were the Stygiann's comments about my behavior. These were the last words that passed between us for more than a week.

One good thing came of the Stygiann's duties with the Dhar'jeem. Even Rheif had to admit this was true. There is no changing Nicean law, and once a sentence of any sort is pronounced, it is dutifully carried out. Thus Rhief was condemned to lose a limb because he had touched the royal person of the prince. This seemed ludicrous now, but the law is the law.

Rheif's sentence could not be commuted, even by Lord Tharrin himself. However, it appeared there was some flexibility within Nicean law—as there is in the law of all lands, when those who make the law wish this to be so. Rheif must lose a limb, but there was no point of law that stated exactly where that limb must be severed. The elbow or the shoulder seemed likely spots to Rheif, who lived in terror of the event. Lord Tharrin, though, seeing that his nephew had taken a fancy to the Stygiann, did not wish to suffer noisesome tantrums within the royal compound. Thus he decreed that Rhief's arm be severed from his body on such and such a day, the severing point being just below the first joint of the little finger on the Stygiann's left hand. The job was done quickly and with care, and the clean wound was treated daily by Tharrin's own physician.

Rheif stated that he did not miss the joint at all, that it had never served a useful purpose. He boasted to me that he had, after all, gotten the better end of the deal, and that it was not uncommon for Stygianns to best other races when it came to trading. The gold chain with its red stones might not be worth an arm, but it was surely worth half an inch of worthless finger. . . .

"Aldair," Lord Tharrin announced, "we must be gone from here within the next week—or the week after that at the latest. You will give instructions in my name that the excavations will be brought to an end as quickly as possible, and that all work areas will be properly sealed against the weather."

As Lord Tharrin spoke these words, he pulled a heavy robe about his shoulders and bent his back against a gust of cool wind. A fire was kept burning in the work tent at all times now. I did not see that this was needed, but the Niceans are cold-blooded creatures, and much affected by temperatures both Rheif and I find greatly invigorating.

To my mind, the weather and the long hours had taken their toll of Lord Tharrin. While he was in good physical condition, he was also many years past his prime. He tired easily, and frequently became irritable and impatient. He was a proud man, though, and stubborn to boot, and would admit none of this to himself. Still, though he complained of the short days and poor light, I think he was secretly relieved that he would soon be heading for the warm waters of the south.

"We will busy ourselves," he told me, "and not waste the coming weeks. There's much to be done, both indoors and out." We were closing up the tent at the end of the day, and he was shuffling idly through his charts and sketches. In the midst of this, some impulse seemed to take hold of the Nicean and he took up the carafe of wine on the table and poured cups for us both. I was deeply touched by this gesture, for it is not a common thing for a master to host his slave. He raised the amber liquid and looked into it, then turned his eyes on me.

"You have done well, Aldair. More than was required of you."

"I'm grateful that you think so, Lord."

He laughed lightly. "Not *grateful*. You have not done the work to please me—though I am pleased. You have done what you have because you love what you are doing, as I do." He paused a moment. "Is this not so?"

"Lord, I freely admit to a great curiosity."

"For matters ancient and historical?"

"Yes, Lord."

"And things of a religious nature, perhaps?"

"To—some extent, Lord."

Tharrin smiled easily. "And this great curiosity has brought you to slavery, has it not?"

I was somewhat puzzled at that, and the Nicean caught my expression. "Aldair. You well know that I have acquainted myself with your background, as gathered by Linius. And while my worthy steward is exhausting and has no sense of the relevant, he is at the same time quite thorough. You were chosen to work with me because you ask questions and seek true answers. There are not many who do. Particularly among your own kind, I think. The Rhemians do not encourage innovative thinking—unless it serves to extend the borders of the Empire. And those borders stretch fair to bursting, "I'll tell you, for the rulers of Rhemia are ever—"

He made a face and shook his head. "But that has nothing to do with you, does it, or how you came to be where you are. I was only half jesting, Aldair, when I said that the search for knowledge has put an iron collar about your neck. It's a poor joke, I'll admit, but there's truth in it—for neither history nor religion treats a man kindly. Ills and mistruths have ever flocked about those lofty pinnacles of learning, and you're not the first to be caught in a bitter glance between the two." He stopped and sipped his wine. "Tell me —do you still believe in this Church of yours, after the misery it's brought you?"

"Lord," I said, quite honestly, "I believe the world was made by a Creator. But I am no longer certain the Church always serves the Creator's will, or speaks in his voice."

Tharrin nodded. "Well said. There is hope for you yet, as I'd imagined. And history, Aldair? This still intrigues you? It's a subject dear to us both, but one so nicely sugared with the needs of the present, it's near impossible to uncover the truth of the past."

"The end's worth the effort, as I see it." The words blurted out unbidden, and I stopped short. "Lord, I've hardly the knowledge to say one thing or the other."

He waved this off with a scowl. "Never apologize for your opinion."

"Even if you've nothing to back it up, Lord Tharrin?"

Tharrin laughed and poured us more wine. "That never stopped a learned scholar or churchman, Aldair. Why should it muzzle a man who truly *wants* to learn the truth?"

I thought about that for a moment. Truth, it seemed, was not held in great esteem by many. Often, it was merely a worrisome hazard on the road to wealth, power, and other things a man held dear. "Could it be, Lord," I asked, "that truth's not to be found on this world?"

"Where, then—on another?"

"Perhaps, sir, it's a gift that comes with dying."

Tharrin looked at me. "Does your Church tell you this, Aldair?"

"Not that I know, Lord. At least, I've never heard it said. But it stands to reason, does it not? That there's truth in the Afterlife? I couldn't see the purpose of dying and taking your soul to Albion, then finding there's still more things to guess about."

The Lord Tharrin didn't answer me for the moment, but the smallest part of a smile crossed his features, He busied himself turning a stone over and over in his fingers, then looked up and blinked into the fading day.

"This Albion, then," he said, still peering toward the evening. "You believe, as your people do, that it harbors the souls of the dead?"

I nodded, remembering those gray shores with a chill. "I think it must, Lord."

Lord Tharrin looked up. "We know of this Albion in Niciea, too. Does that surprise you? It's a sacred place to us as well, but in a somewhat different manner." He shook his head, and I thought it was a peculiar gesture— somewhere between amusement and resignation. "I fear your northern isle is a bit too cold for a Nicean paradise, Aldair. In our teachings, the blessed of Al Wajir are freed of their burdens and journey to a warm and sunny clime in the Afterworld—a place much like Niciea, I suspect, without royalty or taxes. The doomed, however, are sentenced to suffer forever in the chill of Albion."

I was startled at this, and Tharrin laughed and pulled his robes about him. "One man's heaven is another man's hell, is it not? And what does this say about truth, Aldair? Is there one truth for your race, and another for mine? And still another for your Stygiann friend?" He leaned forward and pushed his wine aside. "No, there may be little truth in the world, as you say, but I don't believe we have to die to find a fair piece of it. Out there"—he gestured toward the ruins—"is a truth as real and untainted as you'll likely find in this life."

The statement gave me pause to wonder, and Lord Tharrin noted my expression.

"The Earth hides its secrets, Aldair, and the years cover them with a cloak that's hard to puzzle, as you know. But when you draw that cloak aside, what you find there is clean and real. The ages show themselves naked and unashamed to any eye that can see—and there's no historian been there to mend the past and make finer cloth of the present. Nor a meddling priest who'd color the years to show his own particular god to good advantage."

I listened to Lord Tharrin, and looked past him to the rubble of the great city. It was much as I'd seen it the first time, only the sun made bloodfire from the other side of the sky now.

"I read your thoughts," the Niciean said evenly. "This is not overly hard to do, for they mirror my own. You wonder what it was like, then, and who the beings were who walked those streets. . . ."

"And what passed through their minds," I added. "Yes, Lord, and however much I dwell on this, my head still spins with the wonder of it. Even though I've seen what time can do to stone, it's not an easy thing to fathom the passing of so many years." I glanced at the Niciean. "How many, Lord? Is it possible to say? To the dawning of life, perhaps? After the Darkness?"

Lord Tharrin's head came up, too quickly. "What? What's that?" The warmth of a moment ago was gone, and his voice was cold with disdain. "What can you know of a Darkness," he asked, looking straight at me, "or the dawning of *life?*"

"Lord—" What had I said to cause such anger? "I only thought—the ruins being so old, or seeming so to me, that is—that they must surely date back the full three thousand years of history, after man came out of the Darkness—"

Tharrin laughed harshly. "Whatever those fools in your Church or any other may say, they know *nothing* of the passing of the ages. Beings walked *those* streets *a good five-thousand years before this Darkness of yours, Aldair—this I know for certain!*"

FOURTEEN

Even the featureless face of a Nicican betrays its emotions to another of that race, or one who has learned to understand these creatures. I knew at once that the Lord Tharrin had said more than he meant to say, for the color fled quickly from his face and left him near bloodless. He stared, rigid as stone, then reached out and pulled me to him in a savage grip.

"No word of what I've spoken, Aldair," he said darkly. *"Nothing, you understand? On your life!"*

"Lord—"

The Nicican came suddenly to his senses. The glaze left his black eyes and he stared at the fingers still caught in the robes about my neck. He flung himself from me as if my flesh had turned to hot iron and fled from the tent without a word, leaving me in near darkness. . . .

Needless to say, I found no peace that night. Lord Tharrin's face was ever before me. I would have put the incident away if I could—I tried, for certain, to convince myself the Nicican was overwrought from the long hours; that his years of devotion to the study of the past had adversely affected his reason.

What else was I to think? That in an unguarded moment a master had told his slave the world was built on false foundations? Where was the reason in that? So I met the dawn determined to think no more on this. Such a thing is easier said than done, however. It is not so difficult to put aside the things a man will say. It is somewhat harder to dismiss what he tells you with his eyes.

The archer who usually accompanied me to the worksite did not appear that morning. This guard was no more than a formality, now, as I regularly wandered about the camp on Lord Tharrin's business. Still, I waited half an hour, then walked up to the royal tent to make inquiry. The guards would not let me pass, of course, but they knew me. In a few moments the Niciean's Rhemian steward Linius stuck his head out of the tent and told me shortly that his master was ill, and that Aldair should continue his duties at the site in his Lord's name, doing all those things that needed to be done in order to properly close down operations.

Linius added that the whole expedition was now waiting upon the pleasure of the slave from the north, and it was hoped that he would see to his work promptly, there being no reason to delay sailing from this miserable land.

I assured him that I would do my best. I had to smile to myself at all this, for Linius had been so long in Tharrin's service that he had come to think of himself as a Niciean. The Nicieans were cold, so Linius was cold, too. All this poor creature needed was a set of green scales on his pink belly and he would have been totally happy. That, and a long straight tail instead of a short curly one.

I was not surprised that the Lord Tharrin had taken to his bed. He had pushed himself too hard, and in spite of his conviction that he was immune to the ills of common men, he was no less vulnerable than any other. Certainly I wondered how much the incident of the night before had to do with his collapse. Probably a great deal, I decided. When a man's body is under stress, his mental faculties don't always function as they should. At any rate, this explanation seemed logical enough, and for the moment, made me feel somewhat easier about what had happened.

What foolishness! Though I was familiar with nearly every task at the ruins, the magnitude of my responsibility didn't occur to me until I arrived at the work tent. The sight nearly struck me dumb! I'd seen it all a hundred times before—but now everything seemed totally foreign. I stared at the hundreds of charts and sketches, the carefully labeled stones and artifacts, the intricate table model I could put together in my sleep. And—Creator's Eyes! I was certain I'd never be able to make sense out of this jumble! I alternately cursed the Lord Tharrin, and prayed for his quick recovery.

The work progressed at a snail's pace. I checked and double-checked everything, then checked it again. I was four places at once, and never where I was needed. By the end of my second day as Master of Ruins, as Rheif had tagged me, I was quite sure I had committed a dozen errors—any one of which would cost me my head. The Niciean overseers sensed my fears, and even the digger slaves grinned behind my back. I was infuriated at this, but I could hardly blame them. At this rate, I would strand the expedition on Tarconii shores throughout the winter.

So I stopped, and backed away, and examined the problem as objectively as I could. The answer was relatively simple. In every case I had been asking myself: What would the Lord Tharrin do? How would he package this, or catalogue that? Would he approve or disapprove of the way I had shored up the south quadrant against further damage? And of course there was no Lord Tharrin on hand, only an Aldair who was in complete charge, whether he liked it or not.

With a great effort of will, I began thinking for myself —and work began to get under way. . . .

On the fourth day of my job I was called to the far end of the excavation to supervise the crating of a particularly delicate piece of an arch. Little work had been done in this area, and I took a few moments to explore the test hole there. This was a common procedure at the site. A preliminary shaft would be sunk in a likely spot, and if anything promising came to light, the hole would be carefully expanded. One wall had been uncovered here—a ten-foot section of solid gray material, which we knew was formed by a process of casting, and was not natural.

The moment I saw this wall it looked strangely familiar, though I knew I had never seen it before. It was some time before I realized it was not the wall that was familiar, but the *markings* upon it. I had seen markings like that before —a tight pattern of horizontal bands formed by the coloration of metals and water. There were bands very much like these in the cave farther down the shore, where Rheif and I had weathered the storm. I had stared at them in flashes of lightning for one long miserable night, trying to forget that the cold and stinging sheets of rain were soaking me to the bone.

I can't say why this second display caught my interest. Perhaps because Lord Tharrin had taught me well—that anyone with a digging tool can remove objects from the ground, but it is the wise searcher who relates each new thing he sees to everything he has seen before. This, as the Niciean explained, is how puzzles of the past are pieced together. So when I had a free moment I brought long strips of parchment tape to the test hole and meticulously recorded the widths and colors of the bands there, and then did the same for those within the cave. And during the evenings, when I worked by lamplight at my cataloging tasks, I sometimes took out the two sets of parchment and studied them, and wondered at their meanings, and scribbled notes on scraps of paper.

I think I knew all along what was working in the back of my mind. And when I finally let myself realize what it was I was doing, the idea sent a chill up my spine and set me bolt upright on my bench. I came very near to tossing the whole business on the fire then and there. But I could no more have done that than stop breathing. I had done something. By myself. I had made something out of nothing.

—Or nothing out of something, I told myself soberly. In the cold light of day, I could not believe my scribblings had any meaning—or none I hadn't wished there myself. I had much to do that *was* meaningful, however, if I wished to keep my head on my shoulders, so I put my papers aside, and promised myself I would burn every scrap before we sailed.

Eight days after I had been given my assignment I sent word to the Lord Tharrin that the site was secured, and that all necessary paperwork and cataloging was completed. Also, that crating and ship's storage of those items that would accompany us back to Niciea had been accomplished. The Lord Tharrin sent word back that an *announcement* of my accomplishments was not sufficient. A complete, itemized account of duties performed by the slave Aldair was to be forwarded before the sun rose the following day.

Clearly, I thought darkly, the Lord Tharrin was on the road to better health. I kept my eyes open through another night, then, carrying out this task—though near dawn I am not sure what sort of nonsense I may have scribbled.

Before first light I supervised the striking of the work tent, and the disposition of the few belongings left there. And when the others had gone, I took time to burn those personal papers I had come to think of as Aldair's Mind Wanderings. I felt greatly relieved when this was finished. Moments later, the steward Linius appeared—clearly disappointed, I thought, that I had managed to meet my deadline. I handed him the thick sheaf of my report and saw him on his way. Then I sat down against a rock near the top of the cliff. I felt the heat of the rising sun warm my backside, and a few moments later I fell into a deep sleep. . . .

I was adrift . . . alone in my small boat . . . a chill fog enveloped me in thick coils of gray . . . the fog suddenly rolled aside, but there was no sun to greet me . . . the sky was black, and the boiling clouds wore an ominous fringe of green . . . thunder rolled across the sea like faraway drums . . . the boat crested a dark wave, and Albion loomed before me. . . .

I knew fear, but couldn't name it . . . something ugly and terrible was about, but always just beyond seeing . . . souls, then? . . . the shades of the dead . . . ?

I walked on Albion's shores . . . but my feet could not feel the ground, and my ears could not hear . . . my eyes were made of cheapest glass and the dark world wavered about me. . . .

A great city rose and fell before me . . . and though I could never see it clearly, or know where it might have stood in the world, I knew it had been warmed by the sun long before the ruins on Tarconii's shores had ground themselves to dust. . . .

The awesome chill of time ate at my bones, and I fled the terrible passing of the years. . . . I ran, but my feet were ever frozen in Albion . . . faces I couldn't see loomed before me and told me things I didn't want to remember . . . voices called me by a name I didn't want to hear. . . .

When I awoke the sun was low in the west and the chill of evening was in the air. I had slept through the day, then, and no one had disturbed me—though I wished that they had. I shuddered, rose, and pulled my cloak about me, and tried to shake the last threads of nightmare. The sweat of fear clung to me like dead skin.

There was very little left below to show the Niceans had made their camp on these shores. The tents were gone. Odd bits of material were scattered about. I noted the permanent winter guard had taken their post at the far end of the cove, away from their departing companions.

The two Nicean ships bobbed gently in the harbor—sleek, green beasts made in their master's image, bright with painted scales from fore to aft, hungry for the sea. As I watched, emerald sails spotted with golden eyes blossomed in the dying sun, smelling the wind for the south.

I turned back once to the ruins of Tarconii, before moving down the cliffside. I let my eyes wander over familiar paths and crumbling columns of stone.

I had come to know this city like no other.

But it did not look the same now.

FIFTEEN

After three days at sea, the dull coast of Tarconii still lay to port, but the seamen informed me it would not be long before we passed through the straits that guarded the Southern Sea. After that, it would be only another five days or so before we reached the royal city of Chaarduz. It was a name I had heard often in the Nicien camp.

Once we passed a Rhemian warship heading north. I was alarmed at this, for I remembered the vessels in the white harbor Rheif and I had passed in our small boat. This ship passed us at a respectable distance, but I could see that it was full of armed warriors, and its decks bristled with terrible siege weapons. I pictured the great fist on this vessel's bow slicing through the smaller Nicien craft like a knife through a melon. The Niciens were greatly amused at my remarks. I need not concern myself, they said, for Niciea had nothing but scorn for these ungainly washtubs. Rhemians feared the sea, and never took their vessels far from shore. They were small boys who pulled toy boats about on bits of string —and a Nicien could sail rings around them with half her sail torn away. Besides, I was told, they did not have the secret of the tiny sword which ever sought the north, and allowed a man to always know where he was, even if there were clouds across the stars. I was doubtful of magic swords that could read directions, but I kept such doubts to myself.

However, what they told me about the Rhemians might well be so, I reasoned. Certainly, the sleek Nicien ships seemed born of the sea, and I spent many an hour watching the seamen go about their business. I marveled at their skills, for they had ingenious ways of moving the sails around so that every breath of wind did its work. I studied how this was done, and asked questions when I could. The Niceans were proud of their art, and would even take the time to tell a slave the many ways in which their vessels were superior to any other.

On our fourth day at sea, Lord Tharrin sent for me.

I was shocked at the Nicean's appearance. He was bent over a brazier in a corner of his cabin, a shrunken figure near lost in his robes. Even the light mantle over his shoulders seemed too heavy a burden. Ordinarily, a Nicean's scaly hide stretches taut across his features, showing points of bone beneath. Tharrin's skin had gone slack, and hung in loose folds about his eyes and across his throat.

"You stare, Aldair," he said ruefully. "That is unseemly."

"Lord—"

"I will save you from a lie. I look like the shade of death."

"You have been ill, Lord."

Tharrin grinned wearily. "You are a fine elixir for the sick, Aldair. It is well that you did not choose to be a physician. Those somber features would send a healthy man to the Afterworld."

I started to speak. Tharrin waved me to silence.

"Sit down, and stop hovering about and wondering how to make amends to your master. You can't. The warm sun of Niciea will bake me back to health and there's nothing else can. I—"

He stopped then, and looked at me most peculiarly—as if he was not sure who I might be.

"Is something wrong, Lord?" I asked him.

He held my gaze another moment, then looked down and studied the backs of his hands. "I'm prattling on about my health, Aldair, because there is another thing I wish to say and I'm damned if I know how to say it." He looked up. "A master has no right to ask a slave for trust. Yet I'm asking, Aldair. Tell me. And think before you answer. Can you give me that? It is not something I can demand, or take—there's no way to put an iron collar about a man's mind, and it would be valueless to do so."

I answered him immediately, because I truly had no hesitation in giving him what he asked. "Yes, Lord. I can."

"Not because that's what you know I want to hear, but

because—" He shook his head and ground one fist into the other. "No, of course it isn't. I do you a wrong." He looked down at his desk, then at me. "Trust is sometimes tested. I promise you this one will definitely be pressed to the limit. You still agree?"

"I do, Lord."

He nodded shortly. "I have chosen well, then." He turned toward the cabin door. "Linius!"

The door opened quickly. Too quickly, evidently, for the Lord Tharrin's liking. "You are prompt, steward," he said darkly.

"To serve you, Lord." Linius lowered his head.

"Take a care how you *serve* me," Tharrin warned him. He gestured toward me. "You have instructions regarding the slave Aldair."

"Lord . . ."

"Be certain those instructions are followed—as they were given. Do you understand this, Linius? Any—embellishments —you feel might better *serve* me will not be tolerated."

Linius kept his silence. I looked from one to the other. Certainly I had given my trust willingly and had no regrets. But this did little to still my curiosity. I couldn't guess what was about, but I sensed it was no small matter. The Lord Tharrin did not concern himself with trivialities.

I soon discovered that this was true. I also learned that the trusting are easily duped and quickly disappointed. Linius led me from his master's cabin directly to the ship's mast, where the Chief Archer stripped the robes from my back and proceeded to flog me into insensibility. The whipping lasted until first-blood reached my knees—so I am told— as this is the Nicean rule in such matters. I was also informed that there is some merit in being short, and I suppose this is so.

I do not remember the end of the matter, at any rate. I awoke on my stomach in the ship's hospital, where Master Pharrios, Lord Tharrin's own physician, was salving my wounds under layers of white linen. My back was an island of pain. Pharrios assured me that the beating had not been severe—that the Chief Archer knew how to apply the whip properly and there would be few scars.

For the first time since I had left Tharrin's cabin, I had a moment to get my wits about me. I had a short moment of wonder, surprise. Then anger drove all other thoughts from my mind, and even numbed the pain in my flesh. I have never known such hatred. I had trusted Lord Tharrin, and he had betrayed me—almost before his words died in my ears! I vowed that I would kill the Nicean. Even if it cost my own life in the doing. My chance would come. Not soon, perhaps. But I was willing to wait. . . .

My chance came sooner than I had imagined—for in less than an hour I was once more facing the Lord Tharrin. I met his gaze squarely, and saw nothing. My face was suddenly hot with shame. What had I *hoped* to see? Sorrow? Remorse? Why, the Nicean had nothing but contempt for me! And he had brought me here before him again to show that contempt. A slave would not dare touch a master, was that it? You could beat them half to death and they'd not raise a hand against you. Well, here was a slave who could remember his freedom better than that.

Lord Tharrin did not look at me, but turned to Linius. "Leave us, steward."

Linius showed surprise. "Lord?"

The Nicean's eyes grew cold. "Does a slave need two orders?"

Linius did not. He knew his master, and read him well. Tharrin leaned back and looked at me without expression. "Well, you have your chance, Aldair. I have given it to you."

I knew what he was saying. But I did not move.

"Why do you hesitate?" he asked. "There is blood in your eyes—surely it is mine."

"There is blood on my back," I said stiffly.

"So there is. Would you kill your master for that, then?"

I felt my face go hot again. "You—asked for my trust!"

"*And you denied it!*" Tharrin's fist came down sharply to accent his words.

"*I* denied it?"

"You, Aldair! I said that trust would be tested!"

"It was tested too far!"

"No." Tharrin shook his head. "You did not have the courage to meet it."

I fought to keep my fists at my sides. "There—is—honor." My voice shook. "I was born with *honor*. I am not—a thing to be—beaten!"

"A slave has no honor," Tharrin said simply. He folded his hands before him.

"There was honor—*Lord*—before there was slavery. I was born with it. It cannot be taken from me as easily as my freedom."

Tharrin raised his chin in question. "You do not approve of slavery . . ."

"It is a degradation. A man was not created to—"

"You do not keep slaves among the Venicii, then?"

"We—" I bit my lip. "That is not the same."

Tharrin nodded. "Perhaps it is, though—if you are that slave."

"They are Cygnians," I told him, not caring for the turn of this converation. "They have ever been slaves. They were born to it. They know nothing more."

"And perhaps Niciea believes the citizens of the Rhemian Empire were—*born* to be enslaved. . . ."

"It is—not the same!"

"Lord," he said sharply. You are forgetting that."

Again, I forced my arms to stay at my sides. What was holding me from gripping that pale throat between my fingers?

"Aldair . . ."

"All right." I swallowed, and tasted bile. "Lord . . ."

"Now." Tharrin leaned forward. "Perhaps we can arrive at some answers, Aldair. It appears that the main objections to slavery lie in *being* a slave—not in owning one. That every creature on Earth, noble or low-born, can, through circumstance, become a slave or a master in his lifetime —or both. That there is no rule of nature which brands any being slave or master. That only the *power* of one creature over another determines who is to serve, and who is to be served. It would be well for you to remember this. . . ."

I could hardly believe my ears. Was this the Lord of Niciea talking? And how many slaves did this worthy own? A thousand? Two thousand? Triple that?

"Lord Tharrin—"

Tharrin waved me to silence. "We will talk no more of this," he said absently. "It is not a subject that concerns you, though I would hope you will not forget what has been said."

I felt my jaws stiffen. "Lord, it *is* a subject—"

"And I say it is not." Tharrin reached under a stack of papers and tossed something on the table. I stared at it, then my hands went to my throat. My slave collar was gone! It lay before me, between the Nicieanʼs hands.

"You did not miss it greatly," Tharrin said dryly. "It was removed while the good physician was—ministering to your needs. No—do not speak, Aldair. It is time for me to do the talking, and you the listening. A moment ago I said that *you* denied my trust. This was not so. You did not deny it. Nor do you believe that you have been betrayed. Do you not see this? You did not let yourself do murder because you could not convince yourself there was a reason for it."

Tharrin paused and shook his head wearily. "The flogging was a thing that had to be done. There are rules that even rulers must keep, Aldair. No Nicieian slave may call himself free until the whip releases him. This is the law." He frowned and faced me soberly. "It may be that you will not thank me for removing your iron collar."

"Lord, I cannot believe that would be so," I told him.

Tharrin gave me a wary smile. "What you can or cannot believe changes nothing," he said. "There are things you do not know." He beckoned me forward, and I went to him, but without understanding. From the folds of his robe he drew a silken green scarf sewn with golden eyes. Quickly he bound the fabric about my neck, then leaned back to look at me. The act seemed to lift some great weight from his shoulders. There was no strength in his wasted body, but his black eyes blazed with a fierce determination.

"You have exchanged one collar for another, Aldair. Iron for silk. In all fairness, I should have given you some choice in this matter—for you are bound to me, now, as no slave could ever be."

He bade me sit, then—but gave me no chance for the questions on my tongue. "What is done is done," he sighed. "I have no one to blame but myself, and no other choice in my actions now. I have revealed to you a secret I have shared with only one other. A terrible, dangerous secret, Aldair. Why I did this I cannot say, but there are reasons for all things. This I know and believe. It may be that I will be given more understanding of the matter one day. At any rate, it has happened. I told a slave I did not truly know, a truth I have guarded with my life—*that the ruins of the Tarconii are far older than they should be. . . .*"

He shook his head and pulled himself forward, drawing his robes closer about his gaunt frame. "You cannot know what this means—now. One day you will. Know, though, that we are bound, my former slave. Bound as few men can be. What *I* have done is more than enough to bring us together. Now, though, there is this. . . ."

I could not have moved if the ship had sunk beneath me. Lord Tharrin reached beneath his desk and held a sheaf of parchments before my eyes. I knew them, of course. They were my own foolish ramblings—the papers I had burned in the work tent with my own hands. . . .

SIXTEEN

For a moment, Lord Tharrin's cabin seemed caught in silence. Time might well have been suspended there. I was aware of my own measured breathing, and the pulsing of my heart. It was as if I stood aside and watched the scene from a great distance. I was a part—and not a part—of these actions.

"Lord," I said finally, "there is much here I do not understand."

The Niciean held me with dark, baleful eyes. "I do not expect understanding. Not even after I've told you the things you need to know. There is much I will *not* tell you. I will withhold more than I reveal—but there is a reason for this. For now, I ask only acceptance of what I say. That, and your loyalty. As I said, Aldair, I have done you no great favor by replacing your iron collar with silk."

He paused a moment. "You will learn the significance of the Niciean scarf. It means more than you think. For now, can you accept this loyalty to me? I can command your body, but I cannot rule your mind."

"You have that loyalty, Lord." I was oddly surprised at my own quick reply.

"Your slavery must be put behind you. Entirely."

"It is, Lord."

"And the scars upon your back. Though I did not put them there, it was, ultimately, my hand that held the whip. This may not be so easily forgotten. Or forgiven."

I stared directly into the Niciean's eyes. So cold. Unworldly. Eyes that masked thoughts I could neither understand nor fathom. His oily hide was scale-bound, like the mail armor of some bizarre warrior. That hide had never

108

known true warmth, yet there was a fire in Tharrin's eyes that belied his chill appearance. And something had reached out from those eyes and spoken to me. Spoken of—what? That, I could not say.

"Lord," I said, "I came here to kill you for what you did to me. You brought shame upon me, and I could not live with that. We are proud men in the north. The pain is as great as ever on my back. But the shame is gone. I cannot say why this is so. But I will tell you that you have my loyalty, freely given."

The Nician studied me a long moment. "I thank you for that," he said finally. "Know that the scarf you wear binds *me* to you as well. I do not take that charge lightly."

He paused thoughtfully, then picked among his papers until he found the bulky report I had prepared before closing down the Tarconii site.

"Now, Aldair," he said, "we will discuss this finely drawn blade you have set at our throats." He smiled thinly and waved my puzzlement aside. "On the surface, this is a remarkable piece of work; you show an uncanny insight into a science you presumably know little about. You blunder now and then, stumbling blithely over contradictions with youthful disregard—but even your blunders are thoughtful ones. You have cataloged well, and presented an excellent summary of the year's work."

Lord Tharrin let out a breath and shook his head. "Would to the Creator that is *all* you had done, Aldair. This, now—" He set the report aside and picked up the sheaf of my own scribblings. "A theory for establishing the age of the ruins of Tarconii," he read dryly, then set the papers down and looked at me. "How did you come by—this?"

"It seemed logical enough, Lord."

"Logical?"

"Yes. Mineral salts and deposits of metal appear to settle on the stones in a kind of banding—as if they had been laid down with regularity. A guard who has been with you some years, Lord, told me the rainy season at the site is most predictable. That the stormy season arrives with uncanny precision. The storm which drove us ashore, he said, was most unusual—it had never come at that time in all the years he'd been there. I recalled, after seeing the bands at the site, that I had seen similar markings—in the cave where Rheif and I took shelter."

"And what have the markings in the cave to do with those in the ruins?" Tharrin asked, though I had covered this matter in my paper.

"They were all of a pattern," I explained, "as if the rains over the years had left their signature. There were similar markings in the ruins that had remained underground down the centuries, and had been subjected to the same water action. Of course, the cave is much older than the ruins. That helped. Through measurements, I could see where the markings in the cave left off, and those in the ruins began. There was a helpful overlapping."

"A helpful overlapping," Tharrin repeated dully. His spidery fingers drummed on the table top. "Continue."

"There is little else, Lord. It remained only to establish how many years it has taken each band to accumulate. Of course, I took the age you had given me as the standard. Thus it appeared that each band represented around two-hundred-years' accumulation. The variance in rainfall over such a time is a pattern in itself, and gives separation to the bands. Counting back, I came to the conclusion that the ruins are, truly, somewhat more than eight thousand years old."

Tharrin held my gaze. "How easily we are undone."

"Lord," I protested, "I did not intend in any way to *prove* the age you had given me. I had no such presumption in mind. To prove implies doubt, and I am much aware of my ignorance in such matters. The calculations were for my own amusement. You did not speak of your own method of reckoning. And of course I did not ask. I assumed it was—of a similar method."

"You assumed wrong," Tharrin said soberly.

"Lord—" My mind was turning in circles, now. Too much was happening—too quickly—for me to comprehend. I had been damned, praised, whipped, and raised to some high station that meant much to the Nicean, but little, as yet, to me. My scribblings were suddenly of grave importance. They had been burned—and still existed. The Lord Tharrin was greatly displeased, but I could not begin to guess why.

"Lord," I told him, "I know I should not have wasted my

—*your* time on such a thing. I see that now. After you told me this matter was not to be discussed, I should not have let it enter my thoughts again. But I must say this—for what it's worth. The papers were never meant for your eyes. They were destroyed—I thought—and I have never been more surprised to see anything in my life! I know, now, what surely happened. Being much in need of sleep, I grew careless. I burned scrap note work instead, and somehow inserted my own papers in the report for you. That they are presumptuous, that they offend, I am—"

"Damn, Aldair," Tharrin broke in, "stop mewling like a slave! You see nothing, yet, of this matter. There's more than my *offense* at stake here. What you've done, unwittingly or not, is worth our lives, boy—and more than ours alone!"

I was much puzzled at that. "But whatever the danger, Lord, or why, it need not *become* a danger. The report is in your hands, and my papers as well—" I stopped, suddenly struck.

"Yes," Tharrin said flatly. "There it is. In my hands. And one other."

"Linius?"

"Linius. Good, faithful steward Linius. He is the dagger at our throat. He and his masters. And while I am pleased you did not intentionally hand him this weapon, the result is the same."

Tharrin searched his palms thoughtfully, then looked at me. "You think the Church of the Rhemians is oppressive, Aldair. You cannot know the dread power of the priests of Niciea. Make no mistake—my brother rules, and all obey his will. He has effectively held the priests at bay, as our father did, and his father. But the priests are ever jealous for power. They hold the citizens in terror, and continually search for hints of heresy." He gazed pointedly at me. "Particularly in the royal family."

I felt a chill at the back of my neck. I was beginning to see the enormity of what I had done—and why Lord Tharrin had bound me to him. "Linius, then. Linius and these priests . . ."

Tharrin nodded. "And how am I to rid us of this threat? Oh, I could have that one silenced. But who can say how many more there are aboard? The strength of the priesthood lies in the thousands of eyes and ears that have been purchased by their gold. I have long known Linius for what he is. And I would rather know the traitor near me than wonder."

Light from a small port cast a yellow circle on Tharrin's desk, following the easy sway of the vessel. It cut across the Niciean's bony fingers, stabbed crisp parchment, and began its slow arc all over again.

"Even a patch of the sun gives life," Tharrin said absently. "You see, Aldair, what this paper of yours can mean? And make no mistake. Linius has had ample time to read and copy what he has seen. He misses little that might be of value." He shook his head grimly. "What you have done, Aldair, is to effectively disprove Niciean scripture, as well as your own, with this 'logical presumption' of yours. Nothing more earthshaking than that," he added wryly. "Religious leaders do not overly care for such logic, as you can imagine. Not that they would accept it as such. In the eyes of the priests, it is no proof at all—*except that you, and I, and the royal house of Niciea are in league with the damned. . . .*"

I could hardly believe what Lord Tharrin was saying; yet I could not doubt him. Though it seemed inconceivable that a youth from far Venicii might topple an empire with a few thoughtless scribblings—while all the legions of Rhemia dared not face the might of Niciea. Yet, when I remembered the gray specter of St. Bellium's, the cold heart of Father Tinius . . .

"Lord," I cried suddenly, "I can't right this wrong—though I would if I could! But—*knowledge*—is it not a more powerful weapon than fear? If the priests of Niciea can use this weapon, why can't it be turned against them? No one likes to live in fear, Lord Tharrin—neither Niciean nor Rhemian. The world is *not* as it seems. *Five thousand years* of history have been hidden from us. Years that have disappeared, or been thrust into darkness, for some reason I can't begin to imagine. If that past could be laid bare, through your proof, and whatever help my findings might be . . ."

Tharrin sat up stiffly. For a moment he seemed to pale beneath his green hide. "Aldair," he said hoarsely, "you do not know what you are saying. You do not understand this. *History must not be laid bare. Not now.*"

"Lord?"

"And this 'proof' of mine you speak of?" He shook his head. "There is no proof, Aldair. Other than yours. I have no proof and need none. I know. I simply *know*. And because I do, I know that nothing could be more deadly to the world than *what* I know. Or worse still, what I can only imagine . . ."

SEVENTEEN

It was a difficult thing to do, but I put aside my conversation with Lord Tharrin. This is not to say the subject was not ever on my mind. Doors had opened that could never be closed again. It was as though all the events of my life had been recorded on some ghostly scroll. That scroll was finished now, and sealed away forever. A new parchment had been prepared, and the first spidery letters inscribed the moment I left the Niciean's cabin.

And while it was not a rational thing, I was certain that if I allowed the small knowledge I now possessed to play too much upon my mind, the priests of Niciea would lift the thoughts cleanly from my head—and I would again put Lord Tharrin in dread danger. If I feared to think upon what I knew, I dared not dwell upon those things I did *not* know.

Though I did not understand the full meaning of my new status, others made it clear to me. All aboard the Niciean vessel saw me through new eyes—it was as if the old Aldair had vanished, and a new creature born. Slave and freeman alike treated me with deference. I often heard the words *rhadaz'meh* when I passed, and learned, later, they meant the "master's hand." I could bear weapons again—and, indeed, it was required that I do so. I now wore one of the wicked curved swords the Nicieans favor, a fine blade sheathed in colorful fabric and leather. This blade was lighter than iron, and stronger than bronze—tempered by some process unknown to the rest of the world. I marveled at the keen edge, which the Nicieans swore would cleave through Rhemian and Tarconii armor like a scythe through grass. I did not doubt that this was so.

My rough slave robes were exchanged for new raiments of linen. These had a green band sewn about the right sleeve—and above that, a golden eye. A heavy golden chain inset with green stones was placed about my neck, and Lord Tharrin gave me an intricately engraved silver ring from his own finger. It was too large for me, but the royal gem-smith reworked it to size.

One thing I insisted upon: I would not wear the Niciean boots, but retained my own. I might be the *rhadaz'meh* of the Lord Tharrin, but I was also still a Northman.

No one questioned that a slave had been suddenly brought to such heights. If the Lord Tharrin, brother of the Azhaar himself, wished to anoint one of the squalling gulls that followed the ship—why, that was his royal privilege, and none would be foolish enough to speak against it.

The nobles who followed Tharrin now noticed I was alive. A few were coldly polite—some sought me out with a friendly greeting, as if we had known one another for many years. These latter I trusted not at all. I had, of course, earned the everlasting enmity of the steward Linius, but there was nothing new in this. We had never gotten along, and my elevation over this agent of the Niciean priests served only to strengthen a hatred Linius could barely contain.

The day after I gained my freedom, I sought out the Stygiann. I found him with his charge on the shaded after-deck reserved for the royal household.

"This unworthy slave is honored, young master," Rheif said solemnly, and I caught the glint of amusement in his red eyes.

"Take care," I warned him, "or I will not allow you to fetch me wine and honeycakes."

Rheif laughed, but a curious frown creased his gray brows. "Truly, Aldair—what does this mean? I am totally without understanding of these creatures. First I see the skin peeled from your back, whereupon you are dragged below decks —for good, I imagined. Next, you emerge a young prince!"

"Hardly that."

"Hardly less, Aldair—considering you were next to nothing before—which is the status of one who wears this damnable collar."

I stared out over the sea. "What are they saying, Rheif?

About me. That will tell us a great deal more than either of us know."

Rheif made a face. "You mean you're in the dark, too?" He shook his head and rubbed a furry hand across his muzzle. "As I say, Aldair—these are most peculiar creatures. One wonders how they can share the same world with rational beings such as the Stygianns—and your own people, of course."

The young Dhar'jeem played on the deck nearby, attached to Rheif by a silken harness and a long gold cord. Whenever the child waddled too far away, or neared the railing, Rheif grimly pulled him back in line. The Dhar'jeem seemed to love this game, and repeated it again and again with squeaks of delight, much to the Stygiann's dismay.

"The other slaves have never been overly anxious to share their thoughts with me." Rheif grinned. "They complain that I look at them hungrily—which is not unlikely for a Stygiann who has been consuming vile bug stews for longer than he cares to remember. I have heard things, though. They say the Lord Tharrin only lives to putter about among old stones, and that you are a clever slave who recognized this, and led the Nicean to believe you shared his interests. Some of them are quite put out, as they have learned some skills in this art, too. They are angry with themselves because they didn't think of such a scheme themselves."

I was somewhat relieved. It was the story I'd hoped would be told—and believed. There was enough half-truth there to gain acceptance. I realized, however, that it mattered little what slaves and nobles thought. If Linius had truly had the chance to view my ruinous papers, the priests of Niciea would know for certain why a slave had become the *rhadaz- 'meh* of Lord Tharrin.

"Now," Rheif said thoughtfully, "I would know what this new status means to *you,* Aldair. What thoughts are in your mind?"

I knew what he was asking. "You mean have I bound myself to the Lord Tharrin? Yes, Rheif—in a way I have. Though it was not of my doing, as you well know. And it's a thing that could serve both of us in the future—though I could not speak of this to any but yourself."

"It is al*ready* serving me well," Rheif said dourly, "or so these creatures think. It is known we are companions, and I now receive a larger helping of insect porridge. It is meatier, with fewer legs floating about, and I suppose this is a blessing."

I grinned at his discomfort. "Perhaps there will be larger benefits as well. Two slaves have little chance of ever seeing their homes again, Rheif. *One* slave and a freeman might find a way."

The Stygiann straightened, and his red eyes gleamed. He gazed out over the sea, turning instinctively toward the far-away north. "I had not forgotten, Aldair." There was grim determination in his voice. "I am much pleased that you are remembering, too. . . ."

The green sea turned a brilliant blue, and the slim Niciean ships cleaved dazzling white foam through the wide strait and into the Southern Sea. An enormous stone sentinel guarded these waters to port. The dark mountain was pitted with caves, and rocky palisades and walkways perched pre-cariously on its sheer walls like blemishes on the hide of a great beast. This was properly a Rhemian stronghold, and red-sailed warships could be seen in the harbor below.

The Nicieans, though, sailed past this fortress with great disdain, so close beneath the rock that its shadow blotted the sun. This was not entirely an act of courage. A seaman told me we were safely out of range of the Rhemian siege engines— the helmsman had made the trip many times be-fore, and knew the proper distances.

The bulky Rhemian ships didn't bother to try to catch us. It would have been the armored turtle chasing the dolphin, and both the Rhemians and the Nicieans knew this.

A few hours later, four warships from the Niciean side of the sea moved swiftly out to intercept us and form an escort for the rest of the trip. They were larger than the two vessels in Lord Tharrin's party, and nearly as fast. All were well armed, and painted fore to aft with the green-scale pattern. These ships were killers of the sea, and I thought them a match for anything the Rhemians might set against us.

I had one task to complete before we made port. Lord Tharrin would keep the original record of our year's findings, but a presentation copy had to be prepared for the scholars of Niciea. The presentation copy was somewhat abbreviated, and I assisted Tharrin in the editing of this document.

"It is innocuous enough, I suppose," he grumbled finally. "All that really matters over the years is locked up in this head of mine, and can't be set to paper. The university will bestow its usual honors on me, no matter what the wording." He laughed sharply. "What else can they do? I'm the king's brother, and have no little power of my own."

He slapped the report and laid it aside. "But they will not *read* it, Aldair—be assured of that. They're dullards, for the most part, who purchased their masterships through money or position. There are wise men among them, for certain—but they're scarce as bug down."

As usual, I had many questions whirling about my head. I knew better than to ask them, but this did nothing to still my curiosity. Lord Tharrin, though, gave me little time for dangerous thinking. There was much to do in preparation for reaching port—and in truth, I was glad enough for the chance to keep busy. And on the dawning some two days later, the sails of the Nicean vessels were furled, and the hull slaves—who usually had little to do on these swift green sea-runners—took to their oars and guided us into the blue harbor of Chaarduz. I was up well before the sun on that day, and high in the bow to watch the morning pink the white towers and domed temples of the heart of Niciea's empire.

EIGHTEEN

The dockside bustled with activity. Slaves went about the business of unloading the expedition vessels, though there was little enough aboard after the long months away from port. Most of the cargo consisted of artifacts and samples from the Tarconii ruins. And since the safeguarding of these items was my charge, I was busy through the morning.

Sighting the relatively small stack of sacks and boxes in the hold, the slaves decided they had an easy day ahead. After hefting a few of these bundles, and discovering they were full of stone, they changed their tune. The overseer's whip sang more than once that day.

The ship was emptied before morning turned to midday, but the royal party didn't go ashore until well into the afternoon. I guessed the reason for this. An escort of horsemen in finely arrayed capes and armor was waiting for us on-shore, and one officer clearly of high rank swung aboard even before we were secured and closeted himself below with Lord Tharrin. By the time they emerged the blazing sun had turned both the land and sea to brass, and near stifled all aboard.

Tharrin spoke to no one after this meeting, but it was clear the officer had brought bad news. The Niciean's face was strained, and the strength he had regained on the voyage had deserted him. I learned later that all was not well in the capital, and that there were problems in other parts of the land. The king was not on hand to greet his brother as expected—he had left the city hurriedly nine days before, when rebel tribesmen who had kept the peace with only minor transgressions for some years had suddenly come out of the desert in great hordes to ravage villages, burn crops, and murder the citizenry. More than that, an incident had occurred that threw an ominous shadow over the king's mission. As the army left the city, it was said, a large gray bird had fallen dead from the skies, plummeting to earth only a few paces ahead of the king. The king's mount was startled, and nearly threw its master. Rumors swept through Chaarduz, claiming the bird was of a kind never seen before, and that it had no eyes at all, and was bloodless. A bird had indeed fallen, for whatever the reason, but it was neither of uncommon breed nor eyeless, and had an ample supply of blood. But, as a Niciean officer complained, the people care nothing for the truth of the matter, the lie being of greater interest. If gossip was the theater of the idle, he said, there was no greater stage for such drama than Chaarduz. . . .

I was glad enough to get off the ship and through the city —and, finally, near nightfall, to Lord Tharrin's villa. Even in the fading light I was staggered by the size of my master's estate. It occupied an entire hill overlooking the city and the harbor. At first sight, I thought surely this was the palace of the king itself, and that Tharrin lived in some part of it. Not so. The palace covered several neighboring hills, and met Tharrin's grounds in places, as did the estates of all members of the royal family. The whole was sheltered by a high, common wall, which offered protection and privacy for members of court. Much of the royal grounds was covered by gardens, fountains, and other pleasures designed to delight the eye. The palace, with its surrounding villas, was a city unto itself, and more than three thousand slaves, soldiers, craftsmen, gardeners, and workers of all sorts labored there to serve little more than three dozen members of the royal blood.

The Nicieans are bizarre creatures, and strange enough in their ways. But I came to know that these are surface differences only. In most respects, they differ little from other races. There are poor all over the world—more of these than any others. They exist, it seems, to meet the needs of the royal family of Niciea, and the rulers of the Rhemian Empire—and those other persons these worthies permit to become wealthy and powerful. It has ever been so, I reasoned, and I could not picture what other manner of living there might be. There were masters, and those who served them—freemen or slaves. That appears to be the order of things. As it was with the wooden puppets in the Market of Silium, so it is with the world. I had never questioned it before. But then, I had never been a slave before, either. And that state, even for a short period of time, gives a man a new perspective on the nature of things.

In the household of the Lord Tharrin, the women were set apart, in the Nicican manner. They kept to their own quarters and were never seen. Shortly after my arrival I learned one fact I could hardly believe: the Nicican females do not give birth in the normal manner, but lay eggs, as do the birds. A Rhemian slave informed me that this was a subject that was never mentioned, even among the Nicicans. There was, it seemed, some religious significance or prohibition attached to the process of birth—though I never learned what that might be. Be that as it may, I overheard more than one ribald joke in which eggs, and the getting of them, played a significant role.

To my surprise and pleasure, Rheif was also quartered in Tharrin's household—it being the custom among royalty to raise the young in homes apart from their parents. Tharrin himself told me this tradition was as old as Niciea, when the land was ruled by rival houses, and offspring were traded to keep the peace.

"Perhaps it is still of some value in that respect," the Nicican said amusedly. "Though the kingdom is now united under one family, there are various cousins and nephews who would have more to say in court if their children were not my brother's wards. . . ."

The king had only one child, the young Dhar'jeem, but if he had had a second, it, too, would have been entrusted to Tharrin's household, and none other. Tharrin had no ambitions to the throne, and the king would not have been foolish enough to tempt some wily relative with dreams of power.

Though Rheif and I were housed in the same quarters, the estate was quite large, and both of us were occupied with our duties. Thus it was a two-month before we saw one another for more than a passing moment. I thought the Stygiann looked well, and content, and told him so. But

Stygianns distrust two things in life: compliments and water.

"There is no need to pretend with me," Rheif said dolefully. "It should be clear to you that I have little time left on this world. My health is fading, Aldair. The young prince is a mightier foe than any warrior I have faced in battle, and it's certain he will best me soon enough."

I had to laugh at this. "The dinner devours the diner, to coin a phrase—which, if I am not mistaken, was first said in the Market square of Silium, when a caged Stygiann warrior—"

"Aldair . . ." Rheif looked warily over his shoulder. "I *know* where the phrase originates. It is not necessary to remind me, nor any others, that my relationship with the prince Dhar'jeem did not necessarily begin as it might have appeared. Though I have long suspected the Lord Tharrin knows very well what happened—and that in his eyes I am being justly punished for the simple crime of hunger—which as I see it, is no crime at all."

My duties kept me busy, and I was scarcely aware of the passage of the days. Often, I worked into the night until my notes blurred before my eyes and I dozed beside my papers while the oil lamps burned themselves dry. The excavation of ancient cities, I learned, was only a small part of this science. The key to the city's secrets lay ultimately in countless samples, notes, and data that had been gathered over the years.

I seldom saw the Lord Tharrin. As much as my master protested his lack of interest in "politics and things of business," he was actively engaged in other pursuits. What these might be, I couldn't guess—though I was aware the Niciean often closeted himself during the day, and left the villa at odd hours of the night. What sort of business called a man from his bed at such hours? It was none of my concern— but I knew the Lord Tharrin, and found it hard to dampen my curiosity.

I heard things. There were always rumors in the royal compound. The king had returned and the rebels had been beaten, but not without heavy losses to the royal forces and damage to the king's standing. The rebels would try again, it was said. The king was privately furious with the priesthood, because they had made much of the bird omen—clearly but subtly insinuating that the incident was a true foretelling, insomuch as the royal forces *had* suffered losses at the hands of the rebels. The priests piously added that they were earnestly praying for a better omen for Niciea's ruler. Their true feelings were not lost upon the people, who read the worst into such things, and the king again lost prestige in the land.

There came a night when I ran into a particular knotty problem concerning correlation of current data with that which had been gathered in the past. There being no records on this subject in my workroom, I sought out a seldom-used storage area in another quarter of the villa. Tharrin had wryly termed it a library, but admitted it was a dumping ground for those things he couldn't decide what to do with, and didn't dare throw away.

I had been to this room once before, with Lord Tharrin, but thought nothing about going myself. The Niciean had given me full rein to carry out my duties as I saw fit, and the brass key to our "dumping ground" hung openly on a peg in the workroom. So I opened the heavy door and thrust my lamp before me and saw Lord Tharrin sitting in near darkness. Lord Tharrin and one other.

I stopped, caught the Niciean's startled expression, and backed quickly toward the hall.

"Aldair!" His voice was sharp, commanding—but not loud enough to carry. "Come in quickly, boy, and lock that door behind you!"

"Lord," I began, "I—"

"I know you didn't. I gave you the key and authority to use it. It's *my* mind that's drifted." He glanced at his companion, then back at me. I couldn't help but stare. By the Creator—a Cygnian! A *slave*, sitting big as you please beside Lord Tharrin! And more than that, wearing freeman's clothing.

The Cygnian caught my glance, and turned dark, placid eyes on the Niciean. "He's surprised to see me, Lord. Perhaps as much as I, to see him. . . ." His eyes stayed on Tharrin, and his question, as well.

Tharrin let a slight grin leave the corners of his mouth. "A fellow slave, Aldair—or formerly so, as yourself." He spoke to the Cygnian. "Rest easy, friend. Aldair is the one I spoke about."

The Cygnian nodded. He was fleshier than most of his breed—his wool was shorn for the hot climate of Niciea, and he wore a plain, heavy gold chain about his neck. I found it difficult to meet this creature's gaze. Damn, I wondered, what kind of Cygnian was this? The familiar, docile expression was absent from his dark eyes—if it had ever been there. There was something else, though. . . .

"Aldair," Tharrin said pointedly, "do not add more guesses to that inquisitive mind of yours. You've another secret to guard now—and this one as deadly as the first." He ran a weary hand across his face and shook his head in resignation. "By the Creator, Aldair—you'll do us all in yet. . . ."

NINETEEN

I did not look forward to meeting the priests of Niciea. But, as the Lord Tharrin explained, this was not a thing to be easily avoided.

"It's a ruse, of course," he said grimly, "but a good one. I expected your name to come to their attention. Linius has done his work well. This is why you were given the *Qua'shar,* our holy scripture, and commanded to familiarize yourself with its principles. The priests will not expect you to know a great deal—but then that isn't the purpose of your visit to the temple."

The Nicien told me this was one of the many methods used to gain power and retain a hold over the people. Ostensibly, Aastar the Creator himself spoke to the priests in dreams, and called out the names of persons who were to be honored by "special blessings and instruction." These persons might be noble, freeman, or slave, Tharrin said wryly—but they always seemed to be individuals who were in some position to give information of value, or perform some service.

"Such as spying on the royal household," the lord added. "I'm certain that's how the faithful steward Linius was added to their ranks. Through fear, flattery, or the smell of gold —which, it doesn't matter. Take a care with these fellows, Aldair. I need not remind you they are no special friends of this family."

"They will find, Lord," I told him, "that I know nothing of interest. I'll see to that."

"You'll do nothing of the sort!" Tharrin exploded. He gripped my arm fiercely. "Know, my young friend, that these are not men to be toyed with. They are masters of deceit

125

and cunning, and if you seek to match wits with them they'll have you in their hands!"

He let out a breath and spoke more gently. "I know you seek to serve me, Aldair, but have a care how you do it. The priests know me, and are aware that I would not take a fool into my household. Do not pretend to be one. They will not expect to gain much from you, but they cannot afford to pass up the opportunity to try. They will already know a great deal about you, through Linius. Do not be surprised at this."

The Niciean paused and ran long fingers across his face. "Remember, too, our traitor has given them a weapon to use against us. They may bring it into play soon, or they may not. But they will know your part in this, and they will search for a way in which you might be used against me." He smiled then. "I know they will not find one, Aldair. This does not concern me. But the priests do not understand that loyalty and friendship can be based upon finer currency than gold. . . ."

I took the Lord Tharrin's words to heart. He was right, of course. To play the dolt would only call further attention to me, and my master's household. I would be natural, then —not clever. Cooperative, but not overly eager. Still, I slept little the night before my appointment at the temple. By morning, my mind was full of things I must *not* do— and I was certain I would do them all.

A mount awaited me in the courtyard. It was a tall, slender steed—coal black and glistening like new silk in the morning sun. I thought the animal a handsome creature, but felt ridiculous in the saddle. I was sure everyone who saw me laughed at my stubby legs, which reached only halfway down the beast's flanks. I would have preferred one of the short, stocky ponies of the Venicii, which could be guided by the slightest pressure of a rider's knees or the movement of his body, leaving him free to use his bow to best advantage.

Still, the mount was a present from Lord Tharrin, an honor shown to me, and there was little I could do but climb aboard the giant as if I were scaling a small hill, and hope for the best.

The roadway from the villa to the gates of Lord Tharrin's

estate wound beneath rows of high cedars planted long ago to shade royal travelers. The trees filled the air with pungent odor, and the sun filtered through dark boughs to mottle the path with golden coins of light.

I was enjoying this sight when a sudden noise broke the silence. I came alert in the saddle; my mount snorted nervously, pawed the ground, and skittered his buttocks about in a half circle. I tightened the reins, spoke quick words to gentle the beast.

The noise again. Louder, this time. Like a great beast in pain. The horse plunged forward, but I was ready this time. I jerked the animal off the roadway and broke through the trees and into the clearing beyond. The sun was was bright and I squinted against the glare. Slowing the mount, I listened, then turned him sharply downhill. Past a stand of trees the meadow opened into a rocky clearing. A great wheel had been built there, horizontally to the ground. Its axle was buried, and twenty or more slaves were yoked about its rim. I knew the purpose of this device was to carry fresh water up the hill.

I paid little attention, though, to the wheel itself. The source of the disturbance was to my right—a slave had been chained to two posts, and Niciean overseers were flaying him unmercifully. His broad, furry back was laid open and raw flesh was bared to the sun.

I was not surprised the creature's pain had near shaken the leaves from the trees. This was no ordinary slave, but a being farther from home than either Rheif or myself. I had met Vikonens before, in the northern ports—great, burly creatures with broad chests, short muzzles, and thick cinnamon pelts that protected them from the cold of their frigid islands. They brought their longboats in to trade with the Venicii, and kept the peace for the most part, since it was profitable to do so. Their true calling, though, is not in trade. They are raiders of the sea, and this is the way they prefer to live. The Rhemians seek them out halfheartedly, when coastal cities cry for help, or ships fear to take to sea. But Vikonens pay little attention to Rhemians, and do not deign to run from them, unless it is absolutely necessary.

I sat my mount and studied the scene. My gaze stopped on one of the Vikonen's tormenters, and held there. Good steward Linius, and I was not surprised to find his hand in this. I urged the horse forward, though he wanted no part of the event, having smelled the Vikonen. No beast likes to be near these creatures.

Linius saw me, and his face clouded, then fell into a practiced smile. I glanced at the Vikonen. He returned the look with hatred, and growled deeply in his throat.

"What have you here, Linius?"

"A slave of your Lord Tharrin," the steward said easily. He slapped the whip across his palm and grinned at me. "He does not feel it is necessary for the Nicieans to have fresh water. We'll convince him, though, that this is not a seemly attitude."

"You cannot convince him, Linius, if he is dead."

Linius's smile only widened. But his eyes spoke his mind. "If he does not choose to work, he will, indeed, be dead. It is the free choice of any slave."

"I'll take your word for this," I told him. "For you have a longer acquaintance with slavery than I."

Linius stiffened. "I do my job," he snapped shortly. "Which is to see that my master's work is done."

"You do your master's work with much pleasure."

"I do what I am required to do, Aldair. The Lord Tharrin sets my duties, and I perform them."

"Then the Lord Tharrin has instructed you to beat his slaves until they cannot work. He has told you this."

Linius's grip tightened on his whip. "Aldair, this does not concern you."

"Not Aldair," I corrected. "You forget your place."

"And you forget yours!" he raged. "You have been a slave yourself!"

"I have. But I am a freeman now. You are not."

"I am steward of the Lord Tharrin," he said stiffly. His eyes glanced quickly to those about him. He was losing status in their eyes, and knew it.

"You are steward," I said. "And a slave."

Linius bit off his words.

"What, steward?"

"I—said nothing."

"Perhaps the *other* slave is willing to work now, Linius. Why not try him and see? In this way, you can better serve your master." I did not look at Linius again, but urged my mount away, bringing him as close to the Vikonen as the skittish beast would allow. I paused there, and leaned down and patted the horse's neck, pretending to speak to it soothingly.

"Have a care," I said in the Vikonen tongue. "Do not appear to hear my words, sea raider, but listen well. That one will relish killing you. He will, if you refuse to work. This is not your day, but his. Stay alive, and perhaps you'll feel ice in your fur again."

I moved on, then made my way back to the cedar-lined pathway. I would be late for my appointment with the priests, but there was nothing for that now. I could feel Linius's eyes on my back until the trees closed behind me.

"Well, how did it go, then?" Tharrin regarded me over the tips of his fingers.

"Well, I think, Lord. I followed your sound advice."

"The names of the priests. You remember them?"

"I do, Lord," I told him. "And I'm not likely to forget them. One, the worst of the two, was called Rhazish. The other, not so bad, Chamrin."

Tharrin said nothing. He made me go over the entire session twice, asking questions now and then. Finally, he sat back and regarded me thoughtfully. "They didn't try too hard. And you did well in your answers. It was a testing, and it may be that you will be called again." He shrugged. "We will handle that when we come to it. Now. This other thing. With Linius. I'd hear of that, though I know much already."

I made certain my eyes met his. "Lord, I never intended not to tell you myself. There has been no time."

Tharrin waved me aside. "I know that, Aldair. I don't chastise you for it. Linius goes too far. He takes much upon himself, and this is a sign of something in the wind, is it not?" He frowned to himself. "It is almost as if he —flaunts himself before me. And he would not dare this unless he has some reason for believing he will not be punished for it." He ground one palm into his fist. "And this could easily be so—if I were not free to do the punishing. . . ."

I sat up straight and looked at him. Tharrin shrugged. "He's a coward, Aldair. Whatever may come will not come from him. Do not guard against a noisy enemy, lad, while the silent assassin thrusts a blade in your back."

"Who, then?"

"Who can say? The brother of a king has more enemies than friends."

"A few moments with steward Linius," I told him, "and he would gladly tell me all that's in his heart."

Tharrin shook his head. "I could have that done myself, if it were an answer. No, he has already shown his hand and given us warning. We can thank him for that."

He turned to me and grinned wryly. "We had a conversation once, aboard ship. You recall it? About slavery, and how its acceptance appeared to have a great deal to do with who is the slave, and who the master."

"I recall it well, Lord."

"It appears, from your actions, that you do, indeed, Aldair. . . ."

There was unrest in the city that night. A religious procession sponsored by the priesthood—supposedly in observance of some obscure event mentioned in the *Qua'shar*—wound its way through the streets. The citizens of Chaarduz took full advantage of the event, and before the night was done the procession turned into a riot. Some were killed—for the most part, those not engaged in the festivities at all. Several shops were burned and looted. In the morning, the western section of the city was a shambles.

Tharrin noted that the priests, like Linius, were showing their strength. That there was, for certain, more to come. And the next night I rode out with the Niciean to a secret place far out of the city, almost to the edge of the Great Desert. Other robed figures arrived in silence, and though their faces were covered, the breed of their horses told their masters' blood. I suspected the king was there himself, but I did not ask. I felt there was great significance to this meeting. It would have been far easier to meet in the palace itself. Clearly, though, there were some within the court itself who could not be trusted.

Two days after this meeting the king declared a holiday —naming his own obscure moment in Niciean history as the reason. The king appeared at the head of a colorful parade through the city, and the Niciean treasury brought forth great bags of small coins to shower upon the people.

There was food and drink in the public parks, and it was known that all these things were gifts of the king himself.

The citizens cheered their noble ruler as loudly as they had praised the priests, and for the moment there was quiet in the city. No one, though, believed that it would last. It was a method of buying time, and nothing more. The people of Chaarduz had short memories, and when the food was eaten and the coins spent, they would grow restless again, and listen to whoever offered to distract them from their dull lives, or fill their empty bellies.

TWENTY

It was still an hour before the dawn when the Lord Tharrin sent Mehzaar, who was the captain of his personal guard, to bring me to his quarters. I was both surprised and concerned, because the Niciean had never done this before. That, and the fact that he had sent Mehzaar instead of a house slave on such an errand, said a great deal.

I knew I was right when I entered the small study; Tharrin's features were somber and strained in the light of the single candle on his desk.

"Rest, Aldair. There's wine beside you and you may pour for us both." He didn't wait for the cups but went straight to business. "There are priests outside the gate. Mehzaar thinks one of them is Cha'saam, who is third only to Bhurzal himself. There is also a detachment of the Huizim temple guard in tow. A most impressive party, and you should be flattered, Aldair, because it is you they came to see."

I spilled a drop of wine on my tunic. "Me, Lord?"

Tharrin made a tired gesture. "You, in body. But me, of course, in spirit. They are not quite ready to come for the king's brother, though they are as much as telling me they intend to get around to that. This"—he held up a long parchment, then let it fall to the table—"this tells me a great deal. It is signed by Bhurzal himself, and that holds some significance. The most of it is priestly double-talk, but in essence it says one Aldair of Venicii, *rhadaz'meh* of the Lord Tharrin, etcetera, lately blessed and instructed under holy auspices, is again requested"—Tharrin raised a hairless brow—"'requested,' eh? It means, Aldair, that they want you back. Permanently, this time. You are to bear witness

132

against me for whatever heresy they have in mind—then, I'd imagine, you will take a draught of poison which you have cleverly secreted upon yourself, and leave a note confessing remorse over your complicity in my misdeeds."

The Niciean's face clouded. "Well, they've gone too far this time." His fist struck the table sharply. "I won't have it —and neither, by the Creator, will the king!"

He turned to me and shook his head. "I was a fool to send you the first time," he said darkly. "I'd no idea how far they meant to go. . . ." He stood and paced to the far end of the room and turned. "They could have taken you then. They weren't ready, though, and thought they could come for you when they liked." He grinned determinedly. "Well, they won't. Be damned with them!"

Lord Tharrin picked up his wine cup and drained it, then pointed the vessel at me. "Go to your quarters and stay there until I send for you—and go with no one who comes but Mehzaar himself. It's beginning, Aldair. As Nhidaaj said it would. It is beginning. . . ."

I did not know the name he spoke, but I perceived something in his manner, and knew in my mind it was the Cygnian slave who was not a slave.

I kept to my quarters as commanded, but saw no one but Mehzaar until the following day. The captain, though, kept me well informed. Much was happening about the city: Bhurzal himself had sent emissaries to the king demanding that Lord Tharrin release me for further "honors and instructions." I was, it seemed, merely wanted for questions concerning religious matters, which had nothing to do with the ruling of the Niciean Empire. Thus, the king's brother had no right to interfere in such things.

It was said that the king had put a great deal of pressure upon his brother—that perhaps the priests would be satisfied if their request were granted. He did not need additional problems, having all he could bear from that group at the moment. Tharrin, however, stood his ground, pointing out—according to Mehzaar—that if I was given to the priests, it would only hurt the royal family, not help them. The king had relented in the end, for he did, indeed, rely greatly upon his brother's judgment.

There were other stories, too. Rumors flew about the

city. The Creator himself had been seen outside the palace gates at midnight, pointing an accusing finger at the royal enclosure. A Niciean guard had looked upon his face and turned to stone. . . . It was said that the king was a madman, and had ordered the temples burned and the priests put to the stake. . . . A mouse with no head had been seen alive in the granaries—the priests said this meant the wheat would die in the fields next year, and there would be famine in the land. . . . There were many such tales bandied about, and Mehzaar said wryly that it was likely the people believed them all.

I knew, though, that while most of the things we heard were fanciful yarns, there was a reason for their being. Fear was stalking the streets of Chaarduz, and we'd see worse sights than headless mice before the week was over. No members of the royal family now ventured outside the compound, and even slaves bearing the green Niciean livery were afraid to be seen in the streets.

Late the next morning a proclamation was handed to the king's guards. It stated that a soldier who had accompanied the expedition to Tarconii had confessed to the temple priests that he had witnessed demonic rites performed at midnight in the bowels of the ancient city. Engaging in these rites, and consorting with one another in a shameful, unmentionable manner, were Aldair, *rhadaz'meh* of the Lord Tharrin, Lord Tharrin himself, and the Stygiann barbarian known as Rheif. This latter, who was now guardian of the young Dhar'jeem, had been seen to devour the prince and substitute a demon in his place. This demon, in the guise of the king's son, would one day rule Niciea, and thus damn all who followed its calling.

"That's it, then," Tharrin announced woodenly. "They have come into the open and declared themselves against the king—though little of the rabble out there will make the connection, or care."

I had mentioned to Lord Tharrin that it appeared Bhurzal had used every weapon at his disposal—except the one we might have expected.

"I did not truly expect that he would—not directly," the Niciean told me. "The danger to us, Aldair, lies not so much in exposure of your notes, as in the priests' knowledge that they exist. Be assured they play a part in this. But give Bhurzal his due—he is a madman, but not a fool. He *will* use every weapon at hand in his fight against the royal family. And he will use this, too—but not necessarily in the manner you might expect." Tharrin paused and stared into his wine. "He's let me know he has the evidence at hand. He made certain of that."

"Lord?" I was puzzled at this.

"The proclamation, Aldair." The Niciean grinned wearily. "It's a little game, you see—or so it is to Bhurzal. It's all there—demonic rites on the site of the ancient city . . . unmentionable practices. . . . We well know what it is that's 'unmentionable,' don't we? And so does Bhurzal. In one way, he and I think much alike. Neither of us would care to make public the knowledge of a 'lost history' of the world. For different reasons, though. For far different reasons . . ."

I would have liked to pursue this, but I knew better than to question the Lord Tharrin when it came to certain subjects. Still, I wondered. At one time, much had been made of my Tarconii scribblings. Largely because of that business, I had been elevated to a lofty station. Now it seemed the matter was not overly important—not in the light of other events. But I could not forget that Tharrin had argued with the king himself to keep me out of Bhurzal's hands. Wholly because he was fond of me? Because he honored the bonds between a master and his *rhadaz'meh?* Perhaps.

But I could not forget that the Niciean had once made it clear that when it came to ancient cities and lost years, he would likely reveal a great deal less than he knew. Certainly I believed this was so.

Later that same day, I came upon Lord Tharrin again, this time after his return from a conference with the king. "We can expect the worst, Aldair," he said darkly, "and all that that entails. And when it comes, we can blame ourselves for it. We, the noble house of Niciea. And the rulers of the Rhemian Empire, too. For what happens in Niciea today could easily crumble that world of yours across the Southern Sea."

I puzzled over that. I could see how the priests of Chaarduz could create enough mischief to make the city suffer, or even all of Niciea. But more than this . . .

Tharrin sensed my questions. "Change is in the making, Aldair," he said cryptically, and left me with that.

Tharrin and the king's nobles seemed to be ever in conference of some sort, though what came out of these meetings I couldn't say. While they talked, though, the priests incited a riot with a "rumor" of poisoned grain, and before the army could restore order a three-months' supply of valuable food supplies was burned and dumped into the sea. This act—which they themselves had performed—so angered the rioters that they set fire to three warships in the harbor. A high wind picked up burning bits of wood and fabric and wafted it into Chaarduz, starting a dozen smaller fires in widely separate parts of the city.

From a high balcony atop Tharrin's villa, Rheif and I watched this spectacle into the late hours. Neither of us had much to say. It had been a wearing night, and who could say what the dawning might bring?

"Aldair," Rheif said finally, "what is to become of us?"

"How do you expect me to answer a question like that?" I asked him.

"It is hot here, Aldair. Even at night there is no wind. And if there is, chances are *it* is hot, also. I expect there is a great deal of snow in the north, now. Snow with hare tracks, don't you imagine?"

"Yes. I imagine so."

"And fat owls that beg to be knocked from the trees with stones. And—"

"Rheif," I said, "It's getting late. It is time to go to bed. We may need our rest tomorrow."

"It is already tomorrow," Rheif announced. "If you had wanted to sleep, Aldair, you should not have brought us up here to watch Chaarduz burn—though I admit it was as splendid a fire as I have ever seen. . . ."

TWENTY-ONE

As the Lord Tharrin had noted, Bhurzal the high priest was a man of cunning who knew the temper of the people. Many had perished in the fires that partially destroyed the royal granaries and gutted numerous buildings near the dockways. By midday, the square before the temple was a sea of angry green faces. A great cry of anguish rose from the citizens of Chaarduz, and many waved ragged pennants of yellow, the color of death. Though perhaps a hundred had died the night before, these banners soon numbered in the thousands, until it seemed everyone in the city mourned the loss of a loved one. So infectious was this bereavement that wives called out for dead husbands, who, in fact, stood beside them crying for the mate who would never share the marital bed again.

Bhurzal knew that if this crowd took it upon itself to surge forward, it might well take the temple apart stone by stone, and any who stood in its way. Therefore, he donned the yellow robes of death and appeared before them. He spread his arms to the heavens, and the great robe billowed about his gaunt figure, and his terrible eyes touched them all. The crowd stilled and held its breath, for Bhurzal was seldom seen by common folk.

And when he had them in his sway, he told them that those who had died the night before had earned a special place on the right hand of Aastar the Creator, for they had, truly, perished for him. Chaarduz howled its approval, but Bhurzal had more to say, and raised his hand for quiet. None of these honored souls, he explained, could yet enter the Afterworld. The way was barred to them. This was because certain unclean acts had been committed against the

137

Creator, closing the nether gates. Those gates could only be opened after those acts—and the demons who had performed them—had been properly exorcized.

The people needed no further enlightenment. They knew who the demons were, though Bhurzal had been careful not to name them. As a body, they turned their wrath from the temple, and made for the great wall that surrounded the royal grounds. . . .

"He will not act," Tharrin stormed. "He does nothing, even after that maniac has called his son a demon and turned the people against him!"

His counselors, nobles, and high officers said nothing. They stared at their hands, or blinked past the shaded portico at the towers of Chaarduz below. Many, I noted, still wore the stains of their own blood upon their fine robes. None felt these were badges of honor—for they had driven their own people from the walls that morning, leaving half a thousand dead or wounded. There was sorrow on both sides of the wall that day.

"Tharrin—perhaps he feels there is nothing he *can* do," an elderly cousin said finally. "He said to me, 'How can I call myself king, and father to Niciea, if I slaughter my children?' "

"They would slaughter his," Tharrin muttered. He gripped the curved blade by his side, and his dark eyes swept about the circle. "I do not advocate killing Nicieans. It is that nest of traitors within the temple I'd take to the sword."

I heard a few quick breaths, and several counselors exchanged looks across the room.

"You'd take a priest's life?" asked the cousin.

"He'd take mine," Tharrin said shortly. "And yours."

"I'll not damn my soul," the man said.

"Then you'll soon have it to yourself, Lord, to do with as you will." The one who spoke was a grizzled old soldier who had served Niciea more than half a lifetime. The noble cousin flushed, and turned upon him. "You've no right to speak in that manner, Dhaarim!"

"I fight for you, Lord," Dhaarim said simply. "I have the right to die on the walls, keeping the priests' mob from your throat. . . ."

"All right!" Tharrin broke in. He half stood, hands flat on the table before them. His motion toppled a cup of dark wine, and I watched the narrow crimson thread search the edge of the table, then disappear in hungry stones below.

"We are not here to fight among ourselves. Nor condemn the words of the *Qua'shar,* which are holy to us all. But I suggest, gentlemen, that it is not our Creator who incites our people against their king, or names us demons and heretics—but *earthly* beings, who destroy in Aastar's name. For their glory, not his!"

Most of those present nodded vigorously at this, and mumbled angry assent. And though they were in general agreement something must be done, that action must be taken immediately to stave off disaster—the meeting ended with nothing accomplished. For none of them was a king, and none could put action to his words.

I had little time to consider what might befall us next. There was more than enough to do within the compound. The assault on the wall had taught us a somber lesson. That even with the army behind us, the royal family was dangerously vulnerable. Unarmed citizens—if there were enough of them—could swarm into the grounds and sweep the soldiers aside. And once the army was gone, nothing would stop the mob until the palace itself and all the rich estates around it were in ruins.

Fear was almost a visible specter behind the walls. And I thought it strange that of all the foes an empire faced, the one within its own borders was the only one that truly held the keys to its destruction.

Many of us knew there was an even greater danger at hand, within the compound itself. For the priests had done their work well, and now they pronouced damnation upon any officer or soldier who raised a hand against the people, or a priest of Aastar. Some had deserted already, and it was feared that others remained quietly in their ranks at Bhurzal's instructions, ready to do his bidding. The royal family, then, sheltered potential assassins under their own roofs.

Lord Tharrin was turning his villa into a fortress, and I aided in this task. Many nobles, however, were too proud to take such precautions. It was unseemly to show fear, they said—particularly against the rabble. I knew, though, that many held this fear secretly in their hearts. Tharrin had no sympathy for them, and openly called them fools.

That night, the streets were again in the hands of the mob. There were more fires in the city, and the army was powerless to stop more than a small part of this action. Many officers and soldiers loyal to the king were slain by the black-robed Huizîm. Officially, these troops were guardians of the temple, but it was well known they performed other duties as well.

At some time during the fighting, the steward Linius disappeared. When Lord Tharrin learned of this, he expressed his sorrow that he had not had the opportunity to personally slay the devil. I would have gladly taken the task for myself, for this traitor had done more than his share of mischief.

Three events of import occurred before the sun was high the following day. Each made a distinct and lasting mark on the pages of Niciean history. At dawning, Bhurzal showed his strength by formally proscribing against the king and all members of his family—branding them as heretics and criminals. Any citizen, soldier, or slave who brought a noble to "justice" would receive a heavenly reward amounting to near sainthood. And, Bhurzal added, there would be earthly compensations as well.

The king had no choice, now, but to act. He closed the temples and sentenced to death any priest who continued to follow Bhurzal. A few priests did desert, and asked for royal sanctuary. They reported that Bhurzal was indeed mad now, if he had not been so before, and that many of his closest followers feared him.

The king's actions brought an unexpected benefit. Citizens loyal to his rule who had feared to act before now came into the open and fought beside the army.

The most fearsome news, though, was yet to come. It arrived on the tongue of a courier whose horse died beneath him in the courtyard. The rebels had risen again in the south. This time, more than a few isolated tribes were involved. The whole of the desert, it seemed, had united under under one leader, Fhazir of the Sha'fel. He was an ambitious chieftain who sought power, Tharrin told me—a beast in the robes of a man. "We are in for it, now," the Niciean said somberly. "Bhurzal has played his hand. This is what he was waiting for. Now it has come."

I was more than astonished at this. "Lord, you're certain this is the priest's work? I can't believe—"

Tharrin waved me aside with a weary hand. "It makes little sense, Aldair, I'll grant you that. Not unless you're a madman. Fhazir's strength has been purchased with temple gold. And you have seen what Bhurzal cannot, or *will* not, allow himself to see—*that he has given that fiend the keys to Chaarduz, and will have the devil's own time getting them back. . . .*"

Mehzaar, Tharrin's captain, brought this point home to me later in the day when we met at the walls. I was trying to teach loyal court tradesmen the art of the bow, with little luck.

"It is difficult to recognize the city," he sighed, rubbing grime under his bronze war helmet. "I was born here, Aldair, and know the city like the palm of my hand. Yet, there are streets which have simply disappeared. The people have become savages. It is neighbor against neighbor, now, and friend against friend." He leaned against the wall and stared up the hill toward the villa. "Some, as you know, have turned against the priesthood. They are too late, though, and too few, to stop what is coming. They know they have sold themselves for nothing—that if the army cannot stop Fhazir he will murder them all, and level what is left of the capital."

The king left the city again, in pursuit of the rebel forces, and little order remained in Chaarduz. The soldiers who had not gone to face Fhazir—and there were few the king could spare—now lined the walls of the royal grounds. We could not spare patrols to keep order in the city. The mob ruled there, and the Huizim. Even these black-robed assassins, we understood, had their hands full.

"I admit that when you take us adventuring it is no small matter," said Rheif. His red eyes had that faraway look again, and I warned him that if he mentioned snow in the Northlands, and the tracks of hares, I would never speak to him, for certain. . . .

I was with Lord Tharrin at the walls late the next day when he was suddenly called back to the villa. I rode with him, for as *rhadaz'meh,* I was ever at his side now. I was as surprised as the Niciean to find Nhidaaj the Cygnian waiting for us in the courtyard.

Nhidaaj seemed to read his master's expression. "There is little need for secrecy now," he said soberly. "At any rate, this is not information that will keep."

The Cygnian spoke rapidly, and his words drained the color from Tharrin's face. The slave who was not a slave had many ears and eyes in Niciea. One, well-trusted, had come from the desert to report that the king had been tricked. There were, indeed, rebel forces in the south—but these were only decoys to draw the army far from Chaarduz. The true attack would come from the east. Ten thousand tribesmen or more were approaching rapidly along the coastal plains, with Fhazir of the Sha'fel at their head. All this, while the king chased ghosts in the desert . . .

TWENTY-TWO

"There." Mehzaar pointed. "The dune that is shaped like the wing of a bird. Just above the crest of that."

I followed the Niciean's hand, but saw nothing. Nor could I believe it was possible to see anything in this vast emptiness except sand.

I glanced back at Mehzaar. He lay still as a stone beside me. Only his black agate eyes were visible between the folds of his desert robes. The sun was far to our right, already below the horizon. The sand was still hot beneath us, but a light evening breeze picked up grains of sand from the tips of high dunes.

"They are there," Mehzaar said without turning. Four of them. Possibly another below, tending the mounts.

"How can you be sure they are Fhazir's? Couldn't they be—wandering tribesmen? Herders?"

"They are Fhazir's," he said simply. The dark eyes caught me for a moment. "Fhazir is no fool. He knows he cannot move ten thousand men up the coast toward the city without being seen. He knows *we* will do just as we are doing— send riders to bring back the king's army." He tapped his chin thoughtfully. "That is what these men are for. To stop us."

"It's a big desert," I said. "We can ride around them."

The Niciean smiled wearily. "Indeed, Aldair, this is what they would like us to try. Waste our time and our meager forces, and use up our water and mounts. And there will be others, of course. Beyond these." He shook his head, glanced over his shoulder at the ten Niciean warriors mounted silently below our dune. "You will get a chance to try that bow of yours, my friend. Make your northern arrows count. . . ."

Fhazir's riders spotted us quickly, for Mehzaar made no effort to evade them. He trotted our forces straight across the hard-packed sand in two columns—lancers to the left, archers to the right. Fhazir's men waited until the column was almost upon them. Then they howled over the dunes ahead, long robes straight behind them in the wind, weapons flashing in the fading light.

Mehzaar stopped the column with his hand. The rebels circled widely to the left, then turned sharply to hit that side of our forces. They sought to avoid our archers, of course—but Mehzaar would have none of that. The Nicean soldiers stood their ground easily, not moving. When the riders were no more than thirty yards away, the captain signaled again. The two columns faced left, archers skittering quickly through the lancers. Bows sang at targets only mount-length away. Three riders tumbled to the sand. Lancers kicked their horses forward past our bowmen and made short work of the remaining two rebels.

It was over in minutes. "Get their water and weapons and retrieve your arrows," Mehzaar commanded. "Never mind the mounts. We haven't the time to chase them. . . ."

There were no encounters during the night. We rode swiftly, taking advantage of the dark hours. We would not be able to maintain such a pace when the blazing sun caught us again.

At dawn Fhazir's scouts found us, and this time the column did not fare so easily. There were twelve of the desert raiders and they whipped through the column from all sides, making poor targets for the archers. They closed quickly, forcing our bowmen to take to their blades.

Somehow I sensed this danger a second or so before the others and jerked my mount from the press of bodies, plunging for breathing room. A near-naked horseman loomed up before me. I met the curved blade with my own. The ring of steel on steel numbed my fingers to the bone, and the blow nearly sent me to the ground. I was outmatched and knew it. There was enough weight in my foe's arm to cleave me in quarters if I let him. His blade whistled past my ear again and I buried heels in my mount. The beast cried out and left sand behind us.

The rider was still with me, but I didn't turn to look back. In seconds I'd half-circled the cluster of battle. I didn't dare wait longer. Pulling the horse savagely to a halt, I turned him about at the same time. An arrow was in my bow long before that, and the Fhazir rider had a moment of surprise before my shaft went neatly through his chest.

Another rider moved from the pack, leaving a Niciean soldier on the ground. I drew another arrow and tumbled him from the saddle, then trotted about the circle looking for more targets. The fight did not end until all Fhazir's riders were dead.

"They are good fighters," said Mehzaar, "though without discipline, for the most part. Normally, they do not like to stay around when they are losing, but prefer the chance to kill and run." He shook his head grimly. "These are of a different breed, Aldair. They will not run, for Fhazir has chosen them for this task. There will be no honor for them in returning alive, for he would know, and woul' reward them with a thousand deaths." He looked at me searchingly. "This is what we are up against. You may regret, *rhadaz'-meh*, that the Lord Tharrin allowed you this privilege."

"Mehzaar," I told him, "I regret nothing."

The captain nodded and looked at his hands. "I meant no dishonor upon you. The men know you accounted for yourself, and so do I. Three of the kills are yours, and only one other was taken by the bow. They will not tell you this—but next time my archers will have the wit to run from battle, as you did." He looked up, and grinned at my expression. "Yes. They thought you were fleeing, and they are properly shamed. Another such 'coward' as yourself, and I would have more soldiers left to sit a saddle. . . ."

Two Niciean soldiers had died in the fray, and another two wounded. The wounded, of course, were as worthless to Mehzaar as the dead. There was little we could do for them, and they were left upon the desert with a jug of water, though both refused this offer until Mehzaar ordered them to do so. We also left them with mounts, for we had taken extra horses from the rebels. We knew, of course, that we would never see our comrades again. The rebels would take care of them as soon as we were out of sight.

Four more of the desert fighters were met at noon, but we easily dispatched them. Mehzaar had wisely changed the riding order so that a skirmish line of archers formed a protective crescent before the lancers.

An hour later, though, we were hit again. There were eight riders, matching our own. They were fierce warriors, prepared to kill, and ready to die. When it was over, only five Niciean soldiers were left alive. Mehzaar himself was sorely wounded. There was an ugly slash across his thigh; green flesh was laid open and the captain had lost a great deal of blood. Though his face was ashen gray, he grimly sat his horse and we moved out once more.

The sun was unmerciful. I was certain I would not have the strength to raise my bow if they came again. I was not sweating anymore, and knew this was a bad sign. My skin burned, but there was no moisture. I could not see clearly; though my inner vision saw rebels behind every dune.

After the first deaths in our troop, it had come to me almost as an afterthought that I would doubtless not return from this adventure. This knowledge carried no fear for me, only anger at myself, and at the Nicieans.

Why, I wondered, had I been so anxious to throw my life away? Only a fool would fail to see that we were dead men from the beginning—that Fhazir could engage us at his will, sending one or a hundred against us. He was merely playing with Mehzaar's expedition. It would not have mattered if our column had been fifty or a hundred strong. *None of us would get through to the king. No one expected us to. . . .*

I felt Mehzaar's eyes upon me. "You see it, then, master bowman."

"I see. And you knew this."

"I knew. My Lord Tharrin knew as well."

"But you are here."

"I am here," he said wearily. "Even the impossible has to be attempted, *rhadaz'meh.* You can see that this is so."

And I could. But it did not make dying any easier.

"You are not a Niciean, although you are bound to my master," said Mehzaar. "There would be no dishonor for you if you returned. As a matter of fact, you would be doing us a service. They should know, at the palace, that the king is not coming."

"What good would such knowledge do, Mehzaar? None, as you well know."

Mehzaar laughed, and choked upon his laughter. "Northman, I offered you life only because I knew you would not accept it. I have had time to know you."

"I thank you for that."

"You have served your Lord well," he said, and fell into silence. I did not look at him again, for I knew his wound had brought pain to his face. It is not seemly to watch a warrior at such a time.

The brassy sun was an all-consuming power, pressing us into the sands. Hot air seared the lungs and set a man gasping for a single breath. I smiled wearily to myself. Not like the Northlands, as Rheif was fond of saying. No wintry snow to drape the high limbs . . . no hares to follow . . .

I heard a slight sound behind me, the beginning of a sigh, and turned in time to see Mehzaar slip easily from the saddle. I was off my mount, then, and beside him, but the two soldiers were already there and it was clear the Niciean captain was gone.

In late afternoon one of the mounts collapsed at the bottom of a dune. The rider followed on foot for a while, but when I glanced back some time later he was nowhere to be seen. The sun would set in another few moments and it occurred to me that it would be far more comfortable to die in the cool of the night than under the blistering sun. I vowed I would hold out, then. I would keep life within me until there were stars above and the beginning of a night breeze. A little water to drink, and darkness. Not so bad, really. If it were dark. If there were no sun—

My mount jerked to a stop and brought me to my senses. The lone Niciean in our column was beside me. The sky was orange, the desert a deeper red. The soldier pointed, and I squinted in the proper direction. The land swept upward to the crest of a high dune. Fhazir's riders lined the ridge, side by side, as far as the eye could see. I shook my head and blinked. There might have been two hundred warriors. Or twice as many. I didn't bother to count.

As we watched, one warrior detached himself from the others and rode down the dune toward us, leaving a fine plume of sand behind. A white rag fluttered from his sword.

"I expect they are surrendering," I said, but the Niciean soldier didn't bother to answer.

The Fhazir rider stopped a bare twenty yards away, danced his horse about, then tossed something to the ground and raced back up the dune with a great deal of flourish.

I looked at the Niciean and he dismounted and walked over and picked up the object and brought it to me. It was a water jar, and clearly full to brimming.

"This is difficult to believe," I said.

"Not truly," said the Niciean. He took the jar from me and pulled the wooden plug and sniffed. "Horse pee," he said, and looked disdainfully up the hill. "They are of Fhazir, for certain. . . ."

TWENTY-THREE

The Niciean patrol found me just outside the city. I was afoot, for three mounts had died beneath me, the last nearly a full day before. And while I was more than a little the worse for wear—dried and parched by the sun, and the mere shadow of a healthy Northman—I could not bring myself to complain. I was alive, and the bones of my companions marked the leagues behind me.

It was an irony of fortune that I encountered loyal soldiers, for in my absence Chaarduz had become far more dangerous to cross than the desert itself. There were few safe routes, and these known only to those who had fought in the battle for the city. Most of the streets were closed, or blocked with rubble. There were still fires burning in the western sector, and the harbor was in ruins. The very air now, was tainted with the sweet odor of death.

Some said Fhazir's army was less than a day away. Others claimed the rebels were already in the city, but few believed this was so. Still, all of the city east of the palace had been virtually abandoned, and no one dared venture there except looters and bands of army deserters. These men were a danger to any citizen, because they owed allegiance to no one. They had been corrupted by the priesthood, through promises of gold or fear of damnation—but the priests were no more than outlaws themselves now, and could offer no protection. The king, of course, had put a price on all their heads.

I found a familiar figure just inside the royal walls— Dhaarim, the aging soldier who had attended those useless sessions on Lord Tharrin's portico. Now he was perched on a high peak of rubble, shaking a stone from his boots. The white wall behind him was blackened, and I noted this supposedly impassable barrier had already been breached in several places. Soldiers and slaves alike labored to repair the damage before nightfall, for Dhaarim expected greater troubles to come.

"Fhazir will be somewhat disappointed when he gets here," the soldier said wryly. "The good people of Chaarduz have near taken the city apart, and there's little even a desert raider would care to steal." He studied me thoughtfully a moment, then let out a small breath. "No need to ask, is there, lad? Your silence tells me much. You didn't reach the king."

"Sir, as far as I can see, we came nowhere near him."

Dhaarim cursed and wiped his hands on his tunic. "I should have sent a stronger force—maybe more than one. If a single man—"

"It wouldn't have mattered," I told him. "One man or a thousand." I told him quickly what had happened. He listened, and his weary frame seemed to crumble in upon itself as I spoke.

"Mehzaar was a good soldier."

"He was, sir. He gave a good accounting of himself."

Dhaarim looked up. "And the others?"

"All dead. And all brave men. One stayed with me nearly to the city. We rested last night. This morning he was gone. There was very little water between us, but he didn't take his jug with him. His name was Thareesh, and he was an archer, like myself."

Dhaarim nodded, as if he might remember the man, and perhaps he did.

"The rebels didn't bother us," I said, "though they were about. It's my guess they let us live so we could bring this news to Chaarduz." I looked at Dhaarim, then past him. "Sir, if you'll tell me where I can find the Lord Tharrin, I'll make my report. Though I've little heart for it, it's a thing he'll need to know."

Dhaarim looked up at me, blankness in his eyes. "You couldn't know, of course, lad. . . ."

"Know?" I sat up. "Know? Know what?" But I knew. Dhaarim reached an old hand for me. I shook it off. I didn't want to touch it.

"He fought beside me on the walls last night," said the

soldier. "There. Just above you. And though I shouldn't say such a thing, Aldair, the citizens of Niciea had few among the royalty who cared whether their bellies were full or empty. It's a sad thing they've slain the one who loved them best. . . ."

I did not grieve for the Lord Tharrin. There was an emptiness in my heart for the man who had been both master and friend. I did not wish to fill that emptiness. . . .

I was too weary to even fling away the filthy garments I'd worn in the desert. I merely fell upon my couch and slept until the sun was gone. The mob had cut off the water supply to the royal grounds, but this had been anticipated, and everything that would hold water had been filled to brimming. More than enough, I thought grimly, for all the time it'd be needed. So I washed as best I could, and dressed in the garments I'd not worn since I'd become a slave of the Nicieans, and even after that. I felt much better when I had donned the red-and-blue patched tunic again, and the cape and baggy pants clasped at the ankles. Whether I lived or died now, I would do so as a Venicii—though it was unlikely anyone this far from home would recognize my colors, or care where I came from.

Rheif grinned at the sight of me, for he, too, had become a warrior again. Lord Tharrin had given all his slaves their freedom before he went to the walls, and many had joined him there of their own will, and fought beside him. It said much for the Nicean that few had abandoned him even when they had the right. Though, in truth, there was little else they could do, for it was worth your life to venture from the royal compound.

"Battle is a great leveler," I mused. "Even a noble is no better than a slave in Chaarduz today, for all will be slaughtered equally by Fhazir."

Rheif made a face. "Your fine nobles have been noble to the last, Aldair. Though you cannot know this, for much occured during your absence. Those members of the royal family who have not taken poison in silver cups have tried to buy their way through the mob out there with gold—and I'd be greatly surprised if the rabble kept their end of the bargain."

"You can be sure, though, they kept the gold," I added. From the heights of the villa we could see beyond the walls that guarded the royal grounds. It was most fortunate, I decided, that the citizens of Chaarduz could not see what I could see—that there were pitifully few soldiers manning their posts. Dhaarim was doing his best, but it was a near hopeless task. Many of the Nicean warriors saw little reason to give their lives defending empty villas and fine furniture. And who could blame them? In all fairness, most of these men would have given their lives for the king in battle— but we all knew it was not that kind of a fight anymore.

"What of us, then?" said Rheif, voicing the thought that was in both our minds. "I am not overly anxious to die for Niciea."

"Nor am I. But what would you have us do, Rheif? There is no place for us to go, or none that I know of. It goes without saying that we would not get far in the streets of Chaarduz."

Rheif rubbed his muzzle thoughtfully. "You came *in*to the city. From the desert."

"With soldiers who knew the way," I reminded him. "Through streets that are likely closed by now. No. There's nothing for us in that direction. Only the desert. And the west is much the same. I've tried my hand at fighting the sun, and would not care to do so again. To the east there's Fhazir and umpty-thousand rebels. To the north, the sea. Which do you favor, Rheif?"

"I strongly favor the cold winds of Stygia," he said stubbornly. "But I doubt I'll ever feel them again. . . ."

The sun was fading when a soldier found me at the walls to say it was urgent that I return to the villa. Why, I asked, knowing full well there was no one there who'd want to see me. The soldier would say nothing more—only that I should accompany him and see.

It was a part of the big, rambling structure I'd never seen before. From the main courtyard, a narrow hall with neither windows nor doors twisted interminably and finally ended at a stout wooden portal plainly built to stop intruders. The portal opened onto a small, circular patio. There was a pool there, made of colorful tiles in the Nicean manner. Its fountain was silent, but the pool itself was still full of clear water.

The courtyard was paved with pink stones and covered with lush greenery that twined itself onto lattices and formed a shady canopy overhead. It was near to evening now, but I imagined how it would be here in the full light of day, when the sun filtered through and filled this quiet place with green-gold light and shadow.

The portal closed quietly behind me and I was alone. I seated myself on a stone bench by the pool, and wondered what this was about. I was strangely content, though, to merely absorb the peace of this place. It was hard to imagine that there was little outside this sancuary but death and violence.

"It is lovely, is it not?"

I turned at the voice, and half rose from my bench.

"No. Sit, please. I am Shamma, Aldair. You do not know me, but I know you. I am the wife of your Lord Tharrin."

"Lady—"

"This has ever been a favorite place of mine. He came here, too—though not as often as he liked. He said that in this spot he sometimes felt our world was very close to another. That if one could bring his mind to the proper turn of things, he might find a special passage to those lands we see only in our dreams. Do you not feel this, too?"

"Lady, in truth I do," I told her. And it was as she said. There was a feeling here that defied description. A silence that was not a silence. If there was magic in the world, I decided, surely this was a place it favored.

From the Lady Shamma's voice, I knew she was somewhere behind me, past one of the carven lattices clustered with green. But I did not turn to see.

"You must know," she said, "I am breaking a great many traditions by speaking to you like this. Such a thing is forbidden in our scriptures—though to be quite honest, I have always regretted that this was so. Is a man so different from a woman?" She laughed lightly, but the laugh was touched with sorrow. "I suppose many of our ways are changing today. As the world is changing, Aldair."

"The Lord Tharrin said this," I told her.

"Did he? Yes, I expect that he did. It was a matter much on his mind." She was silent a moment, then, "Aldair, he thought a great deal of you."

"And I, Lady, I— I'm—grieved that I could not have

known him better. He was more than a master to me. He was a friend as well—he opened my eyes to a world I hadn't known before. Lady, may I say that I share your sorrow? That if there is anything . . ."

"Please," she said softly, "there is nothing you need say. He is gone, but not truly so. And I have learned patience, Aldair. In Niciea, this is a thing a woman learns well."

She was silent then, and for a moment I thought that she was gone. I imagined I could hear shouting beyond the villa, near the walls.

"Now," she said finally, "listen, Aldair, for there is little time, and much I have to say to you. Know that the Lord Tharrin put a great trust in you—greater than you imagine. There were matters he shared with you. Things you were told. And there were things he could not tell you, but asked you to take upon faith. I know, since he has chosen you, that you are worthy of his trust—that you are his *rhadaz'meh* still, though he is no longer here to command your loyalty."

"Lady," I told her, "be assured of that."

"Hear me, then," she said quietly. "There is a ship. It is at sea now, but not far away. It was sent from Chaarduz by your Lord, when he foresaw our ruin. The ship is for you, Aldair. It sailed the day you left for the desert, with instructions to await your return." The Lady Shamma laughed lightly. "It is darkening, but I do not need the sun to read your features. Yes, the Lord Tharrin knew you would return. He would not have sent you upon such a mission if this were not so. He knew, truly, that it was not your time to perish in the desert. . . ."

The evening was warm, but I felt a sudden chill in the wind. "Lady—how could he know such a thing?"

"Know that he did, Aldair. I can say no more than that. You will sail. You will take the Stygiann with you, and the king's son—and one other. This last is not known to me, but it is as the Lord Tharrin has instructed. The guard who brought you here is Khyliir. He knows your mission and will be your guide. And Aldair"—her voice fell almost to a whisper—"this is perhaps the most important part of your charge. There is a packet. Just below your bench. Pick it up, please."

I reached below me and my hand touched a soft bundle

of leather. It was tightly sewn, and covered in a slick, waxy substance. "I have it, Lady."

"This has been entrusted to you by the Lord Tharrin. You are to give it to only one other."

"Who, Lady?"

"You will know."

I was somewhat bewildered at this. "Lady, perhaps I will, but I can't see how this could be. Might the Lord Tharrin have entrusted me with too much? Maybe there were things he meant to tell me, and didn't!"

"No," she said gently, "if there were such things, they would have been said."

"And the ship. Where does it take us, Lady?"

Shamma was silent a long moment. "I shared a life with him, Aldair. Our days and nights were woven together like the threads of one color. But that is a secret he could never share with me. . . ."

TWENTY-FOUR

I found him near the slave quarter. He was squatting in the dark, his broad, furry back near bending a small tree. I stopped a short way from him, for I am a Northman, and not so foolish as to startle a Vikonen.

"Do I know you?" he growled. The wide, flat head raised slightly and the short muzzle sniffed the air. "I think maybe I do."

"We have met," I said. "You were less at ease, then, as I recall."

The Vikonen did something to his throat. "You're the one, then. You're not a Rhemian. Like the other."

"No. A Venicii."

He nodded. "A hard people in trade, and not easily cheated. What are you doing in this miserable place, Venicii?"

"I could ask the same as you, and I will—but there's no time for it now. I told you once there'd be a better day. Perhaps this is that day. I take ship tonight and would have you with me. I can tell you nothing more than that, and I must have your answer now, one way or the other."

The creature's small eyes narrowed. "To sea? You have a ship?" He heaved his great chest and scratched his stomach. "I need no time to give you answer. There's nothing but death here, and I'm not ready to meet it."

"You might well meet it at sea."

He gave me a strange, quizzical look. "And what's the harm there, Venicii? I was *born* for that. . . ."

The thought struck me some time later, and brought a chill wind with it. *"You'll take the Stygiann and the king's son . . . and one other. . . ."* Is that why I'd sought out the

156

Vikonen? Or was it a thing I'd have done myself? There were too many things already unexplained, and I didn't care to think on another.

The air below the ground was cold and smelled of age. I could see nothing but torch-glow in the darkness, and the dim shadow of the soldier Lady Shamma had called Khyliir. The passage began at the base of the palace wall itself, and for a while we followed the line of that structure, then burrowed deeper; now I sensed we were well beneath the streets of Chaarduz.

Rheif was behind me, the young prince in his arms wrapped tightly against the night. Further back was the giant Vikonen, whose bulk gave him scant clearance through some of the tighter turns and angles.

"Wait," Khyliir said softly. I came up against him and he laid a hand on my arm. "We will leave the tunnel in a few moments, and I cannot say what is beyond. Nothing, hopefully, but we can't be certain. There are rocks above, and the beach. We dare not risk a torch there."

I nodded in the darkness and the soldier's torch hissed against the wet stone floor.

The night was hot and still above, but a light breeze drifted in from the sea. The Vikonen breathed salt air and grinned at me. Rheif stilled the Dhar'jeem, who was beginning to stir, and I silently asked the Creator to keep the child sleeping soundly.

From the rocky cove we could see torchlight in the harbor, and beyond, a blood-red stain upon low clouds which said the city still burned. There was noise behind and to the east —harsh cries and the clash of metal on metal. I exchanged a look with Rheif. Fhazir, then. It could hardly be anyone else. He was in the city, and we were listening to the death knell of Chaarduz.

Khyliir moved beside me. "This is a risk," he whispered, "but it cannot be avoided." He reached beneath his cloak and sparked a small candle. The tiniest moth might have scorned such a pitiful flame, but it seemed to me the sun had blazed over the horizon.

The Vikonen growled deeply. Khyliir looked at him, then to me. "I am only to give the signal once," he explained.

"Once may be enough," said the Vikonen. "If those devils have half an eye between 'em . . ."

I shook my head at the big creature and he fell silent. Khyliir masked the flame with his hand. One . . . one . . . three . . . one . . . Then his fingers squeezed the wick to darkness.

"Now what?" asked Rheif.

"Now we wait," said Khyliir.

And it was the Stygiann, with his keen night eyes, who spotted the dark craft offshore a near eternity later. There were two oarsman, and they made no attempt to beach the boat, but back-rowed beyond the light swell, and waited. Khyliir looked at me once, then disappeared the way we had come. It was the first I'd known he wouldn't be joining us, and I wondered what would become of him in the dying city. Then there was no more time for wondering, and we waded silently out to meet the small craft.

With the longboat aboard, the trim Niciean vessel wasted no time off Chaarduz. Dark sails billowed, and the bow pointed swiftly to the east. I would have liked to stay on deck, for I had acquired a keen love of the sea. A seaman, though, led us below and left us, in a small cabin aft. The room reminded me of the one Lord Tharrin had occupied on the voyage from Tarconii—an age ago, it seemed to me.

An oil lamp swung brightly behind colored glass, but the ports were tightly sealed, for the vessel was showing no lights.

"Ah, we are truly at sea now!" exclaimed the Vikonen. He had spotted wine and food set out for us, and his big hands promptly closed about a quantity of both.

"I trust there's enough for your needs"—Rheif sniffed—"for the rest of us are not greatly hungry, and suffer no ill from crawling about wet tunnels in the night."

The Vikonen paused, red dripping from his muzzle, and peered wonderingly at Rheif. "I have never seen a Stygiann before—not with his pelt on, at least. You are a curious creature, and from the breadth of you I don't imagine you eat a great deal."

"I do," Rheif said between white teeth, "when it is possible." He squeezed past the big creature and found a place, setting the young prince beside him. The Niciean had come awake, and was delightedly pulling great tufts of hair from Rheif's chest.

I laughed, and joined them. We had nearly finished all there was to find on the wooden table, when the cabin door opened behind us. I turned, and the Cygnian who was not a slave met me with dark, placid eyes. For some reason, I was not overly surprised to find him there.

"I trust you are all comfortable." He smiled.

I held his gaze a long moment. "I felt we would see one another again."

"And I, Aldair, believed the same." Black eyes peered over the curve of his fleecy nose, past me to the others. "I am called Nhidaaj. I know you, Rheif, or know of you. And I have not met your new companion."

"Nor have we," Rheif grumbled. "He has been too busy filling his great gut to give a name."

The Vikonen grinned broadly. "I know not who you be, sir, or why I am here. But I'm not unhappy to be aboard. I am Signar of Haldring, in Vikonea, and if there is fighting or seamanship needed on this voyage, I'm at your call, for in these things I excel above all others."

"You forget eating and drinking," said Rheif.

The Cygnian smiled and took a place near the table. "There is more than enough food aboard, and none of us should starve—even with so great an appetite among us."

"Nhidaaj," I asked, "can you tell us where it is we are going? I was not told a great deal, as you are no doubt aware. Not that we are ungrateful," I added, "that the Lord Tharrin has given us a chance to live. Few others in Chaarduz will have the opportunity, I fear."

The Cygnian looked at me thoughtfully. "I must ask you all to shelve your curiosity a little longer," he said finally. "I assure you there's a reason for this."

I glanced at Signar and Rheif. "Of course," I said. "Our trust goes easily to a friend of the Lord Tharrin." True enough, I thought—but we'll wonder no less for that.

"Fine." The Cygnian rose. "The seaman who brought you here will find quarters, and we'll talk in the morning. Rheif, if you will, I can take the young Dhar'jeem from your care now."

Rheif glanced sharply at me, and I nodded approval. I could not distrust the Cygnian in any way. A man learns to

know another, and there was no deceit in this creature.
Rheif handed the child over, and the young prince immediately buried tiny fingers in fluffy wool.

"You see," Nhidaaj assured Rheif, "he knows me. We are
old friends, the Dhar'jeem and I." And both Rheif and I
could see this was so.

Still, Rheif cast me a puzzled look in the corridor. "It's
all right," I told him. "He's to be trusted. I can say no more
than that."

Rheif frowned and picked at his sharp teeth. "I *know* he's
to be trusted, Aldair. I can read the creature as well as you.
Still, no one ever tells me anything," he grumbled. "I am always in the dark."

"No more so than I."

"I can't believe that," he said. "It is nigh impossible to
know less about his fate than Rheif the Stygiann. I do not
even know where I am."

"You are in the Southern Sea. East of Chaarduz."

Rheif made a face. "I am not ignorant, Aldair."

"One wonders."

"One need not, I assure you. But Southern Seas and cities
named Chaarduz mean nothing to me. All I know is that I
am not under northern stars, and that I cannot track the
snow hare 'cross wooden decking. There are no forest ponds
covered with new ice, or—"

It all happened quickly. The seaman scuttled to a bulk-
head and froze there. I looked past him—saw the figure facing us.

"Linius!" The word stuck in my throat.

The Rhemian studied me a moment and smiled. "Al-
dair," he said, almost gently, "I have something for you. . . ."

There was a part of a second when I saw the blunt cross-
bow at his side. Then the weapon jerked, and a bolt sang.
Rheif was already past me—gaunt form a gray blur of motion. I cried out. The Stygiann went rigid, crumpled like
paper. My blade flashed. An arm big as a small oak swept it
aside, and I looked up and met Linius's eyes—saw his face
go slack with fear. He kicked frantically at the end of
Signar's powerful arms. Then the giant's hands closed, and
I do not think they stopped till they met one another
again. . . .

TWENTY-FIVE

The Niciean vessel cleaved blue water and tossed white wreaths of foam against the painted bow. There were storms behind, in the west, but none touched the ship, and only served to fill the green sails with a fair, strong wind.

The seamen said this was a good omen—that when favor rose from a great force of destruction, the Creator Aastar was telling his children that the words of the *Qua'shar* were as he had spoken them: that neither good nor evil blazed from his golden eye, but only the pure green brilliance of eternity.

I did not comment on this, for at the moment I could not see that we had been touched with fair omens. Others might gaze across the waters and find truth there, but I saw only emptiness.

Perhaps I should have been more than grateful. Rheif was still alive. He had hovered near death for three days and nights, but Nhidaaj assured me he was much improved, now—though it would be some time before one could say what the Stygiann's future might be.

The wound itself was not overly serious. It had penetrated between shoulder and chest, and had not severed any of the major veins Nhidaaj said carried blood through the body. The danger, he said, came from the bolt itself, which was obviously unclean. And while many physicians did not realize the truth of the matter, he informed me, there were unseen things in the soil, and even in the air, which caused poisons to gather in the body.

Nhidaaj was a wonder to me.

I had not even suspected he was a physician until Rheif was felled by Linius's bolt. I could hardly credit the fact now, though I had seen his skill with my own eyes. It is difficult to break lifetime patterns of thinking. In my experience, Cygnians were indolent, dull-witted creatures who could perform only the most menial of tasks. How, though, could I fit Nhidaaj into this picture? He *looked* like a Cygnian— white wool from head to toe, dark, placid eyes, and near expressionless features. Yet he was not the same. There was a light in those eyes I had seen in no Cygnian before—nor in any other creature, for that matter. Fires burned behind that calm visage, and all about Nhidaaj seemed to feel this power. It was not his way, though, to command through fear. His quiet presence was his only badge of authority. The Niceans aboard had nothing but respect for this Cygnian who was not a slave. And though everyone knew the ship sailed by order of the Lady Shamma, Nhidaaj was clearly in charge of our voyage. He commanded the crew, and charted our destination—none, though, could recall that he had ever issued a single command. . . .

I was always careful to keep a smile on my face before Rheif—though it was painful to look upon my old friend. His lean, powerful body, all cord and muscle, seemed to have caved in upon itself. His gray fur had lost its luster and lay flat and dull against his gaunt frame. The red eyes were dull, and seemed to see nothing.

"You are looking fine," I lied. "No doubt you will soon be up chasing hares about the northern woods."

"You are a poor spinner of tales, Aldair," he said wryly. "I know I am near death, for not even the thought of hares makes me hungry. That is a very bad sign in a Stygiann."

"It means nothing at all," I assured him. "Nhidaaj himself says that he doesn't expect you to be greatly interested in food for a while."

"Perhaps," Rheif sighed, "but it's of no matter, for what little food I might be able to swallow is stolen by Signar here before it reaches my mouth—this great oaf, Aldair, would take meat from his mother's mouth, I'm certain."

"Why, that's not so!" Signar exploded. The big Vikonen came half out of his seat. Then Rheif grinned weakly, and I laughed with him. Signar glared at us both and sank back to the stout keg he carried with him about the ship, as there were no chairs or stools that would hold his bulk.

The cabin door opened behind us then, and Nhidaaj chased us both into the corridor—warning us that his patient was entirely too sick for guests who engaged in frivolity and loud noises. Rheif grinned behind the physician's back.

He doesn't look good to me," Signar rumbled. "In spite of the Cygnian's words."

"He looks better," I said firmly. "He looks a great *deal* better to me, Signar."

The Vikonen looked at me, then turned back to the rail and sniffed sea air. "I will give them their due," he said. "The Niceans build fine ships and sail them well. But they cannot match the Vikonens, of course."

"They would be pleased to hear that," I said.

"No"—he turned to me—"I say it as a tribute, Aldair. A Vikonen does not pass out compliments idly, but we are essentially honest folk. Or as honest as need be. And above all things we admire a fine ship and a good sailor." He paused, glanced over a broad shoulder at the billowing green sails. "I have never fought Niceans, but I'll wager they put up a good fight. Ship to ship, of course. They are too small and scrawny for a battle hand to hand, or—"

He stopped suddenly, and laid a big fist on my shoulder. "You think much of him. I know this. I did not mean that— he would not recover. I am no physician, and I am greatly ignorant of such things and should keep my mouth shut whenever possible."

I could not look at him. "He must get well, Signar." I clutched the railing and stared at the blue water. "I will— not—have—him—die!"

"Stygianns are tough and hard to kill," said Signar. "This is well known."

"He took Linius's bolt for me. He can deny that all he wishes. *I* know it is so." I looked up at him, though I could not see him properly. "Do you know what he said, Signar? 'Aldair, it is your fault I have this great hole in my shoulder where one could easily hide a large oak. If you had not frozen like a hare in the hallway, I would not have tripped over your clumsy feet.' "

Signar chuckled and scratched his chin. "Stygianns are great liars."

"They are. They are also cunning and sly and frequently fall into black moods and become impossible to live with.

They complain greatly about whatever befalls them, and are natural-born braggarts. More than that, they have been the enemy of the Venicii since time began. I am sure Rheif has often roasted distant cousins of mine. No doubt I wear the boots that once warmed the back of his kinsman."

I looked wearily out to sea. "And this Stygiann, Signar, is the only true friend I ever had." I slammed a fist hard against my palm. "Damn Linius! With all the care Lord Tharrin must have taken—that news of this ship would reach the little traitor's ears . . ."

"He will betray no other."

"No, but he has done his deed well, Signar. . . ."

What fools we are, I thought later. We go about our way in our own small corner of the world, and shut our eyes to all that doesn't easily pass our doorsteps. And yet the world's bigger than that. A mountain and a maid are seen through other eyes than ours. A Stygiann warrior looks out upon the day and sees the same sun that warms a Rhemian lord or heats the green scales of a Nicican. And each of these creatures sees truth in his own way, and finds all others false. Yet how can this be? Would one be right, and all the others wrong? Are there many truths—and *all* of them right? Or one truth, perhaps, greater than them all . . .

If that's true, I wondered, where could such a thing be found? Maybe it would be too much to ask one truth to serve all creatures. The Creator had not *made* them all the same. No doubt he knew what he was about. Why, then, should a man expect all men to be of one mind?

The more I considered this, the more unlikely it seemed to be.

A part of my question was answered the next evening, in the cabin of Nhidaaj the Cygnian. . . .

"Here," he said, dropping a finger on a point near the far eastern edge of our chart. "This is Xandropolis, our destination. With good weather, Aldair, we should reach port before nightfall tomorrow."

Nhidaaj's chart was a far cry from the map on Master Pelian's wall in Silium. Lands were clearly drawn, and cities placed where they belonged. Fine compass lines spider-webbed from one corner of the map to the other, and these,

I was given to understand, were used in conjunction with the magic blade that always pointed to the north. There were even numbers along well-traveled coasts, showing water depths as determined by knotted ropes. Thus seamen might safely sail on different hours of the tide.

"Xandropolis is a wondrous place," the physician told me, filling my cup with wine. "It is the furthest point of Nicean conquest—and the same for Rhemia. Neither race finds it of great interest, however. It is too far from Chaarduz or Rhemia to defend—yet both claim it as their own, and neither will bear the expense of asserting their ownership." Nhidaaj grinned easily. "All races are to be found there, then, though they do not mingle with one another, except for trade. This is accomplished across a painted wall which makes a dizzy track across the city."

The Cygnian sighed and shook his head. "It is a picture of man's folly, Aldair—and there is no other place like it, I think, in the world."

I did not comment, but kept my eyes on the red wine in my cup. My face swam up to meet me—an outsized snout and wiggly eyes.

"Nhidaaj." I still did not look up. "We do no sail to this Xandropolis to trade with either Rhemians or Niceans."

"No. We do not, Aldair."

"Am I to know, then, what it is we are about?"

Nhidaaj regarded me thoughtfully. Finally, he eased himself up and walked to the far end of the cabin. "Aldair. Do you have trust in me?"

"You were the friend of the Lord Tharrin. . . ."

"No." He turned quickly and faced me. "No." He shook his head. "Trust in *me,* I asked. *Not* because I knew another."

I looked up, met the blazing eyes, turned away. "Yes. I trust you. For yourself." But there was more on my mind. "Trust, Nhidaaj, works two ways. I have done as I have been asked. I am not ungrateful. Neither are my companions. Still, in all honesty, it may be that we could have escaped from the city in another manner. It may be that if we had, Rheif would not be near to death, now. . . ."

"Aldair." Nhidaaj came close to my side and placed a hand on the wooden table. "Aldair. You are right in all you say. Still, I ask you again. Trust a little longer."

"What choice have I?" I asked.

"Every man has a choice."

"It does not always seem so."

"No. But it *is* so, nevertheless."

I laughed. Harshly, I suppose, for Nhidaaj looked at me curiously. "It's as Rheif said, after all."

"And what was that?"

"No one ever tells me anything. I am always in the dark." I looked up. "It's true, Nhidaaj."

"Yes. Yes, it's true, Aldair. Or mostly true, anyway."

"There's much the Lord Tharrin didn't tell me."

"And much that he did."

"Much more that he did not," I insisted.

"All right. Much more that he did not."

"And you can add nothing. Or will not."

"Only—a little."

I turned away from him. "I am to trust you, then. But—"

"Aldair." I looked at him, then. "You don't see . . ."

"No." I shook my head. "Sometimes I see nothing at all."

"Then know that I can tell you little—because I *know* little."

I stared at him. "Nhidaaj. You and the Lord Tharrin—"

"—Were knowledgeable of many things not known to you."

"That's so. Then—"

He held up a hand. "What you shall know, Aldair, cannot come from me. Nor could your Lord have told you more. *That must come from another. . . .*"

TWENTY-SIX

As Nhidaaj had promised, the Niciean vessel reached its destination before nightfall the next day. Though to me it appeared we had reached nowhere at all. The captain dropped anchor in a dark cove, and the ship was again without lights of any kind. If the fabled Xandropolis was nearby, it was nowhere to be seen.

"As you yourself pointed out," Nhidaaj explained, "we did not come to trade in the marketplace. It serves us best to call no attention to ourselves." More than that, he would not say.

I supposed this was so, since we were sailing a royal ship and there was no way to know who was in power in Chaarduz—the king or Fhazir. And while I doubted news of what had happened there could have reached this end of the Southern Sea ahead of our own swift vessel, there was little point in questioning Nhidaaj further. It was all part of the pattern of my new life, I thought dismally. Many things I had never wished to know were alarmingly clear to me now. What it is like to be pursued by Rhemian soldiers and Tarconii longboats. How it feels to be a slave. To thirst on the desert. Watch a good companion dying. Such enriching experiences were not denied to me. But I was forbidden to know the mysteries of ancient cities, or what secrets lay between Niciean lords and Cygnian physicians.

My role was clear enough, whether I liked it or not. Nhidaaj would hold my hand and tell me which foot went before the other. And if I did my sums nicely, perhaps I would be given a sweetcake. This would occur, no doubt, after I had delivered my packet to whatever personage was destined to receive it. Nhidaaj had never mentioned this errand, but I was certain he knew of it. Further, I had been promised that this worthy was capable of answering questions—even questions that neither the Lord Tharrin nor Nhidaaj could answer. I would believe that, I decided, when it happened.

All right, I told myself, you're exaggerating, Aldair. It's not as bad as that. It only seems so. You *have* been honored and trusted. And neither Lord Tharrin nor Nhidaaj has treated you like a child. The Lady Shamma entrusted you with something that is undoubtedly important—and broke tradition to do it. And if there are things you are not to know, there's a reason for that, too. Isn't there?

No doubt. But was it necessary, I wondered, for life to be so mysterious? Was it truly so—or did people make it that way?

At midnight a warm breeze swept inshore and the quarter moon was veiled behind fleeting clouds. Only Nhidaaj and I went ashore—though the physician had the young Dhar'-jeem in his care. I wondered at this, for it seemed a dangerous thing to me. Both for us and the child. Where were we going, and where was Nhidaaj taking the heir to the Niciean throne? He did not tell me, and I didn't ask.

I wished the giant Signar was by my side on that dark shore, but that was not to be. At least I knew the Vikonen would see that no more harm befell Rheif. How long would we be gone—and what would happen if the Stygiann took a turn for the worse? But he will not, Nhidaaj assured me calmly. I was to believe that this was so.

The two figures who met us in the cove were muffled in dark robes. They spoke little, and only in whispers to Nhidaaj. From their lean forms I guessed they were Niceans. We were given robes, and mounts, and in the night it would have been hard to tell us from any four tribesmen making their way across the dark landscape.

After we left the shore and headed south, I saw a dim cluster of light far to the east, and guessed that was all I would see of Xandropolis. The land was fertile. We passed tall groves of palm such as those I'd seen in Chaarduz. The light breeze rattled their leaves like paper.

Short cotton grew here, too, and the ripe bolls were ghost-white in the darkness. Once I breathed the pungent smell of

"And what were they for? Can you say?"

"No. Not for certain."

The last deserved another question. "But you have a guess, Nhiddaaj. . . ."

The Cygnian shrugged. "It would be no more than a guess. And a fanciful one at that."

"I don't object to fanciful guesses," I told him.

He grinned, then turned his mount and pushed to the south again. I took a last look at the things in the water, but there was no more light in the sky, and there was nothing to be seen.

TWENTY-SEVEN

Much has happened that bears telling. . . .

Though I wonder if I can truly recount these things as they occurred, or whether they are best forgotten. I say this because I am not certain what has happened, and what has not. Some of both, perhaps.

The strangeness of it all bewilders me still—but in the light of what has come after, I have come to think my faulty memory is no accident. Best, then, that I set down what was, and what seemed to be, and make no effort to distinguish between the two. . . .

We made our way south and west. The night was dark, with no moon, but in these climes the stars are abundant. It is the best way to see the desert lands, as I can testify from my trek from Chaarduz to nowhere in search of the king.

I wondered, that night, what had become of the city. No doubt Fhazir sacked it thoroughly and leveled it to the ground. Surely, as is the custom of barbarians and spoilers everywhere, he sniffed out all that sparkles and shines and appears to have value, and destroyed what he could neither carry off nor understand. I would not expect to find the pink walls of Tharrin's villa intact. Nor the clipped gardens and quiet fountains. Of all those wonders, it grieved me most to think about that green bower with its tiled pool, where I met the Lady Shamma. No doubt the magic has fled that place. It would disturb Fhazir that time stood still there. . . .

Perhaps, I thought, the king gathered his forces and reclaimed his throne. Or perhaps not. At any rate, his heir the Dhar'jeem is safe for the moment. He rides ahead of me, asleep in the arms of Nhidaaj—unaware of the trouble that plagues his father's kingdom. Or maybe it is his kingdom by now.

We rode no more than an hour before Nhidaaj brought us to a halt again. I left my mount and scratched and looked about and wondered where we had come to. It seemed no place at all to me. A well filled with sand. A palm and a mud hut. Much the same as we had left before.

It is at this point that things become disorderly in my mind. Things happened.

Or seemed to.

Nhidaaj had a small fire going when I returned from watering the mounts. A fire, I thought. What for? We had ridden only an hour or so. Neither we nor the horses needed rest. It is not tiring to ride across the desert at night.

I did not ask questions. I drank wine that was offered me. Perhaps I drank more than a single cup. It was dry, with a musty odor. Better than most Niciean wines, which tend to be overly sweet.

I am sure, now, there was more to this wine than grapes alone. . . .

This is a most peculiar fire.

Sometimes the flames leap yellow. Sometimes, though, there are tendrils of green within, or fingers of brightest blue. As if a chest of gems had been set afire . . .

There is a city burning in the fire. It is not a thing I care to see. . . .

The city has burned to a fine ash. The ash has turned to stone. Another city has risen there, greater than the first. . . .

The sun rises within the heart of the second city. It is a terrible, white sun, and there is no ash this time. . . .

The fire is gone.

A spark from the fire has set the torch aglow, and the torch casts tall shadows on the walls. The walls are dry and brittle and smell of beetles. The pictures there are painted in old colors. Some of the colors are gone, but their memories cling to the dry walls. They are earth red, sand brown, and raven black.

The steps go down, and down and down again. Their centers are deeply worn. The air here is powder-musty.

The things on the walls have the heads of nightmare creatures. One has the sharp beak and round, cruel eye of a bird. They walk stiffly, like blind gods.

You are a long time coming, Aldair....
Who are you? Do I know you?
I think not. But you are known to me....
It's dark. I—can't see you.
There is a lamp. Touch it with your torch....
Red flame. Dancing on a pool of amber.
The smell of cinnamon.

There is a chair. Enameled in gold and blue with arms like the claws of birds.

The creature who speaks sits in the chair. He is beyond the red flame, and his cloak is shadow-gray. The eyes beneath the cloak are wide, flecked with green and yellow, and the dark pupils are set on end like pumpkin seeds.

Flat nose and blade-black ears.

Fur as sleek as water.

Who are you? You are like no creature I know.
There are few of us. And you have not seen us because we do not go into the world, Aldair....
You stay—here? In this place?
Here. And other places.
What other places?
There is not much time, Aldair....
Time for what?
To know the things you must know ...

I don't understand that. Everyone tells me I must know things and *not* know things. I never know more than—parts of things!

That was not done to deceive, my friend. This is known to you....

All right, it is. But—

Men yearn to have all secrets bared to them, and they become angry and impatient when one holds knowledge that another would have. Yet, when they gain that knowledge before they are ready to receive it, they cry out against the giver, and say that what they have been shown are lies and not the truth at all. . . .

They don't want the truth, but say they do?

They do not hunger for truth at all. Only comfort. Do you recall that you became angry with the Lord Tharrin because he would not use his knowledge to fight the priests of Niciea?

I thought—

—That truth would free the people from fear? A noble idea, Aldair. Do you think, now, that this is so? That even if the people believed their true history had been denied them —that the world is not as it seems—that this would ease their fears? No. I tell you there are truths the people are not ready to hear. Not yet . . .

Am I ever to have this knowledge?

Yes, Aldair. You are . . .

And you will tell me these things?

No. For I am not your teacher. . . .

Who, then? Nhidaaj? Another?

I am Nhidaaj's teacher. His master. Just as Nhidaaj was the master of the Lord Tharrin. But he is not your teacher. Nor was the Nicean . . .

The Cygnian? He was Tharrin's—*master?*

Not as you know the word . . .

But—

Listen well. It is not to be the same for you. You will not learn as others have learned. This is the role of some, but it is not your role. . . .

There it is again! I am to be taught, but I have no teacher. I am to learn things, but only *parts* of things, is that it? It has ever been that way!

You seek your burden eagerly, Aldair. Do you know, truly, what it is you hunger for?

I—don't think a man need fear the truth.

A man might be wise to fear what he doesn't know. . . .

How can I fear anything? I don't *know* anything!

You will know. . . .

How do you *know* I'll know? And if I do any of this— seeking—how do you know I'll *find* anything? I don't even know what I'm looking for!

I know. . . .

How—all right, you know. And if that's so, what's the use in my doing anything at all?

I am told that I returned to the ship alone.

I do not remember that journey, but it is true that the Cygnian is no longer with us, nor the young Dhar'jeem. I have no doubts about the prince's safety. If there is a new king of Niciea one day, I think he will rule his people wisely. No one has told me this, but I am certain Nhidaaj has a new pupil in his care. If this is so, Niciea will not suffer for it.

I no longer have the packet I was to deliver for the Lady Shamma. But I do not doubt it is in the proper hands. Instead, I have another packet. It is somewhat larger than the first, and contains several fortunes in gems. There are stones of all shapes and sizes, and each is finely cut and polished. There are sapphires that put the color of the sea to shame, rubies red as blood, and diamonds with hearts as cold as ice. There are a great many emeralds, too, as this green stone is a favorite of the Niceans, and highly valued in that land.

There is one thing more in my packet. A heavy parchment written in spidery script which states one Aldair of the Venicii has been named sole owner of this vessel, which is described in great detail. The document is witnessed by the Lady Shamma, and signed under the personal seal of the Lord Tharrin.

I cannot say why I have been given a great treasure and a fine Nicean vessel. Nor why I have been taken into the desert to drink drugged wine and speak with strange creatures who never show their faces to the world. What is it I am to seek, and do? The creature with yellow eyes said that I would know. But in truth, I do not. . . .

The captain of my ship has told me he will serve as long as I require him, in the name of Lord Tharrin. He is an honorable man and a fine seaman, but I sensed this was not truly his wish. I asked him, then, to tell me honestly what he would do. He has explained that as long as Niciea is in the hands of rebels, he feels compelled to join his king, if possible, and help bring his country to order.

I respect his wishes. Last night we sailed into a cove

known to him, not far from Chaarduz, and he and a number of crewmen have left us.

I have named Signar captain, much to his pleasure. He tells me there are places where a good crew can be recruited, and the Niceans who stayed with us have been promised passage home when this is accomplished—for we are heading north, out of the Southern Sea, and the climate there is not to their liking.

And after we pass the great stone fortress of the Rhemians, and round the land of the Tarconii?

I cannot say, but I know this: that much has happened to me in a relatively short time. I have been student, heretic, outlaw, slave and *rhadaz'meh* to the brother of a king. Now I am the owner of a fine ship, and wealthy beyond all reason.

I am not the same person that I was before.

Though I am not sure just what it is that I have become.

I know that I am to seek, and to find.

But what is it that I am looking for?

TWENTY-EIGHT

Once more we sailed without incident through the narrow strait and into the Great Ocean itself. I was somewhat concerned, though, until this passage was over. We could outrun the ungainly Rhemian warships, but we dared not meet them in a fight, for we had no men to spare for combat. More than that, the Rhemians knew Niciea was in turmoil, and I feared they might take advantage of this if they could.

"They cannot know our strength," growled Signar, "or the lack of it. And I'll see they're none the wiser."

He said nothing more than that, but eyed the great rock looming ahead with disdain and mumbled something deep within his broad chest. I did not question him. A captain must run his ship as he sees fit, or he is no captain at all.

Signar did not disappoint me. When we passed under the shadow of that mountain, every man aboard was on deck. They moved about like a swarm of bees, going in one place, and coming out another. Sometimes they changed the color of their capes below, or carried items about from fore to aft. If I had been watching all this from the Rhemian stronghold, I'm certain I would have thought the Niciean vessel was *over-manned*, if anything. The crew delighted in this sport, and would have gone too far with it if Signar had not cautioned them with a growl or two.

The Vikonen did not miss the opportunity to show that we were well armed—for every shield and weapon we could find was displayed more than once on our decks.

Out of the Southern Sea the waters became choppier, and the wind had a chill to it, for we were well into autumn now. The ship ploughed northward through high swells—topping one monstrous wave, then dropping quickly into its trough. At the bottom of these depressions there was nothing but water to be seen, looming above our masts.

However, none of this bothered Signar or his crew. For myself, it was comfortable to look to starboard and see the dark mass of the land there. To the west there was nothing but awesome emptiness, stretching away forever. And beyond that, I wondered. Something? Or did the ocean go on without end?

"They say it falls off into nothing," Signar told me. "That there is a great mist near the end, rising up from below. The mist is poisonous to breathe, but Vhinaar sings her song there and beckons seamen to join her. These seamen forget the air cannot be breathed, and sail into the mist and over the edge. Of course, they are never seen again, except in the halls of Rhagnir."

"Rhagnir?"

"It is a Vikonen word. Rhemians have the same term, but call it Hell." Signar shrugged. "One is as good as another."

I looked into the gray waters. "And you believe this, then? That a ship sailing west will fall into Rhagnir?"

Signar filled his chest with sea air. "I am of two minds, Aldair. One should take a care with things that belong to the gods, and not scoff at their warnings. I have known men to laugh at Rhagnir before, and these men no longer sail the seas. Still, one can honor the gods and keep his own thoughts at the same time. And I personally do not believe there is a place a Vikonen cannot go in a good, sound ship. Be it the ice seas of the north, or the Great Ocean itself."

Signar spoke with great conviction and bravado, but I noticed he cast a wary glance over his shoulder—in case a god of some sort might be hovering there to listen.

We made one stop along the barren Tarconii coast, at the site of the ruins where Tharrin had left a garrison to wait for the spring. I did not see that he would have objected to this—he would not be coming back here, and there was no need for the men to die needlessly. They were more than grateful, even when they learned we would be traveling north for a while, and they would not quickly feel the sun.

Rheif seemed much better to me, and I'm not ashamed to say I gave thanks to the Creator more than once. He frequently joined us on deck for a part of the day now, and refused any help from any of us. He could have used a hand, but Stygianns have their pride, and there is nothing for it.

"You are looking your old self again," I told him one morning. "Though you can take no solace in that."

He gave me a hollow grin. "Only a Venicii would insult a wounded man who cannot fight back." The grin fell away then, and his features went slack with weariness. "In turth, Aldair, I am already a pelt set for hanging. There is little more to do but the tanning, and the removal of some poor bones and flesh."

I tried to make light of his words, as I always did now, but he knew me well enough. Talking tired him tremendously —a most abnormal condition for a Stygiann. So more often than not I left him on the decks alone, with a seaman to keep an eye on him. He would sit there for hours without moving, his eyes ever on the north. I could guess his thoughts. They could not have been far from my own. . . .

We left the sight of shore only once, when we neared the big Rhemian port with its pink-and-white buildings climbing a green hill. I could not forget sailing our small boat under the shadow of blood-red sails, with Rheif flattened out of sight below decks. That day seemed long ago, in another life I had lived.

Signar said he knew the port, and that it was called Camelium. Once it had been a fair raiding place for the Vikonen. Long ago, though, in his grandsire's day. The Rhemians had not conquered all of Gaullia, then, and were still confined to the Rhemian peninsula and lands to the east of the Southern Sea.

"We do not come this far south anymore," Signar complained, shaking his head somberly. "Things are not well for the Vikonen. The Reminans have pushed their legions further north over the years, and while we do not fear them, mind you—they are as thick as fleas wherever you look, and it's hard for a man to miss 'em!"

"That is the strength of Rhemia," I added. "Where the legions go, officials and merchants soon follow, and with them, Rhemian ways and customs. In a generation or so, even the children speak Rhemian, and forget their own tongue."

Signar muttered an oath. "Aye, they steal a whole world, Aldair, and think nothing of it. But let them catch a Vikonen with a keg of ale that's not his own, and you'll see a furry head roll in the street!"

It was the end of a chill, gray day; slate-colored clouds hung heavily over the sea. Signar brought the vessel to anchor in a cove that seemed safe enough—we didn't like to do this, as we were already close to the heavily populated coastline of southern Gaullia. Still, we needed fresh water, and it was a risk we had to take.

While the wind moaned about through the rigging, we were warm enough inside the small cabin that had once belonged to Nhidaaj. An iron brazier took the chill from the night, and lent a warm glow to the dark wooden walls. There was wine in copper cups, and the sound of the sea meeting the hull.

Signar had been silent a long while, his cup buried in a great hairy hand. Finally, though, his eyes raised from the glowing coals and met mine. I knew, before that, something was on his mind. Talking is important to Vikonens, and they brood and chew over their words long before they speak them.

"There are things that need to be said, Aldair," he began. "I think perhaps now would be a good time for this."

Rheif looked up and glanced at both of us, but said nothing.

"Signar," I said, "there is never a bad time for companions to talk with one another."

He nodded and looked at his hands. "It is this, Aldair. We are heading steadily northward, and becoming more conspicuous by the day. There is nothing more noticeable in these waters than a Nicean vessel, unless it be a sea monster of sorts. So far, we have been lucky—though I doubt we've gone undetected. A Rhemian warship may well be sniffing us out now, for all I know. They would be most interested in knowing what we are about, so far from the Southern Sea." He paused and rubbed a hand across his short muzzle. "What I am saying, Aldair, is that it is time to think about where we are going. . . ."

"*. . . Where we are going . . .*"

Something peculiar was happening to me, though I could not say what it was. I heard Signar. And I did not. He spoke. But his words were not words that I knew. Something . . .

"Aldair."

I looked up. There was a creature there. I tried very hard to remember his name.

"Aldair. Is something wrong?"

"No. No, there is nothing wrong." But there was.

"*. . . Where we are going . . .*"

I looked at Rheif. Rheif looked away. Signar, then. Yes, Signar. I remembered.

"I—where would you have us go, Signar? Return to the north—and home?"

It seemed a simple enough question. Signar, though, gave me a long and quizzical look.

"Aldair, I am a Vikonen, as you know. "While I am at sea, I am not unhappy. And as for what *I* would do, that is not truly for me to say, is it? The only thing I do not wish to see in my future is capture by the Rhemians. I have not spoken of this, but it is how I came to be a slave of the Niceans. I escaped the oars of a Rhemian galley in the Southern Sea and swam ashore near the strait. Only, it appears that one shore is as bad as the other, and it was not long before I was in that unhappy state of slavery again—only this time, under Nicean masters."

Yes, I thought. I see that, Signar. I do. The thought came terribly hard, though—like a man lifting boots through the northern mud.

What's wrong with me . . .!

"We've all—had our fill of slavery," I said from somewhere. "Yes. Yes, we—"

"Aldair."

"And—" Something. "And we'll have only freemen on this vessel. Only—freemen. When we get to . . ."

"Vhiborg," Signar finished.

"Vhiborg. No slaves."

"Spoken like a true Vikonen, Aldair."

Better. Thoughts coming better. "And—there are things that would change the ship. Make it less easily spotted. Without—reducing its seaworthiness . . ."

"There are. A good painting, for one thing."

"And the sails. You mentioned the sails, once. . . ."

"And not only that," said Signar. "The rigging's set for southern waters. In the north, now . . ."

Rheif laughed. A hollow laugh that near set him choking.

We both looked at him. His once powerful frame was wasted, and his skin hung like sacking to his bones. But from the hollows of his eyes, the Stygiann gaze still burned like red coals in the night.

"You two are fine hunters," he said scornfully. "You've planned a great feast and set cookfires a-burning. All you need do is catch the game and skin it!"

"Rheif!" Signar said sharply.

Rheif looked at him woodenly. "I do not fear you, Vikonen."

"It is not the time. There will—be a time. You can see—"

"No. I'd speak of it. And now."

Signar looked down and ground his palms. I turned from one to the other, but neither would face me. "Rheif. Signar. Whatever this is about, I'd know it. As I said, there should be nothing unsaid between companions."

Signar glanced up dolefully. "Is that what we are, Aldair? Companions?"

I was startled by his words. "You can ask, Signar?" I cried. "You can ask such a thing?"

Signar squirmed uncomfortably. "There was a time when I—would not."

"And now? Now?"

"Aldair. Listen to me. You do not see yourself. Your friends do, but you do not. We see that a change has come over you. That you are not as you were before. I know you for an honest man. Neither Rheif nor I feel that—"

"Wait." I stood up and faced him. "Something is in your mind, Vikonen—and in yours, Rheif. I will tell you that I am Aldair. As I ever was. I am the same Aldair of the Venicii who fled from the Tarconii with you, Rheif. And shared Niciean bug soup. And I am the same Aldair who found you at the Lord Tharrin's waterwheel, Signar, under the whip of Linius." I spread my hands. "What is there about me? Have I grown another tail? Is my snout a foot longer than before? Tell me, so that I will know as much as you!"

"Aldair," said the Vikonen, "we know these things. . . ."

"Get to it, Signar. Please."

"I will, then." He looked up steadily. "We sailed from Chaarduz on some mission. We did not question this. We were away from that place with our lives. That was enough.

Then we saw you go into the desert with Nhidaaj and the young prince. You returned alone. We did not question this. We did not even ask why a fine vessel that belonged to the Nicíean Empire now belongs to you. Or why you are suddenly wealthy beyond a man's dreams. All of these things are somewhat unusual. But we did not question you, Aldair."

"There are—things I do not understand myself, Signar."

Signar nodded. Without conviction.

"If I have been less than a friend should be," I said, "it was not my intention. I—"

"Aldair." Signar rolled his big head in wonder. "You do not really *know* what I am saying, do you? If you do not *speak* to us often, or appear to *see* us—we take no offense. Sometimes a man's eyes are somewhere else, and he cannot bring them to bear on what is about him. I understand that. But, friend, wherever it is your mind has taken you, it has become blind to danger. I will say what I have been trying to say—*that you are not Aldair.* You are a stranger who has taken his place. We do not know you. You drive us northward to Vhiborg. And after that? What, Aldair? You have never said. You will speak of nothing. Perhaps you assume that we know your mind, but we do not. What am I to tell the men I recruit there? That they are to become searaiders? Merchants? Fishermen? Or shall I say that a wealthy ex-slave has acquired a fine vessel and wishes to sail it about the seas for his pleasure—though he does not tell his captain where he wishes to go or what he wishes to do."

"Signar . . ."

And there it was again. I wished to speak. And could not. Signar was wrong, and I wanted to tell him so. I *did* concern myself with these things. I *did* care for the fate of my companions, my crew—

Only—this was not truly so, was it?

"*. . . Where we are going . . .*"

A chill set my body to shaking, and I gripped the arms of my chair until my hands ached. For I realized he was right. I was not myself, but another. What's wrong with me? *What's wrong with me?*

Again, a veil lifted slightly from my mind. Yes. There *were* things I could not share with my companions. Things that were not mine to share. More than that, much that was still beyond my own understanding.

Go ... seek ... and find, Aldair. ...

Find WHAT? Creator's eyes, what is it you *want* of me?

Then: Peace. Silence ...

... Rolling over me like a warm, comforting wave ...

A door had been closed. It was opening, now, and I could see—something.

"Aldair ..."

Signar's dark face above me.

And Rheif: "He is all right, Vikonen. Leave him alone."

Signar turned on him. "All *right,* you say? Do you *see* him, man?"

"I see him."

"Then—"

"He knows now, Signar."

"Knows what?"

"He knows. He knows where he is going. ..."

From somewhere, very far away, I looked at the Stygiann. His voice was not his own. For the moment, it belonged to another. And for a brief, fleeting second, there was something in his eyes. Then, just as quickly, it was gone.

But I felt no fear, now. The door was open. And Rheif was right. I knew. It seemed, now, that I had known all along. ...

TWENTY-NINE

It is easy to see why the Rhemians have never been able to close the port of Vhiborg. It is a difficult place to find, being several miles inland and not on the sea at all. The channel leading to this place is deep and narrow, bordered by steep cliffs which are easily defensible. It is far enough to the north to appeal to Vikonens, but there are other races here, too—Rhemian deserters, Tarconii mercenaries, and even a small colony of Stygianns, much to Rheif's delight.

There was much to be done here, and quickly—for we were late in the season. Many seamen who use this port are content to stay ashore during the winter months, when the waters are high and ice covers the rigging. There is reason in this, Signar tells me, and I can see that he is right. But I cannot be content with that now. And Signar does not question me.

So we have arranged for supplies, recruited the men we need, and made those modifications Signar felt were necessary. We have fulfilled our obligation to the Niceans among us. They have been loyal and unquestioning. A cold death in the Northlands is no reward for such service.

Gaining their passage southward was easier than we had imagined. Sea raiders would rather spin tales than eat, and my Niceans were a novelty—their yarns of rich ports to the east of the Southern Sea found eager listeners. Within the week, two vessels swept down the channel for the open sea. Niceans were aboard each craft, and I am certain they were thankful every league took them closer to the sun.

Signar has done wonders with the ship. He has taken some of the best features of the Vikonen longboat and blended them with the basic design of the Niciean craft. We are stronger, and faster. He assures me nothing afloat can catch us, and that we can take anything the sea can fling against our hull. We had no trouble signing on a crew, for nearly every seaman in Vhiborg wanted the chance to sail with us.

I must say that I viewed none of the events that occurred in Vhiborg. I didn't show myself on the decks, but kept to my cabin until we were well out to sea again. I chose this because I was not fit for the company of men. Signar was right. Something has happened to me. I am not wholly myself. I am Aldair. But I am Aldair changed. I am a part of something that stretches from dark yesterdays to far tomorrows. I am a link in something that must be. As was the Lord Tharrin and Nhidaaj, and the creature with yellow-flecked eyes who does not go into the world.

And what is it I am to do? What am I to seek?

I cannot say. I only know that I must. And that I can no more avoid this seeking than stop the beating of my heart. And because of the task that has been given me, the company of men now seems a fearful thing. Sometimes, even Rheif and Signar seem to speak in tongues I cannot understand. It is as if some of the magic of Lady Shamma's garden has journeyed with me. Often I sense that time no longer binds me to this world. Thoughts ease themselves into my mind, and they are thoughts that do not belong to me. I wake from dreams I do not understand.

Who am I? What is happening to me?

I asked for none of this. I am simply Aldair of Venicii. I come from an insignificant corner of Gaullia that is of little interest to anyone.

Only I am not that Aldair, now. . . .

"We will have to tell them something," growled Signar. "And soon. A crew has the right, Aldair."

I looked at him. Signar. The Vikonen. White gulls circled in a gray sky.

"What would you have me say?" I asked him.

Signar bit his lip. "If you tell 'em, they'll go no farther with you."

"And if I do not, they will desert me anyway. The answer is simple, Signar. Tell them nothing."

Signar shook his big head. "Sailors are not fools, whatever you might think. They've eyes, and they can read the sea, and they'll know soon enough. And they're a superstitious lot, I'll tell you that. Once they find where you're taking us, they'll follow neither your command nor mine."

I looked at Signar with some surprise.

"Aye. Me, too, Aldair. Though I'll not desert you. But I'm a sailor like the rest, remember?"

"No. You're not the same."

"I'm the same, all right. A fair bit meaner than some, and a hair smarter, as befits a captain. I don't see gods and demons lurkin' under every wave, but I don't go out of my way to spit in their eyes, either."

"*. . . Where we are going . . .*"

"I'm—not asking them to follow me to—that place," I said. "It's—after that, Signar."

Signar looked at me curiously. "And where'll that be, then? At least we can tell 'em that."

"*. . . Where we are going . . .*"

I pulled a robe about me against the chill, and stared at the sea. "I don't know, Signar. I don't know that. . . ."

After a moment, the Vikonen let out a deep breath. "This is a thing you must do, Aldair?"

"It is. . . ."

"Then you must. And you will. And I'll not let either ship or sailor stop you, friend."

But I already knew that. . . .

THIRTY

. . . I near the end of this chronicle, and thus approach its beginning. For now I know that I have hardly begun the task that has been set before me. I have opened a door, and I have seen what lies beyond. I have gained new knowledge. And I have learned that knowledge is more precious than spun gold, and deadlier than all the legions of Rhemia. That of all things in the world, it must be weighed most carefully, and shared wisely.

Only three other creatures have read what is written here. One is Signar the Vikonen. Another is Thareesh, a Niciean archer who still lives, though I left him for dead in the desert. The last is Rhalgorn, bloodkin of Rheif the Stygiann, who wields a sword as old as history, and has the gift of second sight.

But these belong to another tale, which is just beginning, and I have yet to record the end of this one. . . .

There was little light on the waters, though it was an hour past dawning. The leaden sky hid the sun and pressed close to the chill sea. It was a morning when every sound is smothered at birth, and a man walks heavily to hear the comfort of his boots.

It was only through the courage of Signar that our vessel stood off these shores. What he told the crew, I cannot say. I only know that though they feared that isle more than death itself, and felt its chill in their hearts, they feared the Vikonen more.

So once again I found myself manning the oars of a small boat off the dark shores of Albion. And again, I was not alone. Why is it a man expects so little of his friends? Perhaps he knows himself too well, and cannot see why another should value him greatly.

Even so, I had barely shipped oars when a gaunt figure eased himself down the side of the hull and joined me. I said nothing. The Stygiann looked at me solemnly, and pulled a robe about his shoulders. "No doubt," he said, "if this gloomy isle of yours is truly peopled by souls of the dead, they will not have devoured all the game about, and there will be fat hares for the taking."

I could not look at him. "Yes. No doubt there will, Rheif. . . ."

I kept my eyes from the Vikonen, above—though I knew what he was thinking. Even that climb down to the boat had cost the Stygiann greatly. And we both knew he had no interest in hares—for Linius's bolt had loosed a poison in his body, and he could not hold watered wine on his stomach. Whatever improvement he had shown on the trip north was short-lived. Signar and I were aware of this, though we did not speak of it. Rheif knew, too, but he was a Stygiann, and a Stygiann lives and dies a stubborn creature.

So I did not look at him, but frowned greatly and bit my lip—as if it was a great struggle to pull the oars over water as still as a duck pond. In this way I was able to keep a wetness from my eyes.

By late afternoon the clouds parted, and an autumn sun took some of the chill. We had come ashore in the mouth of a small river; it flowed with no great force so I decided to follow it inland.

The river was Signar's suggestion. I wanted nothing to do with the crashing breakers Rheif and I had seen from the other side of the island during our escape from the Tarconii. So the Vikonen found us a friendlier shore, just north of the point where the channel narrows between Albion and Gaullia.

We moved for a while through broad, marshy thickets. The water was heavy with the smell of drowned wood. Our bow cut dry rushes and laid them back like summer wheat. There were fish and fowl of all kinds about; great flocks of long-legged herons waited until we were nearly upon them before they took to the air.

The marsh gave way and the river narrowed. We rowed

under the shade of massive oaks, thick with branches of gold and red. The crowns of these great trees tangled overhead, and only thin shafts of light made their way to the water.

The forest on either side was teeming with game of all sorts—so dense with life that there was motion wherever we looked. These creatures had no more fear of us than the big floaks of birds by the sea. There was squirrel, beaver, and otter in great profusion—and more fat hares than Rheif could snare in a lifetime.

Deer were everywhere—round-eyed does and tall stags with enormous antlers. This was a sight I enjoyed, for deer have become scarce in Gaullia, even in the north country. And though my race are not big meat-eaters, such as the Stygianns or Vikonens, a deer roast on occasion is a marvelous treat.

Before dark, I pulled the small punt ashore and started a fire. I did not want Rheif to suffer from the cold, and there was a sharp chill in the air. I had waited until now to think about game. There was no need for caution in this place, and I put arrows through a brace of hares and a small deer only steps from camp. I dressed the hares quickly and put them to fire, then strung the deer so it would catch the smoke of our fire.

Neither Rheif nor I had spoken much during the day. Rheif, because he seldom felt like talking now—and I was busy enough with the boat. He thanked me for the hares and said they were delicious, though he barely touched his portion. It was a sad thing to see, for this was his favourite dish, and he could do no more than gaze at it mournfully—like old men who see a young maiden pass, and remember joys they can no longer experience.

If there were demons or souls about, they made no appearance that day, or during the night. Strange, I thought. At sea and in Vhiborg I had been full of dread fears. I had become a different person. Apart from my companions. My very thoughts seemed to belong to another Aldair. More than that, I was a child of my people, and the Church had filled me with dark terrors of this place. Still, the moment we neared Albion, all my fears had dropped away. How could that be, I wondered. For now there was nothing but peace in my heart. I was myself again. I had set foot on the isle where no man dared to go, and found it a wondrously beautiful place filled with deep forests and great varieties of game.

What was I here for, then?

For a moment, I was certain I had made a great fool of myself. That no strange creatures in the desert had guided me to Albion—only my own imagination.

I knew, though, this could not be so.

We kept to the river the second day, and part of the third. We saw much the same scenery as we had seen the first. The waters led us steadily southward, then veered to the west where the trees thinned and higher ground topped the horizon. The current was too swift to navigate now, and we beached the boat and headed south. I had no idea where we were going, but the narrows between Albion and Gaullia lay in that direction, and it seemed a proper route. If such tales could be believed, blue lights had been seen over those skies at one time. I hoped we would not encounter these, or the spirits that were supposed to dwell there.

"You do not fear this place, do you?" Rheif asked me some time after we had left the boat behind.

"No," I told him, "I do not. Though perhaps I should. But if this place belongs to the dead, Rheif, they do not intrude greatly upon the living." I looked at the Stygiann. "Does this land hold fears for you?"

Rheif grinned wearily. "Nothing holds fear for me now, Aldair. I am somewhat beyond fearing."

I did not answer, but glanced quickly about, as if something in the copse of whitethorn ahead interested me greatly.

"I will say this, though," he went on. "I am not much of anything anymore, but I am still a Stygiann. And you must know that we have senses not given to other races. I have heard the footsteps of wood elves deep within the forest of the Lauvectii, and these creatures tread more softly than spiders. Once I heard water music from the depths of a black pool, and saw a single dark eye there—though no other warrior could discern these things. I was greatly afraid, then, and knew I was in the presence of spirits of some sort. So you can see that a Stygiann not only hears the hare tremble in the bush, and can count the mites on a hawk circling above. He is also aware of any soul creatures and demons that are about. I have neither seen nor head any of these things on this isle, Aldair, though there are more *live* creatures here than you can imagine. Animals that you cannot hope to notice with your limited senses, though this is no fault of your own."

With that, Rheif leaned back against his tree, near exhausted from this effort. It had been a great while since he had said as much. And while I could not yet conjure up any great fears for the spirits of Albion, I still jumped at every other hare that leaped across our path. Rheif's words did little to comfort me, for Stygianns are great liars, and I have no doubt he truly believed he could count the mites on a hawk if he cared to.

Late in the afternoon we came to a green ridge covered with short grasses. It rose just above the top of the forest and it was not overly steep, but I could see it extended for some miles and could not be avoided. We climbed this obstacle slowly, and Rheif did not seem too exhausted from the effort—though he sat down against a big tree and stated solemnly that this was a good place to rest for a moment. I walked to the far side of the ridge and peered down, and saw the thick forest on the other side—and the white bones of a dead city thrusting through red-and-gold foliage.

It had been a great city.

Many thousands must have lived there, for it stretched as far as the eye could see. I had gained some little knowledge from the Lord Tharrin, and there was much here to show what had gone before. Heat, cold, and the press of centuries had taken their toll. Even the hardest of stone eventually goes to dust. I could see, though, what might have been. A few skeletal fingers were still twice as high as the great oaks beneath them, and I was struck with the meaning of that. If this city was even as old as the ruins at Tarconii, many of these buildings might well have risen four or even five times their present height!

I could not imagine such a place, but it must have been the most majestic city that had ever risen from the earth.

Edging into the city was a flat, marshy plain that disappeared to the southwest. It was no more than a day's ride away, and it curled lazily through the ruins as if it had once

been a river flowing to the sea. If this was so, time had long
since leveled its banks.

I stood watching this wonder until the sun fell away in
the west, and I greatly wished the Lord Tharrin could have
been there beside me. What a sight for him to see! And how
much his experienced eyes could have read there.

Behind me, Rheif sniffed the air with his gray muzzle. "Is
this what you came to see, Aldair?"

"I don't know," I told him honestly. "It is certainly not
what I expected to find."

Rheif took a labored breath. "I will tell you this, though
I know nothing of things of the past, as you do—but I am
certain that whoever stacked so many homes one atop the
other, it was not the souls of the dead."

The sun disappeared and a cold chill struck the high ridge.
Rheif had spoken for both of us, and left a question that
kept me sleepless a great part of the night. Souls had not
built the long-dead city in Tarconii, either, or the two ancient
things in the waters below Xandropolis. And if they had not,
who had accomplished these things?

THIRTY-ONE

In the morning I left the ridge and went down into the city.

I told Rheif that while I would enjoy his companionship that day, we were in a strange land and it might be well if he could find his way clear to stay on the ridge and keep watch—at least for the time being. That if I needed aid, I could signal with a streamer arrow. Rheif agreed that this was wise. He promised to keep watch for my call.

We both spoke these things as if they were so, though we knew he could not have lifted his gaunt frame from the ground. I left food and water close to hand and turned quickly to my task. I could feel his eyes behind me. And I could not turn to meet them.

There is little I can say about the city. A lifetime of work might uncover its secrets, but they were safely hidden for now. Cold earth and the roots of great oaks guarded its grave.

I walked among silent trees through broad ferns still wet with morning. I followed a line of stones until it vanished under a mossy hill, and imagined a great avenue beneath my boots. Toward noon I reached the shore of the saltwater marsh. There were ruins near its center, barely topping the surface. I studied them for a moment, then moved quickly away. I didn't care for the smell of the place, and it is said that such areas where water stands still breed killing fevers.

Back into the forest, then. I rested there, and considered. Where the Good Fathers of the Church saw the spirits of the dead, there were only the bones of the past. An important discovery. Lord Tharrin would have thought so. And Nhidaaj.

And the creature with yellow-flecked eyes? What would he

think? Had he drawn me to Albion for this? *Had he drawn me to Albion at all?*

I was suddenly angry with myself, and ashamed. Where had I gotten the idea I had some mysterious part to play in dark and secret dramas? It all sounded very well with drugged wine in your gullet and yellow eyes peering at you from a shadowy cloak. You'll be a seeker, Aldair . . . there are things to be done, Aldair. . . .

Well, they had wasted their "terrible secrets" on Aldair of Venicii. I had found a lost city. I knew that wherever the Afterworld might be, it was not in Albion, which was a land much like any other. The world *was* truly older than the Good Fathers or the priests of Niciea cared to admit. So men had lost a piece of their past. Was that a great wonder? If Silium and Culivia and even Rhemia itself someday crumbled to ruin, would not other cities take their place?

I was suddenly very tired. I belonged in Venicii doing a man's job, where men are always needed. Wandering about on meaningless adventures gained a man nothing. There was, indeed, an answer to all these "dark secrets," I decided. It was the nature of man to seek knowledge—and if there was no knowledge to be found, to make himself *believe* there was. Thus, Good Fathers and Nicean priests became more than they might have been because they "knew things" forbidden to others. And Lord Tharrin and Nhidaaj and his mysterious friend? Their secrets merely differed from the secrets of others. There was nothing here for me, though. I had no desire to add another religion or secret society to the world. I had let myself become caught up in false dreams. I had never been "another" Aldair—only an Aldair who wanted to believe there was something more to the world than there seemed to be. . . .

A spark of color caught my eye and I followed the quick, nervous flight of a tiny red bird through the foliage overhead. He was no bigger than a mite, but he had taken this giant oak for his own. I watched him move from one branch to another in short, jerky flights. He made several trips to the ground and back, circling about and disappearing for a while in a section of rubble.

I watched this action several times, then forgot the bird and studied the rubble itself. It was peculiarly shaped, more circular than blocky, as most of the ruins appeared. Moving to it for a closer look I saw that it was indeed unusual. Round, somewhat wider than a man, and half as high. It was hollow, like a pipe, and made a sharp right angle at its top. It was not made of stone, but constructed of the gray, mortarlike substance I had seen in Tarconii. It was a remarkably durable material—this piece was barely pitted by the years.

I walked around the object, wondering what it might be. I found its opening, and peered into darkness—then backed quickly away, startled. A wave of warm air had come out of the hole to meet me!

I stood well clear of the thing. A sudden chill touched my spine. *Warm* air? I had already decided it could be a chimney of sorts. Such a thing could bring cold air from some hollow in the city. *But not warm air. There could be no warm air down there. . . .*

I found step-holds built into the shell of the thing. I did not hesitate—if I had, I would never have done what I did. Gathering several dry branches for torches, I lowered myself through the hole and started down.

It was a long while before my boots touched bottom. And that was odd, I thought. The street level shouldn't have been that deep. Then I remembered Tarconii. There had been some rooms there built *under* the ground. Water usually took its toll in such places, and there was seldom anything to find.

This was no ordinary underground structure, though. I knew the distance between each step-stone, and kept count. I was more than a hundred feet below the surface.

A piece of cape served as a wick. I wrapped it about one of my sticks and struck a flint to it. The bottom of the tube was littered with leaves and soil. This debris may have been a foot deep—or fifty. More likely the latter, I decided. A great deal of rubble can collect over the centuries. *Fifty centuries? Sixty? More than that?*

There was a round door just above me, grilled with slit-like openings and big enough to crawl through. The warm air was coming from there. There had been a metal handle once, but only rust stains remained. I pried the edges with my knife, and it came away easily enough. The flow of warm air was somewhat stronger now.

I crawled through a narrow passage for twenty yards or so. There was another of the stonelike doors at the end. I dropped, this time, some eight feet or so. The torch nearly went out and I quickly made another.

I decided at that point not to go too far in my explorations. The idea of finding my way back to the surface in darkness was not appealing.

I was in a small room. Slitted on all sides for air flow. The room was clean. Not even a layer of dust on the floor. I could not imagine how this could be. The inhabitants of the city might have left it only yesterday! *That* thought gave me a most uneasy feeling.

There was a metal door, still intact. It was painted gray, like the room. It opened smoothly, without a sound. I stopped, sucked in a breath, touched the blade at my belt. A dim red eye stared at me from above. My heart slowed, finally, as the eye did not appear to moving for me.

I studied the thing cautiously. It was no eye at all, but a small red sun attached to the ceiling just beyond the door. I stared for a long moment and marveled at this thing. It was brighter than any gem, and burned without a flicker. It was a dim fire that smoldered steadily, like no lamp in the world. I felt suddenly cold again. Perhaps the Good Fathers were right after all. Who else but the Creator himself could make such a thing?

I passed hurriedly under the red sun, and down an empty hall. There was nothing in this passage—only another small sun at the end, and a narrow stairway leading upward. At the top of the stairs was a door. It opened onto darkness. My torch was only a small circle about me, and I could see nothing.

I took a step. Then another.

And froze. Heard my own voice cry out in fear.

For the room was suddenly filled with brightness. There was neither torch nor candle in sight, nor any of the small red suns.

There was light, and it was just—*there.*

Darkness. Then light.

And in the light, my old world died. It could never be the same. Nor could I be Aldair of Venicii again. I would be something else, ever after. And no other creature on Earth would be what he was before. . . .

Epilogue

I have given much thought to this.

How it should be said and what it is I wish to tell those who read my words. A year ago, after these things happened, I know I would have described all I saw in great detail. I'm certain I could not have avoided bringing my own emotions into play.

Now I am finishing this chronicle on the deck of my ship, far to the south of Tarconii, past the straits of the Southern Sea. The small cove where we are anchored is lush with green plants and tangled growth. This is the same land that holds Chaarduz, and the Niciean Empire, but those places are far to the northeast of us, and might well be on another world.

So from this point in time, I am better able to see the events of the year past. I know that many things I might tell about would not be understood. I know, too, that the fear, loneliness, and sorrow I felt at the time cannot be conveyed to another. Those who read this account will experience their own emotions. They cannot share mine. This is why I will tell only what I have seen. My feelings will not be reflected here. There is enough to be told without that. . . .

When light flooded the room I stood at the border of a great hall which seemed to have no ending. The floor beneath my boots was black, hard, and shiny. The walls on either side were faced with a thousand gray windows that looked out upon nothing. Near the far end of the hall were cases of the finest glass, and within each case there were things to be seen.

Like the small room below, there was no dust of the ages here. How this was accomplished, I cannot say.

The gray windows were not empty after all. When I stood directly before one of these, miraculous pictures appeared. They were not pictures as in a painting. They moved and could be heard, and were true images of things that had happened. As each window came to life, I watched tiny pieces of history taking place, as if I peered over the shoulder of those who had been present. I cannot guess how this was done, but it was a marvelous and terrible thing.

I will only relate a few of the scenes I watched, for there were countless pictures to be seen. Battles fought long ago by warriors who carried primitive weapons and wore no armor. People who lived by the sea in crude earthen huts. I saw small villages grow into stone fortresses. These places were guarded by men in shaggy clothing who defended themselves with shields of hide and wood.

Later, there were hundreds of stone keeps, each holding small bits of land and coveting the territory of their neighbors. These little kingdoms changed hands often. Finally, I recognized the red pennant of the Hectanic League, and the first confederation of tribes. Under the rule of Vertiginian, this alliance was the beginning of the Rhemian Empire.

There were other scenes, picturing the beginnings of the Niciean and Vikonen peoples. The migration of Stygianns from the east. The enslavement of the Cygnians. The simple lives of the Tarconii.

Some of the gray windows did not come to life, so I cannot guess what stories they told. Often a voice talked about the pictures. The voice spoke in the Rhemian tongue, but was strangely accented, and pitched in a peculiar manner.

Midway down the hall, I saw the first pictures of the creatures. . . .

I said in the beginning I would not let my own emotions color this chronicle. I will abide by this, and merely tell what I saw, though this is not an easy thing to do.

They were creatures like no man has ever seen.

Tall. Nearly hairless. Some with pink skins, some nearly black. Even a Cygnian whose wool has been freshly shaven could not look as bare and ugly! Their faces were nearly featureless. Small, triangular blobs for snouts. Eyes set too close together. Red slits for mouths. Tiny ears set flat against their skulls.

Where had such a terrible race come from? Where had they gone? I could not answer these questions, but it soon became clear to me that it was they who had built this miraculous place—that it was their city that had once stood in Albion.

Many of the gray windows showed pictures that were hard to understand. The creatures riding about in strange devices —both on the ground and above it. Moving in and out of buildings higher than the mind could imagine. Doing a hundred other things that were impossible to fathom.

—And suddenly I remembered. I had seen these beings before, in a dream that was not a dream. Pictured on dusty walls in a place where I spoke to a creature with yellow-flecked eyes.

I come to a part of my story that is difficult to tell. So I can only try to put down the words that come to me, and trust that I will be understood. For it is not easy to keep my promise now—to merely relate what I have seen, and not color this document with feeling.

At one window, I watched the creatures bring their sky-things to the ground and deposit great rows of shiny capsules on a grassy knoll. Where this occurred, I could not say—it could have been anywhere in Gaullia, or further south, at the heart of the Rhemian Empire. For a long while the capsules lay there, with the beings scurrying about between them. Then, as if some signal had been given, the capsules opened by themselves. There were naked bodies inside— still, as if they were dead. And these silent beings were creatures like myself. . . .

The bodies rose. Stepped out of their shiny coffins. They seemed half asleep, as if they did not understand where they were. They milled about, doing nothing, until the hairless creatures opened other canisters deposited by the sky-things. Inside the canisters were primitive weapons and clothing, and various other utensils of a primal race. The voice spoke of this as a beginning. He spoke of the "units" being placed on the hill as representative of a larger action. From this, I gathered that similar events were taking place elsewhere.

When the creatures left their sky-things, the bodies came

quickly to life. They clung together on their lonely hill in their tattered clothing, holding their crude weapons close to their breasts. They looked at each other for a long while, until finally, one of their group pointed excitedly in another direction. The picture soared through the air to show what he was seeing—another group, on a similar hill.

(I learned later that this was the explanation for the blue lights seen over Albion. They were flying devices made for the purpose of transmitting pictures from one point to another. Evidently, some of these continued to function long after their masters had no use for them.)

The two groups studied one another, and talked among themselves. Finally, each hurried down the sides of their respective hills, and hid in the nearby woods where they could not be seen.

My heart cried out in shame at this. For I knew I had seen the beginning of my world. . . .

There were other pictures. I forced myself to watch them. They showed much I did not wish to know. How my race and others were "grown" by the hairless creatures. How things were put into our minds through methods I cannot imagine. I will not describe the pictures of things like myself in tubs of shiny metal and glass. But I will ever recall these scenes in my dreams.

There was more.

Much more.

More than I care to record here.

But I will tell about the glass cases at the end of the hall, which I know, now, was the beginning, and not the end. There were animals in these cases that seemed alive, but were not. Whether they were frozen in life, or clever imitations made to seem real, I cannot say. One could walk about them and view them from all sides.

There was a great shaggy creature on four legs paused beside a stream. It was frozen in the act of sweeping a multicolored fish from the water. Both the water and the fish seemed real, as well as the forest behind.

Another case showed two gaunt and furry animals crouched on the edge of a dark, wintry forest. One creature tore at the remains of its kill, while the other raised its gray muzzle as if it were howling at the sky. Even its frosty breath seemed real.

There were small, green creatures with long tails and scaly hides, basking on a hot stone . . . white, woolly animals with heavy fleece and black faces . . . great spotted beasts with curly horns that chewed placidly on long grasses.

And finally, I came face to face with myself. A fat, round-bodied animal with short, hooved feet and a curly tail. Long snout. Flap ears. I was munching dried corn beside a fence. There was a female nearby, lying on her side, suckling her young.

There were names on all the cases.

They did not say Vikonen or Stygiann or Niciean. They did not call these animals that walked on four legs Cygnians or Tarconii or Rhemians.

They had names.

But I will not record them here. . . .

It is enough to know that none of the races of the world are *men* of different sorts, as we thought of ourselves. We are made creatures. Grown from animals and given hands instead of hooves and paws. Set in motion to match our makers—to repeat their triumphs and follies for whatever amusement might be gained from this.

I know what a *man* is like now. And I do not wish to call myself by that name.

That this terrible thing was done, that we were created to fill the idle hours of men, is a truth that can neither be changed nor denied. *Why* this was done, I cannot say for certain. But things I learned from the gray windows have led me to answers that may not be far from the truth. I know that at one time Man covered the Earth and its seas. The lands we hold now were their lands, as well as places we have not yet discovered. I know that as the centuries passed, the numbers of men decreased, and that time buried their cities. Whether they destroyed themselves, or reduced their number in some other manner, I do not know. But I do know they learned to live to a great age, and that those who were left came at last to Albion.

Why did they do what they did? Perhaps, having wearied of life, they sought to create it, and become as gods. Perhaps the hate or shame within them drove them to mock their race, and make a comedy of their own histories.

That, then, was their greatest sin. To change us, make us parodies of themselves, was not enough. They were not content with that. *They had to pattern us after themselves in every way, and set that pattern in our minds. . . .*

Do you see the horror in this?

We are like the horse that is set in a green field on a length of rope. We can graze where we please—but only to the end of the rope, and no farther. We are reliving their lives, repeating their histories. We have nothing that is really ours. *This is their sin against us: to give us no souls of our own. . . .*

There were other great halls buried beneath the city. Some were still intact, while others had given way to time and gone to dust. I did not explore them all, but I know they were filled with wondrous things—all the marvels of Man's past. I left these treasures in the dust where I found them, and took only two things for myself. One, a very old ornament that now hangs about my shoulders. I chose it in defiance of what I saw in Albion. It is gold, finely done, and encrusted with jewels. It is the figure of some terrible beast, either real or fancied. It has the scaled body of a Nicican, the wings of a bird, and the head of a creature that reminds me of the being I met in the desert below Xandropolis. Its forelegs are great claws, and its hind legs cloven hooves. It has horns upon its head, and breathes fire made of blood rubies.

It is a dreadful beast indeed, and since I, too, am a beast, I wear it proudly. I have also had this figure painted on the sails of my vessel, and set upon the shields of my warriors.

The other thing I took from Albion was a great sword; this, too, set about with gems. Its hilt is of gold, and wrought in the head of the animal from which the Stygianns sprang. I meant this gift for Rheif, but he never felt its weight. Now it hangs from the belt of his kinsman, Rhalgorn.

And good Rheif—an enemy who became a cherished companion—lies yet in the soil of Albion, atop a high ridge overlooking a dead city. I have often wished I could have returned before his eyes closed forever. Though I do not think this could have been. I think that Rheif waited for death only until I was out of his sight. Stygianns are stubborn and proud, as I have come to know.

At any rate, he is with me wherever I go, for the name *Ahzir al'Rhaz* is painted across the prow of my ship, and means, in Niciean, Far Wanderer from the North.

I know many things I did not know before.

I know Lord Tharrin's true fears when he found the secret of Tarconii was in the hands of enemies. He was not protecting the people of Niciea, nor himself—but others engaged in that special mission of his life. I now know that there *are* others. I have met a few of these beings, and we know one another when we meet.

I know what the creature in the desert wants me to do. It is a task that hangs heavy in my mind, and I wonder that I have been chosen for it. It may be that I will not see the end of this work—but it is a thing that must be done. The destiny of Man has been kept alive in the beasts he created. It is a terrible destiny, as I see it—we are chained to both his triumphs and tragedies, for his pattern has been implanted upon our souls.

This is a chain that *must* be broken. If there is a Creator beyond Man, we must find him—and through him, ourselves.

Whatever our destiny, it must be our own—not another's.

We have the bodies of beasts. Such is our fortune.

But we do not need the hearts of men. . . .

JOHN BRUNNER in DAW editions:

☐ **THE BOOK OF JOHN BRUNNER.** A personal anthology of Brunner's multifold talents: stories, articles, poems, etc. A feast for Brunner fans! (#UY1213—$1.25)

☐ **TOTAL ECLIPSE.** The engima of a deserted planet boded ill for the future of nearby Terra. Brunner at his controversial best. (#UY1193—$1.25)

☐ **THE STARDROPPERS.** They tuned in on the cosmos—and tuned out of the world! (#UY1197—$1.25)

☐ **ENTRY TO ELSEWHEN.** A triple treasure of space, time and dimension. (#UY1144—$1.25)

☐ **GIVE WARNING TO THE WORLD.** Are there aliens among us? Are the chariots of the gods returning? (#UQ1122—95¢)

☐ **THE STONE THAT NEVER CAME DOWN.** The final climactic hour of today's world—and a last-minute remedy. (#UY1150—$1.25)

☐ **POLYMATH.** Their leader on that alien planetfall was a genius—on the wrong world's ecology! (#UY1217—$1.25)

DAW BOOKS are represented by the publishers of Signet and Mentor Books, THE NEW AMERICAN LIBRARY, INC.

THE NEW AMERICAN LIBRARY, INC.,
P.O. Box 999, Bergenfield, New Jersey 07621

Please send me the DAW BOOKS I have checked above. I am enclosing $_____(check or money order—no currency or C.O.D.'s). Please include the list price plus 25¢ a copy to cover mailing costs.

Name_____

Address_____

City_____State_____Zip Code_____
Please allow at least 3 weeks for delivery

Presenting JOHN NORMAN in DAW editions . . .

☐ **TRIBESMEN OF GOR.** The tenth novel of Tarl Cabot takes him face to face with the Others' most dangerous plot—in the vast Tahari desert with its warring tribes, its bandit queen, and its treachery. (#UW1223—$1.50)

☐ **HUNTERS OF GOR.** The saga of Tarl Cabot on Earth's orbital counterpart reaches a climax as Tarl seeks his lost Talena among the outlaws and panther women of the wilderness. (#UW1102—$1.50)

☐ **MARAUDERS OF GOR.** The ninth novel of Tarl Cabot's adventures takes him to the northland of transplanted Vikings and into direct confrontation with the enemies of two worlds. (#UW1160—$1.50)

☐ **TIME SLAVE.** The creator of Gor brings back the days of the caveman in a vivid lusty new novel of time travel and human destiny. (#UW1204—$1.50)

☐ **IMAGINATIVE SEX.** A study of the sexuality of male and female which leads to a new revelation of sensual liberation. Fifty-three imaginative situations are outlined, some of which are science-fictional in nature.
(#UJ1146—$1.95)

DAW BOOKS are represented by the publishers of Signet and Mentor Books, THE NEW AMERICAN LIBRARY, INC.

THE NEW AMERICAN LIBRARY, INC.,
P.O. Box 999, Bergenfield, New Jersey 07621

Please send me the DAW BOOKS I have checked above. I am enclosing $_____(check or money order—no currency or C.O.D.'s). Please include the list price plus 25¢ a copy to cover mailing costs.

Name_____

Address_____

City_____State_____Zip Code_____
Please allow at least 3 weeks for delivery

☐ **STRESS PATTERN by Neal Barrett, Jr.** Marooned on the
strangest planet of all!   (#UQ1143—$1.25)

☐ **THE STORM LORD by Tanith Lee.** A panoramic novel of
swordplay and a man seeking his true inheritance on an
alien world comparable to DUNE.   (#UE1233—$1.75)

☐ **GATE OF IVREL by C. J. Cherryh.** "Never since reading
The Lord of the Rings have I been so caught up in any
tale . . ."—Andre Norton.   (#UY1226—$1.25)

☐ **THE LAND LEVIATHAN by Michael Moorcock.** Stark peril
in a world that might have been and maybe still is . . .
Adventure by a master fantasist.   (#UY1214—$1.25)

☐ **THE HERITAGE OF HASTUR by Marion Zimmer Bradley.**
Unanimously acclaimed as the master work of the Dark-
over saga . . . and a potential Hugo nominee.
                                  (#UW1189—$1.50)

☐ **DON'T BITE THE SUN by Tanith Lee.** A far-flung novel
of the distant future by the author of **The Birthgrave.**
Definitely something different!   (#UY1221—$1.25)

**DAW BOOKS are represented by the publishers of Signet
and Mentor Books, THE NEW AMERICAN LIBRARY, INC.**

THE NEW AMERICAN LIBRARY, INC.,
P.O. Box 999, Bergenfield, New Jersey 07621

Please send me the DAW BOOKS I have checked above. I am enclosing
$_____(check or money order—no currency or C.O.D.'s).
Please include the list price plus 25¢ a copy to cover mailing costs.

Name_____

Address_____

City_____State_____Zip Code_____
Please allow at least 3 weeks for delivery